"Sometimes it takes fiction, more than facts, to h[...] Lord's *pH*, a cli-fi (climate fiction) novel about climate change and its evil cousin, ocean acidification, we meet likeable and quirky characters dedicated to science and art while trapped in a system seduced by money. I learned a lot from this daring novel. And I laughed. Not a bad way to spend one's time: buried in creativity, learning and laughing."

—KIM HEACOX, author of *Jimmy Bluefeather* and *John Muir and the Ice That Started a Fire*

"Nancy Lord is an entrancing naturalist writer and a captivating storyteller whose factual knowledge of her beloved Alaska is impeccable. So fascinating to see how she weaves a fictional tale to remind us of the ecological and cultural issues we face on this planet."

—JEAN-MICHEL COUSTEAU, Founder and President, Ocean Futures Society

"Very few novelists remember that we live on an ocean planet, and none, as far as I know, have tracked the emerging science of ocean acidification, a threat of almost unparalleled dimension. That Nancy Lord does all that and still provides a superb story is testament to her great powers as a writer!"

—BILL McKIBBEN, author of *Eaarth: Making a Life on a Tough New Planet*

"Widely respected and beloved Alaskan essayist Nancy Lord has written a dazzling novel, filled with wry, sly humor, wondrous science, and intriguing characters—all driven by some of the most significant questions of our time. How can scientists defend the truth in a university corrupted by petro-chemical profiteers? How can the lovely, life-sustaining creatures of the seas survive the corporate plunder of the planet? And this—how can a book this important be such a joy to read?"

—KATHLEEN DEAN MOORE, author of *Great Tide Rising* and *Piano Tide*

For Janeen!
Love the pteropods!

pH

A NOVEL

NANCY LORD

Bainbridge
2·20·18

W

WESTWINDS
PRESS®

Text © 2017 by Nancy Lord

Library of Congress Cataloging-in-Publication Data
Names: Lord, Nancy, author.
Title: pH : a novel / by Nancy Lord.
Description: Portland, Oregon : Alaska Northwest Books, [2017]
Identifiers: LCCN 2016054873| ISBN 9781513260686 (paperback)
| ISBN 9781513260693 (ebook)
Classification: LCC PS3562.O727 P42 2017 | DDC 813/.54—dc23 LC
record available at https://lccn.loc.gov/2016054873

Edited by Tina Morgan
Designed by Vicki Knapton

Published by WestWinds Press®
An imprint of

www.graphicartsbooks.com

PART 1

Chapter One

It was cold, standing at the ship's rail that early on a September morning, without a hat. Ray's annoyance at having left his wool cap in his cabin only added to his general peevishness about all things Jackson Oakley.

"Puker," he said to no one in particular, as the smaller boat approached their ship.

"Huh?" Colin, as usual, stood attentively close—too close—as though mother-of-pearl wisdom would fall from Ray's hard mouth and he would be there to catch it.

"Puker boat. You know, what they call those sport boats that take tourists out fishing, and everyone spends the whole trip puking over the side." He gave the gangly young man with watery eyes a sort-of grin, as if to say: *Not like us, serious seagoers doing serious work, nothing so trivial as slapping around for sport.*

He was trying as much as he could to make the best of a bad situation.

He and the others who had roused for the transfer watched as the boat, its white cabin roof bristling with an array of fishing rods, slowed. The opening into the Gulf of Alaska was righteously calm, with just the rise and fall of its oceanic swell. The mainland behind them formed a dark line like a charcoal smudge between the blue-green sea and paler sky. A couple of gulls, trailing the puker boat, flapped sullenly.

Their captain, up on the bridge wing, faced the ship into the swells as the smaller vessel jockeyed to its side. On the boat's bow, a man in clean yellow fishing bibs dangled a pink buoy over the side to protect the precious puker boat from smacking. Yellow, pink, white fiberglass—it was all very Easter-egg bright on a blue morning.

Ray avoided looking at Oakley, who was giving some final instructions, presumably, to Helen, his (Oakley's) star student. Ray was trying to mitigate his anger with relief. While on the one hand, Oakley's abandoning ship and his duties with the chemical ocean-ography part of their research was unforgivable, the man would be gone. As his daughter, Aurora, might have said about a school bully, "good riddance to bad rubbish."

The two vessels came together with barely a bump: a sea louse nudging the side of a salmon. Oakley's duffel was pitched through the open gate, and then Oakley himself stepped through, down onto the smaller boat's bow. The vessels separated, and Captain Billy tooted his horn. Oakley, heading for the cabin, raised his hand in a gesture that was somewhere between a Marine's salute and a queen's wristy wave.

The last thing Ray saw as the other boat turned toward port and sped up was someone reaching out of the cabin to hand Oakley a bottle of beer. Or at least Ray chose to believe it was a bottle of beer. It wasn't orange juice. He resisted the temptation to perform his own good-bye wave, which would have been a middle-finger salute.

"Well, that sucks."

Colin again. Ray wasn't sure how much Colin or any of the other students knew about what had transpired in the last few hours, less than a day out on their weeklong cruise. The official story—

what he and Oakley had announced in the galley—was that Professor Oakley had been called back to the university. They'd assured the eight students that nothing would be disrupted. Oakley had arranged for a boat owned by a friend to pick him up so they wouldn't lose research time returning to port. Helen, who'd been on several cruises already and knew the sampling protocols, would take over responsibility for the chemistry work. Alex, of course, was still overseeing the wet lab. They'd be a little short-handed, but everyone would chip in.

And they would. In his nine years of co-leading the University of the North's twice-yearly research cruises on the Gulf of Alaska, Ray had never had a problem with student slouches. They might occasionally pause to vomit over the side in rocky seas—it did happen—but nothing would keep his team from filling their bottles, netting their specimens, counting their copepods, getting the work done. Joyfully.

In Ray's opinion, nothing would be lost by losing Oakley. Nothing they couldn't do without.

"We'll make the best of it," he said to Colin.

If things were a little more complicated, and perhaps more personal, than the official explanation—well, things always were, weren't they?

For years, Ray and others in the School of Ocean Sciences had been advocating for more attention to ocean acidification. With more coastline than the rest of the United States put together, it only made sense that Alaska institutions should lead the science. Not just in understanding what happens to ocean chemistry as the ocean absorbs carbon dioxide from the overloaded atmosphere, but across all the scientific disciplines. Biology, certainly—you can't change ocean chemistry without affecting what lives in the ocean. Even physics is affected by chemistry; pH influences how sound travels underwater. So when the university president expressed an interest and came up with money to fund an office dedicated to the subject, Ray and his colleagues were thrilled—or as thrilled as a bunch of science nerds could be. The next thing they knew, the president was bragging about the "top-notch" chemist he'd recruited to head the new office.

That would be Jackson Oakley, the man from Texas. The press release that went out praised his "pioneering work in developing calibration instruments for measuring ocean pH."

Ray liked to think that he was open-minded, liberal in the best sense of the word, but he couldn't help it if his thirty-six years in Alaska had put him off Texans: their clichéd but ubiquitous cowboy boots, their syrupy drawls. If oil development had—admittedly—been good for the state's finances, it had exacted enormous costs on the environment and social fabric. Many perfectly nice Texans must have come north with the industry; he just hadn't known any. In any case, his prejudice was not something he generally shared. Only his wife, the eye-rolling Nelda, ever had to listen to him.

It had been just over a year since Dr. Jackson Oakley— "Oakley" like the tree, Ray always thought—came to campus, and Ray still wasn't sure what he did in the new Office of Ocean Acidification Science. The man rarely had anything to say in meetings when the departments came together, instead seeming preoccupied with his laptop or tablet or phone, scrolling and tapping. He was younger than most of the professors—the aging boomers, like Ray, who had started at the university during its own boom time, when oil money had first gushed loose. He wore nicer clothes—shirts with collars, lambswool sweaters. (Ray only knew about the lambswool because Nelda had pointed it out, perhaps admiringly.) He had a headful of beach boy hair and cheeks that were always smooth and shiny, the proverbial baby's bottom, as though he'd not only shaved within the hour but then rubbed in some kind of lotion. Ray had noticed that Oakley smelled like coconuts, confirming, for him, the lotion theory.

In the elapsed year, Oakley had not, to Ray's knowledge, spoken out about the dangers of ocean acidification.

Ray had made overtures, on several levels. He'd shown Oakley a few of his pteropod photos and offered them for any publications or posters the new office might produce. He told him about the farmer's market and the ice museum, testing his interest in local attractions. He asked if he liked winter sports, and Oakley said he was a skier, which Ray misunderstood as cross-country (understandably, he thought, since that was what people did in Fairbanks, on the many trails) until he was corrected. "My former wife and I had a place in Park City, but now I go to Banff," Oakley said, which is how Ray learned that Oakley was accustomed to travel and resorts and had, in addition, apparently come to the campus in an unmarried state. Oakley did not ask Ray about himself or his work.

The students seemed to like him well enough. The thesis students said he was smart and that he texted them his comments, very modernly. An older chemistry professor had retired, and no one was sorry to see someone more up-to-date take over his advising.

When Ray complained to a colleague that Oakley seemed "smug," the colleague said, "That's because he knows he's brilliant."

Now, as their ship resumed its course, they all moved back inside. Ray found himself following Helen, the grad student who worked most closely with Oakley and now was left with his responsibilities. The two men had easily agreed on her assignment. Aside from having previous cruise experience, Helen was the epitome of a responsible woman, given to getting the work done without a lot of noise about the fact that she was getting it done. She was also an Alaska Native—part-Iñupiat—and everyone these days was very big on diversity. Ray said to her now, "You can expect a little extra in your pay envelope for this week."

She gave him a confused, brow-lowered look. Pay envelope?

"I'm joking!" Why, Ray wondered, did he always have to

explain his jokes? There was, of course, no pay envelope. There was not even any automatic deposit. The students on the cruise were all volunteers. There were benefits to them, of course. The experiments they conducted, the data they collected—these were for their studies, their theses and dissertations. The cruises went on their vitae. If they worked hard, they also had a great time together. In any case, every May and September, there was never a problem choosing a crew from among eager applicants.

This time, the job of assembling the student crew had fallen completely to Ray, without complaint. He'd been a little slow, perhaps, to realize that Oakley, his putative co-leader, had basically ceded him *all* the work of preparing for the cruise. And Ray had done it, because it was easier to do it himself than to try to work with Oakley, who only became more distant and distracted every time Ray tried to talk to him. "Sure, sure," Oakley always said. "That'll be fine."

Then, when the rest of them made the long drive to the coast in a couple of vans, Oakley had chosen to fly. "To save time," he said. That was the beginning of Ray's awareness that Oakley was not going to have time—to *make* time—for a week on the water, away from his phone and whatever else he deemed more important than data collection and mentoring students. Oakley had apparently thought that he'd have constant satellite communication, and when he learned, not long after they'd gotten underway, that that was not the case, he told Ray he was leaving. He had already called, while he could still reach him on the marine radio, an old friend with a boat. "A fanatical fisherman," he told Ray. "He works now for Shell in their offshore operations. Lucky I could reach him."

Lucky indeed.

"I feel very confident leaving everything in your capable hands," Oakley had said, with false flattery. "And Helen's. She'll do a better job than I ever could." The false modesty bothered Ray only a trace less than the false flattery.

There was no use arguing with him. Ray could only think about the government grants, the ones that included their names and credentials as co-leaders and spoke to the ways they assured best practices in all the data collection and analysis, the strict adherence to protocols, and the importance of consistency and continuity year to year with the time series. Ray had written into the narrative whole paragraphs about the significance of ocean acidification and the need to track ocean chemistry and understand what that change might mean in the cold, biologically-rich waters off Alaska. This year's grants had specifically emphasized student mentoring and all the benefits that students would receive from spending a week with experts in their fields. And now they would have just the poor sucker zooplankton guy.

On top of that, this was the cruise on which he'd decided to bring his daughter, because he hoped she might discover, before she became an indifferent teenager, a love for science—or at least the ocean. He had hoped to spend some time with her.

What was more important than the research cruise? He had asked Oakley this, but Oakley had only shaken his head. The implication was: *Everything about me is important, and this is only a boat trip.*

Ray looked at his watch. They were nearly on schedule, not far from their first station.

The image of Oakley reaching for that beer was really bothering him. There was a reason they jokingly referred to research cruises as "Seahab." Ray preferred to think of them as "cleansings," as he preferred to think of himself as a social drinker, not an alcoholic, although his wife might disagree. Anyone might get headaches when stopping a regular habit; it happened with coffee drinkers, too. And only once on a previous cruise had he even thought about looking for a bottle of vanilla in the ship's pantry. If his hands shook, it was probably from drinking more coffee than usual. The students, with their youthful, small-fingered competence, easily changed the chlorophyll filters in the lab and only kidded him about his inability to work with tweezers.

Still, it was hard not to want that beer. Or at least to want Oakley not to have it.

Back in his cabin to fetch a data sheet and a hat, he glanced at his interrupted work. He'd got the computer set up, photos of his beloved zooplankton swimming over the screen. The general messiness of books, papers, instructional manuals, loose batteries, the cruise plan folded back on itself to the list of personnel—these were the proof of his life.

He found Colin and the three young women in their padded float coats on the back deck. They were leaning against the rail, exclaiming about the Dall's porpoises jetting around the ship. Tina, the funny one, said something that made the others laugh. Cinda, Ray noted, wore new rubber rain pants, still creased from their packaging. The lovely Helen stood just apart from the others, dark ponytail tossed over one shoulder.

They all watched the porpoises for another few minutes, and then the two women who had been working in the wet lab joined them. They gathered around the giant pumpkin of the CTD —the instrument package they would drop to the bottom of the sea—to await Ray's approval and instructions.

Where was Aurora? He thought she would have come out with the women students. She wanted to see this.

"She's in our cabin," Tina said. "Listening to her iPod. Er— I mean reading. Studying."

Aurora was missing a week of school and had brought along more books than the grad students.

"And what about Annabel? I haven't seen her since last night." Annabel was the artist. The government funders liked them to include a teacher, a journalist, or an artist on every cruise. The theory was that non-scientists could help interpret the work and convince the public of its value, and then the public would convince their legislators to provide funding. *Good luck with that,* Ray always thought before writing up his boilerplate bullshit.

Annabel had been recommended by someone in the art department, but he wasn't sure what her art was, other than she called it "environmental." He had not had time to talk to her yet, except to learn that she wanted to be with the night crew and had something in mind that had to do with bioluminescence. He made a mental note: talk to Annabel. And another: have an open mind about frigging modern art.

"We haven't seen her this morning. Last night she was in the kitchen asking for sheets of nori." Tina had removed her hat that looked like a rabbit's head with floppy pink ears to straighten the wire in the ears.

"She had a bunch of chemistry questions," Cinda said. "She'll be disappointed that Professor Oakley left."

Ray looked at Helen. "Did she talk to you?"

"Not about chemistry," she said in her quiet Helen voice. "About drugs."

"Drugs?"

"She had three different kinds of motion sickness pills, plus those wristbands with the pressure points. She wondered if she would need any of them."

Cinda asked, "So what big-deal consulting thing is Professor Oakley doing?" She was picking at something on her new raingear, and Ray couldn't tell which of them her question was addressed to. Helen just looked away.

He felt obliged to say, "I don't know about any big-deal consulting thing." He waited. "Helen?"

"I don't know that it's a big deal," she said, even quieter than before. "He's been getting a lot of invitations to speak."

Everyone looked uncomfortable now, or maybe they were just eager to get on with the work. Ray stretched his face into what he hoped looked like a smile and said, "It's his loss, missing out on all our fun." He would leave it at that, leave his fresh anger in the cold place behind his heart. How embarrassing was it that students knew more than he did about whatever his so-called colleague was doing? And how annoying that acidification was the media's new darling and everyone wanted a piece of Mr. Acidification himself. No one would miss Ray Berringer and his zooplankton expertise for a week, but apparently the world couldn't live without constant contact with His Hotness Jackson Oakley. Apparently, the public could not get enough explanation of instrument calibration.

Only Marybeth, the undergrad helping with zooplankton studies, hadn't worked with the CTD before, so he quickly went over the basics: conductivity, temperature, depth; the collection bottles that would trip closed at different depths; additional instruments; and the communications cable that connected to the computer.

Ray checked that all the knobs were tight and the troublesome wires free, though he knew that Colin would already have done this. He looked at the milk crates filled with sampling bottles. "Is Alex set up in the lab?" Alex was another incredibly diligent student. Not for the first time, Ray wondered why so many of the best students, like Alex, had Korean and Chinese family names. He had his theories, involving stereotypes that were best left unspoken.

"Almost. He says he has to do the rest himself."

"Computer?"

"Ready to fire."

The CTD drop at the first station went well. When the bottles were back onboard, the three women took their places on overturned buckets, like milkmaids around a cow, to siphon off samples— carbonate, nutrient, chlorophyll. In the wet lab, Alex had finished assembling his towers and was setting filters in place. Ray passed through to the dry lab, where Nastiya and Marybeth were back to work with samples from the first plankton tow. On their high stools, they peered into microscopes while their hands fluttered with eye-droppers and tally counters.

Ray had now entered his realm, the world of living zooplank-ton. Though he was dedicated to the study of marine organisms overall, there was nothing that excited him more than the tiny, footed, flagellated, ciliated, bristled, tentacled, transparent creatures, in all their life-cycle stages, all the way up to pulsing jellyfish as large as the reflected moon. It had become a primary goal in his life to encourage as many people as possible to look at his microfauna, to know that they existed. If ordinary people could admire their great beauty, maybe they would want to learn more about them, and maybe they would begin to understand why it was important for such crea-tures to have a home in the ocean. With his photographs, shot through the lens of a microscope, he was able to capture and enlarge the tiny larval forms of fish, the amphipods, the copepods, the microzooplankton radiolarians with their incredibly intricate min-eral skeletons, and the shelled pteropods known as sea butterflies.

Ray liked to tell students, "My goal is to make people want to hug plankton."

"How's it going?" he asked now. He picked up a clipboard, to have something to do with his hands.

"Is very good," Nastiya said.

It wasn't just her Russian accent; it was the off-the-beat syntax that got him every time, and something about the harshness of her consonants. *Good.* My God, how could "good" be such an attractive, even sexy, word? When he talked with Nastiya he always wanted to adopt her own speech. The couple of times he had inadvertently done this, she had looked at him, wounded, and thought he was making fun of her.

Nastiya's great attribute was her ability to sort zooplankton. She had a tremendous eye for the subtleties between species, and she could sit at a microscope for hours.

His inner voice repeated "Is very good," but his outer one said, "I want to set up the carboys on the foredeck after lunch, and we'll try some incubation."

"Okey-dokey," Nastiya said, finally looking up from the scope and straightening her back.

Okey-dokey?

"So," said Marybeth, "the lack of wind equals lack of mixing equals lower productivity? Not so many nutrients up in the water column where the phytoplankton can reach them? And then the zooplankton have less phytoplankton to eat?"

"Precisely." Ray moved around the table to stand closer to her. The room was tight between the lab tables, the big freezer, and the boxes of supplies. "That's the theory. That's the value of all these data sets, the time series, year after year, to match ocean conditions to primary production and to be able to apply what we learn to understanding and managing the species people care about, like salmon. Other people, I mean. People like us care about zooplankton." He was trying to be funny again. *People like us, crazy people like us, wacky scientists.* He wasn't yet sure that Marybeth was one of them, but she seemed an eager student—and had sworn, when he'd interviewed her for the cruise, that she'd been sailing all her life and had never gotten seasick.

"Let me have a look," he said to Marybeth, taking her warm spot on the metal stool. The sample teemed with several species of the bug-like copepods, with their long rowing antennae and plumose setae extending like the horizontal fins on airplane wings. How could anyone not be in constant awe that a critter only three or four millimeters long could be so finely, elaborately designed? He used the eyedropper to pick out a few, one at a time, and squirt them into the adjacent dish. He counted aloud and she clicked the tally counter.

"A few *Calanus pacificus*," he said. This was significant, but not unexpected. He explained to Marybeth: "One of the southern species that's becoming more common here. A warm water copepod, 'warm' in quotes, moving northward. Smaller than our resident species. If it becomes more dominant, the foraging efficiency of visual predators might be affected. And, to the degree that it displaces our larger, fatter, more nutritious northern species, those predators will have less to eat.

He refocused the lens. "What I'm not seeing is *Limacina helicina*. Nastiya?"

"What?" She said this more aggressively than seemed warranted.

"Are you finding any *Limacina* in your sample?"

"No, I have not."

"And, Marybeth, why are we interested in *Limacina?*"

"Because it's a pteropod, and pteropods are a keystone species. Lots of other things eat them."

"That's right. And pteropods have shells, so they're vulnerable to ocean acidification. That makes them an indicator species as well. There's two species we should be finding in these waters—the more common *Limacina helicina* and the less common *Clione limacina.*"

"The naked one," Nastiya added.

"Right. The naked pteropod, because it only has a shell in its embryonic form and loses it a few days after hatching. It becomes a predator itself, and eats the shelled pteropods."

Nastiya again: "*Clione* suck those suckers right out of their shells." She laughed wickedly.

"Yes, it's specialized that way. It uses its buccal cones to grab and turn the little snails and its hooked proboscis to extract the bodies. OK, I'll leave you two to your work."

Was he concerned about the lack of pteropods in their first tow? Not really. One tow wasn't significant. One season wasn't even significant. That's why they needed tow after tow, year after year, along with all the temperature and other data—the time series that showed trends and long-term change.

The chemistry. The ocean's chemistry—its pH—was going to be significant.

Coffee cup in hand, he went looking for his daughter. He had hope for her inquiring mind, which seemed more promising than her brother's. At sixteen, Sam loved driving fast machines but seemed to have no interest in how they worked or what to do when they stopped working, and he avoided the natural world except as a playground for said machines. Of course, science recognized that the adolescent brain, especially the male one, was incompletely formed. Hadn't he himself been an idiot, in multiple ways, during his teenage years? Aurora, on the other hand, was watchful and attentive to detail, and she loved animals.

But where was she? Not in the galley. He headed for her cabin, a vision of a disapproving Nelda hurrying his steps; you didn't just leave your eleven-year-old to fend for herself in a strange place! What if she'd gotten disoriented and fallen down a ladder into the engine room? What if the ship's crew, whom he knew from previous cruises to be incredibly nice guys, really weren't? What if she was barfing her guts out? If she was seasick now it was going to be a long week's cruise.

But there she was on her back on her top bunk, still wearing purple pajamas. She was plugged into her iPod, jiggling one leg, and staring into another electronic screen that he'd never seen before.

"There you are," he said, pretending that he hadn't just panicked. "Would you like to get dressed and come see what the others are doing?"

"No."

He waited a couple of beats while the electronic device beeped. "Hey," he said, "I'm going to get my binoculars. Let's go up on the flying bridge and see what birds are around. And porpoises. There were porpoises a little while ago. I should have come and got you then."

"OK."

They passed onto the deck where the carboys—those glass incubation jugs they'd hauled from Fairbanks—would be set up, and up the stairs to the pilothouse where Captain Billy refilled Ray's coffee cup with an earth-friendly blend. It was already afternoon in New York, and a Mets game was playing on the radio. Billy showed Aurora the GPS and the depth finder and then the paper charts that marked their course straight out from the mainland to the edge of the continental shelf. She feigned interest, politely. He let her sit in the captain's chair. Ray could tell that Billy really wanted to listen to the Mets game. He thought he'd like to hear the game, too, but he had the wrong job for that.

"Let's go, Nanook," he said. "We've got contracts to fill, eggs to hatch, and cats to kill."

Aurora frowned at him but was already through the door, a fairy princess in an oversized hoodie that reached almost to her knees.

They climbed the ladder behind the pilothouse—Aurora as fearless as a monkey, Ray spotting from below. Topside, she took a seat on the padded bench where biologists on survey cruises sat to record their marine mammal and bird sightings.

Ray's boyhood fascination with birds had never worn off, even as he'd learned that his eyesight and temperament were better suited to small things he could capture and control. That was like so much in his life, starting off large and getting smaller—dinosaurs, then gorillas and bears, hawks and owls and the wood ducks of his

Michigan youth, down to passerines he could hold in his hand, drag-onflies and beetles, the nearly invisible world of microorganisms. Not that there was anything inherently "better" about the larger and more charismatic species, but he had seemed to know at an early age that he himself would not be large—in the sense of attainment—or charismatic. He'd recalibrated his ambitions several times along the way, through school and in the romance department, where he'd somehow lucked out with a wife who exceeded his expectations—but who also knew this and sometimes reminded him.

He raised his binoculars now, setting on a single kittiwake that winged lazily across the bow. Off to one side, three glaucous-winged gulls, two of them juveniles with muddy-looking feathers, rode a half-submerged log.

"Where's the porpoises?" Aurora bounced on the bench.

"You know what to look for?"

"What?"

"Rooster tails. Water will be spraying from their backs when they break the surface. It'll be just quick splashes, they swim so fast. Here." He handed her the binoculars, placing the strap around her neck. "Look at those gulls on the log. Oh, and look! There's a puffin, a horned puffin." The football-shaped bird with its white front beat past; he could just make out the orange bill with his bare eye.

She was slow to track the bird, to lift the glasses and aim them in the right direction. He could tell she was only pretending to see it, for his benefit. It was too far away now.

A retired bird biologist had told Ray, just a couple weeks earlier, that he used to do surveys along the coast behind them, and that the numbers of birds today were mere fractions of what he'd observed in the 1970s. Especially murres. They used to be as thick as flies, he'd said. Now tourists saw a few murres and puffins, maybe a red-faced cormorant, and thought they were looking at abundance because they didn't have anything to compare with. They couldn't begin to imagine the thickly packed and cacophonous cliff colonies, the huge rafts of seabirds covering the nearshore waters, the darkened skies when they flew. Ray had also heard from a tour guide that the guides never said anything to their customers about diminution. If they saw just one puffin or one orca, they exclaimed over it: *You're so lucky to see that!* The tourists went away thinking they'd just had an amazing nature experience in a pristine, undisturbed, Serengeti landscape. Because really, the guide had said to Ray, these people paid a lot of money to go on their tours and cruises and you wanted them to think they were having the best wildlife experience *ever.* Why would you want to depress them by mentioning climate change or that there was oil under the beach sand or that the reason a group of birds was resting on the water in the middle of summer was because they'd had a complete reproductive failure?

And now, on top of all those other insults, an acidifying ocean.

A picture of Jackson Oakley crowded back into his mind—that shiny smooth face that reminded him of the smiley faces people sometimes used, annoyingly, in their e-mails. Who was the man consulting with? What was he saying in his apparently many speeches? Was it all about his precious calibrating instruments and the need to study, study, study more ocean chemistry?

Ray looked at his daughter, her uncombed hair blowing back in the breeze as she held tightly to the binoculars aimed at the sky, at feathers of clouds farther out over the Gulf. The Gulf stretched to the horizon, an achingly beautiful scene if you didn't know better. He was the cup-half-empty guy, the realist, but he knew he ought to let others—children at least—enjoy some innocence. He would bite his tongue. He would not say, "You should have seen this place when . . ."

He did the best he could under the circumstances, which was to say nothing.

Chapter Two

Helen was ravenous after working on the back deck all morning, sampling and hauling plastic totes of glass bottles to safe storage. By the time the cruise was over, she'd have roughly six hundred filled bottles to take back to the university lab. She was facing months of measuring alkalinity and dissolved inorganic carbon. As unreasonable as it seemed, even to her, this anticipation thrilled her.

In the galley, most of the others had already helped themselves and were sitting around the three tables. She served herself a bowl of chowder and a humungous roast beef sandwich oozing caramelized onions. There was pie for dessert.

She slid in where she could, next to their leader. She liked Ray Berringer—a man devoted to his "bugs"—although beyond the cruises she didn't see much of him. Biology did its thing, chemistry did its. This division of departments had always seemed peculiar to her. What they were now calling "Western science" was just beginning to grasp that everything was connected, something Alaska Natives had known forever.

Ray, mouth full, nodded to her. His Sealife Center cap sat a little askew on his head, and graying neck hair merged with his untrimmed beard above a frayed T-shirt collar. She knew he loved the cruises, was clearly more comfortable as a salty sailor than a tweedy professor. Every year different faculty and students came on the cruises, but Ray was a fixture. He was the one who made sure the research happened, who wrote the grants and filed the reports.

She was still not entirely sure why Professor Oakley—Jackson, as she now knew him—had left. He had work he couldn't do from the ship. He and Ray didn't get along, for whatever reason—two alpha dogs, she suspected. But he'd also told her he was finding the whole thing "awkward."

"The whole thing" she understood to include her. In recent weeks their relationship had passed from advisor and student to something she hesitated to call "love," but included spending nonacademic time together and, yes, sex. "Chemistry," they had joked. They had good chemistry, were drawn together by—what? It wasn't just physical attraction; they interested one another. Perhaps it was their differences. In any case they were both adults—she had taken her time getting through school—and they had been discrete. She had felt confident that they could continue to be adult, discrete, and professional on the ship. Apparently he hadn't shared her confidence. Or something.

She played the scene over in her head. Their few minutes in the ship's lab, where he'd found her labeling jars. "I'm not staying." Her confusion; they were already halfway down the bay. "You know this work better than I do." Her protests. "I already told Berringer. It's done." Her questions. His answers, his excuses. "It's not about you," he said at one point. The whole thing, he said, was awkward.

At the end, he'd reached out and cupped the side of her face, and she had felt the heat. He said, "You'll do a great job."

Now, squeezing in among her colleagues, she tried being cheerful. "Unbelievable weather."

Ray swallowed. "It will be interesting. I don't think I've ever seen such stratification so late in the year."

Across from them, Tina and Robert were trading Sven and Ole jokes. In Tina's joke Ole was doing a striptease in front of a tractor. Helen guessed it was OK to tell bigoted jokes about Minnesotan farmers. They were not a protected minority, not that she knew of. People were more careful about telling Eskimo jokes these days; at least they didn't tell them so much in her presence. Her own sense of humor tended to be less hah-hah, quieter, culture-based. The small teasings and subtle ironies of the Iñupiat weren't always obvious to others, but Arctic cultures wouldn't have lasted long without them. They'd needed ways of amusing themselves in the cold and dark. More critically, humor diffused conflict and kept people alive.

Helen grimaced at the ridiculous punch line, Ole's confusion between "attract her" and "a tractor."

On Ray's other side, his daughter picked at her food. Clearly she'd taken more than she could eat, eyes bigger than her stomach. How many times had Helen's grandmother—her *aana*—told Helen and her cousins when they were small about the boy who ate too much? They'd loved that story, which went on and on, the greedy boy eating all the berries and greens and fish until he eventually ate a whole whale and drank an entire lake. It was a funny story, but it also taught a lesson.

Those cousins—most of them—still lived on the North Slope and were married with children of their own, or not married but with children. Helen was old now—twenty-six—to not have children, and she knew some of her girl cousins wondered about her and felt sorry for her. In their minds children were essential; a woman without them was incomplete, lacking, lonely. They would never say this, but they would tease her: *Where is your baby?* At Thanksgiving she would see them all in Igalik, at the holiday feast and the wedding of the cousin who was having her second baby. She was looking forward to that.

Now, with another bite of her sandwich, she watched Ray's

hand sneak over and snatch a potato chip from his daughter's plate. The girl had turned toward the kitchen and didn't notice. Ray did it again, walking his fingers like a spider across the space between them. This time Aurora noticed and swatted at his hand with a little shriek. It must have been an old routine for them. The sweetness of the play caught Helen unawares, and she raised her napkin to cover her smile.

Ray turned to her with mayonnaise on his mustache. "We'll be a fine team, you and me and this bunch of galoots."

After lunch, back on deck, more of the essential monkey work. Helen tightened a last cap, stood to stretch her back. Tina and Cinda were debating something about the bottle numbering system, and she turned from them to watch the ship's wake drawing its long, frothy line across the blue. She could never look at the ocean and see just the surface; her eye wanted to take her down, as though into the illustrations she'd loved in grade school: past the little fish and the magnified plankton near the top to the jellyfish drifting below and then the bigger fish, always sharks, on down to the huge halibut stirring the mud on the bottom and the crabs and anemones and corals, all the waving tentacles and open mouths, marine snow falling, the big whales coming up from a dive, all that hidden world. What was the number? Ninety-nine percent of the living space on the planet is in the oceans? And they knew so little about it, still?

"Oh, man, have I got the farts," Tina said.

"Methane," Cinda said. "Twenty times more potent than carbon dioxide as a greenhouse gas. You're killing us."

"Yeah, me and seven billion other people. Not to mention the cows."

Alex came out and took away more bottles for filtering.

"Dude," Tina shouted after him, "take a break. Save some of that for us."

Cinda looked up at Helen. "That was cool about the press release, how much it made the news. People are starting to pay attention. What seems weird is that no one's screaming about it being a hoax. You'd think the nutcases who oppose climate science would have a problem with the ocean absorbing CO_2 from the atmosphere. What's up with that?"

The press release that Jackson had sent out had, in fact, been drafted by Helen. In Helen's draft, it had explained for those who were still new to the idea what ocean acidification was and raised the alarm about the change in pH that they were tracking in Alaskan waters. In its final form, though, the statement focused more on the fact that ocean acidification was being studied at the university's new Office of Ocean Acidification Science, and it didn't mention that it was a danger, right now, to sea life. Helen had felt a little hurt by this—that she missed the assignment somehow. She was more hurt that Jackson hadn't talked to her about the edits. When she'd asked why he decided to downplay the new data that suggested— showed—that Alaska's cold waters were already significantly affected by acidification, his answer—not entirely convincing to her—was that the point of the release was to announce the new office. He reminded her of the "rule" that a letter to the editor or a press release should be limited to one point; otherwise people got confused. One subject. Next time, another subject.

Cinda's question might have been rhetorical, but Helen answered it anyway. "Maybe because it's straightforward chemistry?"

Cinda rinsed her last bottle. She was filling two at a time now, one in each hand. "I don't know. All the data in the world don't seem to convince people that we've got a problem with greenhouse gases. They still think Al Gore made up global warming to get rich."

Helen had heard exactly that from their congressman, when he'd spoken on campus. He'd claimed that global warming was "the biggest scam since Teapot Dome," and that Al Gore was just out to make money. He'd insisted that just as many scientists didn't believe in global warming as did and that his opinion was just as good as anyone else's. The students in the audience had been stunned by his belligerence, and when the moderator tried to pin him down on the sources of his information, the congressman cut him off, yelling, "Don't give me that," and continuing his rant about how it was all just natural cycles and what was permafrost anyway—just frozen dirt. He'd said, "There's nothing pretty about ice. Ice grows nothing." She remembered those exact words, because he'd said them with such contempt.

That day in the auditorium Helen had sat on her hands, horrified that a person in such an important position could be either so ignorant or so corrupt—and which was it? Even an Alaskan grade school student knew that sea ice was an essential part of the Arctic ecosystem—not just the habitat for species like polar bears and ringed seals but that the underside of it grew—yes, *grew*—algae that fed the zooplankton and supported the food web. So was what she heard ignorance, or was it obfuscation, meant to deny the truth and protect the interests of those who benefited from destroying ice?

And Teapot Dome? Wasn't that a scandal, not a scam? She'd gone home and looked it up. How odd to compare global warming to a bribery scandal, specifically one in which a government official took bribes from oil companies!

What was especially incongruous was that the reason the congressman had been speaking on campus was to take credit for federal funding for the new acidification office. She had to think he hadn't known what he was doing.

The ship slowed, and the captain's voice boomed through the speaker. "Whales at one o'clock!"

Helen dashed for the binoculars she'd left in the boot room and headed for the stairs, close behind Colin and the girls from the lab. From the main deck they climbed the ladder to the flying bridge.

The ship had slowed completely now, the engines a gentle throb through the steel deck. Colin was pointing, and she saw the vapor of a blow trailing off, still well out in front of them. Then another blow beside it, tall and straight up.

"Two of them," someone said. "At least two."

And, "They might be fin whales."

They all strained to look, cameras and camera phones and tablets pointed.

The whales blew again, closer, and their long dark backs cut through the surface. They were paralleling the ship on the starboard side. They were big whales, that was for sure.

"Fins," Colin said under his breath.

Ray was there now, and his daughter, who wasn't dressed for the outside and had her bare arms crossed over her chest. Ray was explaining that fin whales mostly fed on plankton, lots of euphasiids in these waters, and on forage fish. "Two tons of food a day," he said. "They're sometimes called 'greyhounds of the sea' because of their speed, which they use to circle schools of fish to bunch them up before gulping them."

Then the whales were right beside the ship, so close Helen didn't even need her binoculars. The water was so clear; she was looking through the surface and down into it, at the entire bodies of fin whales. The larger one was just feet from the ship now, seeming to look them over. Its spade-shaped head was knobby around the twin blowholes, and whitish chevron-shaped marks stretched down its long back to the elegant slice of dorsal fin. It turned its head, showing the white side of its jaw. It rolled around to face the other way, and she saw the other jaw—the dark one—and remembered this asymmetry of the fin whale, white on one jaw and dark on the other.

"Did you see that?" she said quietly, to anyone who was listening. "Did you see the way it flashed us with the white side of its jaw?"

She could imagine now what she'd only read, that biologists speculated that the jaw coloring had to do with that fish herding Ray had just mentioned. Fin whales were known to circle clockwise, which meant the white jaw would be visible to the fish, could be like a flashing light. But why would they want to circle only clockwise? Why not have two white jaws and be an ambidextrous circler?

The scientist in her wanted a theory, wanted to understand, needed more than awe.

A voice came from beside her. "Can you imagine anyone wanting to kill such a magnificent creature?"

It was the artist, the woman she'd met briefly at the safety orientation when they first boarded and then later had the short conversation with about seasickness meds. Now here she was, googly-eyed about the whales.

"Actually, yes," Helen said. "Native people hunt and eat whales. Not fin whales, not in Alaska, but bowheads and belugas, and in Russia, gray whales."

The woman—petite in an oversized and overstuffed parka, with bleached-blond hair matted into dreadlocks and dangling beads—turned to her. Helen watched her register *dark hair, dark eyes, skin a little yellowish, Mongolian eye fold, whoops.* Now the woman looked embarrassed. "I'm so sorry. I didn't mean that. I meant the Japanese commercial whalers that do it for the meat. The Inuit have a different relationship, I know."

"The whales give themselves to the people." Helen said this instinctively, rhetorically, defensively. It was what she'd been raised to know, and if she didn't actually believe this—she was a scientist, after all—many of her relatives did. While it might not be literal truth, the belief centered on respect; if you behaved well and were grateful for your food the animals would see that you didn't go hungry. She wasn't sure why she'd made such a bald statement to a strange woman, except that she was annoyed by her attitude and her use of the word "Inuit." It was not a name that Alaska Natives used for themselves.

"Yes," the woman said, and Helen noticed she was quite a bit older than she'd first thought. Her face was like a shriveled apple, like the faces of apple-headed dolls some of the grannies sold at Native arts fairs. Helen didn't understand why a woman that age, even an artist, would be wearing at sea spackled tights, pink ballet slippers, and a giant puffy parka.

The woman asked, "Do you think the smaller one is the baby of the other one?"

"I'm not a whale expert," Helen said, "but that's probably a good bet."

The smaller one—the likely calf—was at the surface now, exhausting spray that nearly reached the ship. Helen breathed deeply, hoping for a whiff of fishy breath. The ship was one hundred twenty feet long, and the whales beside it—approaching half that length—made it feel small and insubstantial, as though it were a toy boat and they were little Lego people snapped onto it.

"They're telling us something," the woman said. She held her digital camera at arm's length, shooting in directions and at angles that seemed odd to Helen.

Helen was trying very hard not to be rude. "What are they telling you?"

"They're sizing us up. They're saying, 'OK, you're innocuous.' Or they might be saying, 'Screw you, stop messing up our home and stealing our food.' The water's reflective, so it's hard for me to read the energy field."

Helen resisted expressing an opinion about energy fields. The larger whale was sinking lower, not diving but sinking like a submarine, its blue back blurring into the depths. Then it was under the ship, and everyone inhaled and turned to the other rail. Both whales were leaving them, off to that side and moving away, just the pencil lines of their backs showing as they surfaced, and then just the vapor of their twin breaths.

The ship began to move again. The captain, out on the bridge wing, waved his cap and called to them, "I have never seen whales that fucking good, and I've been doing this for thirty years!"

After that night's dinner, Tina organized two teams for charades. Book and movie titles were popular, as were marine themes. *Silent Spring* was easy. *Twenty Thousand Leagues Under the Sea* was hard. Cinda was surprisingly good at acting, and Colin made up new rules. The artist, Annabel—Helen had finally learned her name—contributed titles and song lyrics that no one else knew and was very loud and random in shouting out her guesses. She had a laugh like a goose cackle and kept, for some reason, repeating "caudal peduncle." Ray joined them, but when the clue from Alex was "jumping jacks," he went from "jacks" to "jack to "Jackson Oakley" and made a snide comment about "our missing colleague who was too important to be here."

Helen covered her discomfort by getting a glass of water. She understood why Ray would be unhappy with Jackson, but she didn't think it was very professional for one professor to criticize another in front of students. She'd never heard Jackson say anything bad about Ray. He didn't talk about him at all.

The correct answer was Jacques Cousteau, which someone guessed after Alex pretended to be a pigeon, cooing.

After that they played Cinda's game, which wasn't really a game. Helen knew it from cultural training sessions, where it was called "values clarification." *If you were a color, what color would you be?* The group was mostly shades of green, and Aurora was purple. *If you were a bird, what bird would you be?* Arctic tern, chickadee, harlequin duck, sandhill crane, peregrine falcon. Helen said she'd be the blue of glacier ice and a golden plover. She was glad she wasn't a psychologist, because even to a non-psychologist the immediate and rather flippant associations the group tossed out seemed to tell more about each of them than they knew. Including herself—was she really like ice? Ray, of course, had to be especially flippant. If he was a bird, he'd be an Eskimo curlew because, "then the Eskimo curlew wouldn't be extinct, which it seems to be, or else, I guess, I'd be extinct."

Ray offered up the next category: "If you were a pteropod, which would you be, *Limacina* or *Clione,* shelled or naked?" Most of them wanted to identify with *Limacina,* the "sea butterfly," because the shell was so jewel-like, as well as protective, and to "fly" through the sea with its winged foot was pretty cool. Only Ray and Colin chose the carnivorous *Clione*—for its own exotic beauty, they said.

"It eats the other ones," Aurora complained.

"We all have to eat," Marybeth said.

"Circle of life," Tina intoned. "Circle of life."

When everyone had gone off to prepare for the night shift or to watch a movie or sleep, Helen settled into a corner of the galley with licorice from the candy drawer and began reading her advanced organic chemistry text, the section on aliphatic nucleophilic substitution. She was still on the first page when Annabel returned— wrapped now in a pink woven shawl pinned at her chest with a green papier-mâché brooch the size of a fist. "I don't want to bother you," she said. "I can see you're studying. But I'm told you're the one I should talk to about ocean acidification. I need to understand the chemistry. Can we talk sometime?"

Helen closed her book on a scrap of napkin. "We could do it right now if you want." She'd heard this at a conference: never pass up an opportunity to educate.

Annabel nodded vigorously, hair beads jangling. *"Formidable!"* she shouted in a French accent. *"Tout de suite* I'll be back."

And she was, as though she had flown to her cabin. She

thumped onto the bench across from Helen and opened her drawing pad to a clean sheet. "Pretend I'm a third-grader," she said. "I'm that stupid."

"I doubt you're stupid," Helen had to say. "But stop me if I start getting too detailed for your purposes. The basic chemistry isn't too complicated. And, by the way, you'll be hearing us shorthand 'ocean acidification'; we call it OA."

She talked, and Annabel, several rings sparkling on each hand, made chicken-scratch notes in green ink.

She wanted to make sure Annabel understood that the ocean wasn't turning to acid, only becoming more acidic, while still being on the alkaline side of the pH scale. "Sea life evolved in a very stable pH situation. We're asking creatures to live in a different environment now, very suddenly. This is the hard part—we don't know exactly how individual species will respond—are responding. We know that corals are having a very hard time. And you heard Ray talking about pteropods, the marine snails. They're very vulnerable. Anything with a carbonate shell is affected."

She drew a carbon dioxide molecule on Annabel's paper, then a water molecule and one for carbonic acid. "This is the thing," she said. "In the atmosphere, carbon dioxide stays carbon dioxide. The carbon and oxygen atoms stay bonded. In the ocean, CO_2 reacts with seawater. It forms carbonic acid, which releases these hydrogen ions and reduces the pH. The hydrogen ions combine with carbonate ions to form bicarbonates. Then there are fewer carbonate ions left to make calcium carbonate, the major building blocks needed by shell builders."

Annabel was studying her crude drawing. Helen hesitated to get into the aragonite versus calcite distinction or to be specific about saturation horizons. She knew how easy it was to pile on too much, to let her passion for the subject overtake another person's tolerance for it. Keep it simple, Jackson was always saying.

Annabel looked up. "So you could say that reduced carbonate ions lower the saturation state."

Helen tried not to be surprised by the non-third-grade reference. "That's exactly what we say. We say the water is undersaturated with aragonite, one of the main forms of calcium carbonate."

Annabel said, "Ray showed me some pictures. His little animals have to work harder to form the calcium carbonate for their shells, and if it gets too bad, their shells actually start to dissolve."

"That's exactly right. In the Arctic we're already seeing corrosive water."

"We really are fucked."

Colin, who'd been noisily poking through the candy drawer, came and stood by them while he unwrapped a Sugar Daddy. "Such language," he said. He glanced at Annabel's pad. "What kind of art do you do?"

Annabel extracted a pair of sunglasses from her purse and put them on. "Just about everything. Drawings, paintings, sculpture, collage, fiber, constructions of various kinds, some printmaking, installations. Sometimes it's ephemeral. Usually there's an element of healing."

Colin did a funny thing with his eyebrows.

Helen said, "I imagine you have a particular project with us?"

"I brought materials," Annabel said. "Colored pencils, paper, some clay, wire. I have to see what presents itself. I don't impose anything. Very possibly there'll be an element of light. I'll leave you to your studies." She started to get up. "Sugar Daddy!"

Colin jumped aside, as though in fear of having his candy ripped from his hands.

"I would *love* to have that wrapper. Just the paper."

Colin peeled off the paper and handed it over. Then Annabel, in her movie-star glasses, was to and through the doorway, waving the candy wrapper in one hand, flapping her art pad with the other, and calling back to them, *"Grazie, grazie,* beautiful people!"

Colin turned to Helen. "Ephemeral art?"

Ephemeral art was the least of it. Helen wanted to know how a person who seemed to understand saturation horizons could also embrace woo-woo energy fields, and why that person would need to add Italian to her enthusiastic French. People thought *she* lived in two worlds.

CHAPTER THREE

When it was sufficiently dark, Annabel joined the crew to watch them tow for plankton. Robert, the kindly doctoral student in charge, explained the mechanics of a bizarre contraption called a Multinet as three other students, in their float coats and steel-toed rubber boots, danced around the back deck to "Let's Spend the Night Together."

The idea was that, under the cover of darkness, zooplankton and small fish rose through the water column to feed near the surface. The tows, with different fine-meshed nets opening in different parts of the water column, would capture what was present at the various depths. The collections would then be preserved in jars and hauled back to the university for analysis—to determine how they compared to other years and how they related to water temperature and other conditions.

"It's mostly plankton," Robert said, as he jerked on the Multinet's frame, sliding it another foot toward the stern. He was a tall man with a freckled face and broad hips emphasized by his blousy, bibbed rain pants. Annabel was sure he was gay, not that she cared about such things. "We won't get many fish," he was saying. "Fish can outswim the nets, so any fish we collect are usually dead or dying. They also get squished once they're in the net, from the pressure."

The ship slowed, and the nearly full moon that had been trailing them began to make tremendous bounces through the dark sky. They were rolling up and over the swells now, as opposed to plowing straight through. Off the stern, fingerling fish leapt from the water like popcorn, flashing silver as they caught light from the deck.

Annabel got out of the way while they deployed the Multinet, and then Ray appeared in his slippers and watched with her.

The cable went out, and where it cut through and disturbed the water a sparkling that was not reflected moonlight surrounded it.

"OMG," she said. Her hands flew to the top sides of her head.

"Dinoflagellates," Ray said. He looked at her, as if trying to see whether she had any clue about what was happening, or if her head might be coming apart. "These are single-celled, microscopic, major producers in the ocean because they're photosynthetic—they deliver the sun's energy to the rest of the food web. Their bioluminescence is a defense mechanism, triggered when a disturbance, like the movement of a potential predator, deforms the cell." He might have been laughing, amused with what he was saying. "The light flash is meant to attract a secondary predator to attack the one trying to eat the dinoflagellate. What a system, huh?"

He went on to tell her more about bioluminescence than she could possibly understand—about oxygen, ions, chlorophyll, cysts. Different organisms used it for different, and sometimes multiple, reasons: to evade predators, to attract prey, to communicate with their own species ("Here I am—come mate with me"), to communicate to other species ("Here I am—get the hell away from me").

She was stuck on the name. "Terrible whips," she said.

"Huh?"

"From the Greek and Latin. Like *dinosaur*, terrible lizard."

"Actually," he said, "I think it's *dinos*, whirling. Whirling whips. They have the two flagella. Their propulsion—one makes them whirl, the other acts like a rudder." He went digging in his pocket, pulled out a crinkly packet, held it out to her. "Ginger?"

She shook her head. She wanted to keep her eyes on the spark-glow, dimmer now, and on the mercuric surface of the moonlit water. All that nearly invisible life was pulsing together in a radiant force, a vital energy. She could feel her Vishuddha chakra heating her throat and spilling into the flow that unites all creation. Her hands took the prayer position over her heart.

"Tomorrow," Ray said, "come by the dry lab if it's not too rough, and we can look at some live zooplankton. I'll find you some ptero-pods. We'll do a ring net tow in the morning and see what we get."

"I'd like that," she said. "Thank you." Annabel would never mention it—not unless he asked—but the man's aura was darker and ashier than a healthy person's should be.

Very early the next morning, Annabel stood alone at the rail, watching the Gulf of Alaska pitching into white peaks that collided with other waves and collapsed. "A confused sea" was the term she'd heard for this, when individual waves come at one another from different directions. She loved this, the way the waves moved, and the language of confusion. She held her camera out over the rail and pointed it straight down, snapped a picture, then studied the image on the little screen. The focus was as confused as the sea, blues blurred and softened into such beauty that she wondered for two seconds why she even tried being an artist, why it wasn't enough to simply welcome what nature already provided, to see it clear or squint-eyed or as though through tears.

But then, it was because she *was* an artist that she had that aesthetic reaction. And if her personal aesthetic leaned to the blurry, abstracted side of things, that was what she could present to the world: the beauty not of nature itself but of sight. She had written in her last artist statement, "I don't copy nature; I reveal it." When Ray had invited her to look at his magnified zooplankton photos, she'd admired them. They were clear, literal, scientific images. The pteropods she was anxious to learn about featured exquisite whirled shells, gossamer wings, buds of antennae like tiny soft nipples. The representations were perfect unto themselves. But they were not art. The most imaginative things about them were what some people saw in them, the common names they'd given the two kinds: sea butterflies and sea angels. So much lovelier than snails and slugs.

Ray had been kind to take the time to show her his photos and to explain some of the plankton studies. His daughter had been with them, looking more interested in Annabel's hair than in the photos and the colored graphs that showed what Ray called a time series. "Are you famous?" she'd asked.

Annabel was used to getting this question from children and had learned that modesty was not her friend. If she said no, children simply wandered off and gave her, and whatever art lessons she might have been teaching, their complete disregard, as though she were no better than a fly, or one of their own parents. But if she said yes, she had their full, admiring attention.

She was nowhere near famous—how many artists were?— but she did have adequate credentials. She'd once, years ago, won an arts council fellowship, and the Anchorage Museum had purchased one of her light installations. She also had several commissioned projects in and on various public buildings, including a wastewater plant. And she had been to two prestigious artist colonies. A medium-sized fish in a small pond, she knew, but what the heck.

"Yes, I'm quite famous," she'd told Aurora, who regarded her with revived interest.

Annabel liked science and scientists; really, she did. She was always interested in the links between art and science. Both required creative minds, speculation and hypothesizing, experimenting, sometimes-tedious detail work, a willingness to fail and try again. She read about the sciences and did her best to understand them, at least in the broad scope of meaning. She appreciated their importance.

She could not say the same for the reverse relationship. What was with the raised eyebrows and rolled eyes, the looks of incomprehension? The worst of it had come from that constipated man who was fortunately now gone. When they'd first boarded the ship and she'd struck up what she thought was a cordial conversation about the chemicals used in papermaking and why she made her own art paper, he'd looked around her as though searching for an emergency exit. Although now that she knew he really *was* looking for a way off the ship, she would cut him some slack. His mind would not have been prepared to consider the ecological shadow of treated paper products and the superiority of hemp paper.

Annabel snapped another picture as a milky jellyfish floated by. Her past was streaming into memory: water lapping at her perfect small toes, the cries of gulls, the salty taste when she accidentally swallowed a mouthful of ocean. Back there, at the Jersey Shore, the child she was had collected shells, of course, and arranged them carefully on her windowsill at home, inspired by their whorls and polished shapes, by their pink and cream colors. She'd brought home starfish, too, and was aghast when they began to stink and she realized she'd dehydrated and killed living creatures.

The intricate designs of bird feet in the sand, the patterns the waves and wind made in the same sand, the different colors of the ocean on different days, the shells and the pebbles and the tiny grains of sand themselves—all of that, she was sure, had shaped her as an artist. She was all about seeing the patterns and finding the sequences, *this* and *this* and *this* going together, and then breaking the pattern, with *that*.

Naturally, she'd been drawn to Alaska. In addition to having incredible light, it was a good fit for her pioneering, anarchistic bent. She'd lived now for a long time in the Interior, attuned to the curves of oxbow rivers and the lines of birch forests, to feathers of frost and the peach colors of winter days. She'd worked with natural materials like birchbark and branches, always careful to collect only from downed trees and not too much of that. She still had a recurring nightmare that involved writhing starfish, legions of them baking in the sun with all their podia flailing.

Here she was finally on a ship at sea! Her entire boating career to this point had been one summer sternwheeling down the silty Tanana past dog yards and expensive log homes. Her, a cruise guide! It hadn't been much money, but more than an artist makes, and the tourists had been agreeable enough, even if they were more interested in the chicken dinner than the river and all began to look alike after awhile, which was a terrible thing for an artist to admit.

The shoreline now was already far behind them, lost somewhere beyond a bank of fog. The bottom was a long way down. She took another photo of the water, and then of water meeting fog, distance.

She remembered, from when she was very young, an annoying uncle joking with her: "Why does the ocean roar? Because it has crabs on its bottom!" He had thought it fun to pinch her skinny butt. He would not have known that her own delight came from somewhere else, from within the language. A bottom was one thing, and it was something else compared to that thing. That might have been the beginning, for her, of visualizing possibility.

Later that morning, when she got to put her eye to the microscope focused on *Limicina helicina,* the shelled pteropod, she was very excited, until she realized she was looking at the fluttering of her own eyelash. This was not easy work—bouncing in a boat while trying to hold still and peer through a lens at a minuscule something that was sloshing around with a bunch of other teeny-tinies. It seemed they were in the wrong season to find many mature ptero-pods, which would be visible to the eye—like a lentil pea, Ray had said. She conjured up the images she'd seen on his computer. In those, brownish snail bodies stretched from their spiraling, trans-lucent shells into the parts that were specialized feet, not made for sliming along trails but for moving—flapping, even—through water. In some of the photos the foot was clearly split in two, exactly like wings. The foot-wings, Ray told her now, with what seemed like excessive pleasure, made a mucous that was cast out like a net to catch algae. "That's how it feeds."

It was good that she had a well-developed imagination, because when Annabel finally thought she could see the little beast she couldn't see any shell at all, just a tubish body and fuzzy twitch-ing parts that she assumed were the mucousy wings. It was entirely possible she was out of focus or still looking at an eyelash.

"Especially in the spring, these guys are usually found in swarms in surface waters," Ray was saying. "Not so much now. The other pteropod we have here, the naked, carnivorous one we were talking about, is larger but much less common."

It was a pteropod-eat-pteropod world, that was for sure. Ann-abel remembered seeing the naked one among Ray's photos, too. It looked to her like a miniature—very miniature—beluga whale, its long bulbous body flanked by stubby foot-wings that were like the whale's stubby flippers. It was largely transparent, with a peachy sac in its center. Ray had made a point of telling her that in a well-fed animal, the sac, which was its digestive gland, would be bigger and darker.

"You are wearing glitter?" the Russian girl asked, with what seemed like alarm.

"*Da*," she said.

"*Da?*" The girl's nostrils flared, horselike.

"Yes, I am wearing glitter." Annabel was not, as a rule, very big on conventional makeup, but she did like to apply a little metallic blush to give her face sparkle. The color in this instance, an orange-gold, was called "perpetual praline." Heck, she hadn't bought it for its silly name or the fact that it was "lickable"; she'd just liked the color, and the discount price. It occurred to her now that perhaps the Russian girl was afraid that flecks would fall into her sample and be counted as a new species.

Annabel was, if nothing else, glad to be in the presence of living, moving, perhaps flailing creatures. The previous night the ones from the Multinet looked, once they were concentrated and "fixed" in jars, like pea soup. "Mostly euphasiids," Robert had said to her, swirling the contents. The deepest tow had picked up a couple of finger-length lantern fish that everyone had seemed excited about. Lantern fish, one of the girls told her, lived in the deep sea and were bioluminescent—except that particular pair were quite dead and squished, their big eyes popping free. But this was cool: each species had its own pattern of lighting up, and males and females of the same species had different lit parts.

"And what is your art?" the Russian girl asked now.

The Project, as she thought of it, was in fact coming together, had all night and all day been forming and reforming in her mind, like a school of fish swimming in circles and grabbing bites of plankton. She hadn't spoken of it, but now both girls and Ray, smelling of ginger, were staring at her, waiting to hear.

"I'm building paper sculptures," she said, although she had not yet begun the actual work of the paper folding and softening she had in mind, nor had she settled on the inscriptions they would carry.

"Sculptures of what?"

These very literal, very concrete, very need-to-know people— they couldn't help themselves.

"We'll see," she said. "Inspired by the sea and its creatures. And by your work," she added pointedly.

Ray looked down his somewhat-reddened nose. "Does it have a title?"

"Titles usually come last for me. You know, given by the work."

He didn't know; that seemed clear. He rearranged his face, a jollier look. "Don't forget our charismatic microfauna."

Huh?

"The pteropods in particular. We love them."

"He is hugging *Clione,*" the girl added.

Annabel again visualized the blobby naked one, the one that ripped the others from their shells. Beautiful, in the way that every being was, but the charisma was escaping her. Some people called it a "sea angel?" She would meditate on that. These fine, obsessive people were indulging her, and she would indulge them back.

For the next few days Annabel worked like a dervish. She was in and out of the dry lab, putting cake pans of water in the big freezer, then popping them free and stacking up her ice floe collection. In her cabin and in the small library where she could spread out, she was cutting, folding, softening, and sculpting her homemade paper. She recruited Aurora to help her massage the paper to softness. Her locker filled with creations. She forgot to attend meals at the scheduled times and lived on fruit and nuts from the bowl in the galley. One day, when she sought the air, she watched an albatross following the ship, its huge long wings scything, and she was so overcome with emotion and exhaustion that she had to lie flat on the deck in the reclining goddess pose until her equilibrium was restored.

The girls in the lab went about their business, counting copepods and incubating batches of various zooplankton species to calculate their growth rates. They listened to music on their iPods and talked too loudly. Once, squeezing past with pans of fresh water, Annabel bumped into Marybeth and spilled water on the floor.

"Oh, no!" Marybeth shouted. "I'm so sorry!"

"*No problema,*" Annabel reassured her. "But could you open the freezer door for me?"

Marybeth pulled out her earbuds and opened the door. "You don't need to remeasure? Is it water?"

"Yes, water, H_2O, neutral pH of 7. See what I'm learning?"

"You learn that freshwater freeze?" said Nastiya. "You are brilliant scientist."

"It's for her art," Marybeth said.

"What art you make from your frozen Frisbees?"

Annabel gave Marybeth a big wink. "The art is incubating," she said.

An hour later she came back with two inch-high sculptures of paper that she'd rubbed and rolled into tender gray softness. The girls were gone from the lab. She balanced each of the sculptures on the microscopes' flat plates, as though they were next to be examined. One, she decided, bore a faint resemblance to a coccolithophore, the incredibly ornate soccer ball she'd been studying in books she found in the library. It was only an alga, she'd discovered, and got less love than the little animals, the way a cabbage got less love than a moose. The other—the one she gifted to the sensitive Marybeth—had appendages that might be wings, though, of course, that wasn't the point—to look like anything. Instead, the sculptures carried an intention. She didn't want to have to explain the intention but to let it simply emanate from her hands through the material and shaping into the universe—a healing gesture. Each one also carried a manifest symbol, folded inside where it would not be seen but might still be felt, like a heartbeat. She'd written the characters in the seal script she'd taught herself during her Chinese language phase. For Marybeth: *sweet* and *happy.* For Nastiya: *kindness.*

The right night, their next-to-last on the water, arrived. Annabel made the announcement at dinner. She stood in the front of the galley in her Nepalese robe and a paper headdress decorated with silver stars and announced, "The spontaneous event that will not quite be spontaneous—because I'm telling you about it now—will occur tonight after dark. You may wish to appear on deck."

They all just looked at her.

When she was seated again with her curried rice, Ray slid in next to her.

"What spontaneous event?"

"My art."

"And what might that be?"

He didn't look well. She would have liked to assist him with his diet.

"The paper sculptures I've been making."

He seemed to relax then. After a minute he said, "It would probably be a good idea for me to know a little more. Do you require anything from the crew? You're going to be on deck? Isn't paper going to blow away? We can't have anything going in the water." He added, "Not that you would want to lose it."

"I was going to go chat with the captain after dinner, about pausing for the performance."

"Now it's a performance?"

She really didn't want to go into detail, especially since the whole room seemed to be silenced (but for the engine noise and the cook's clattering with the roasting pans), not even chewing now but leaning in, toward her and Ray. "Remember when you asked me for a title?"

Ray nodded, but she could tell he didn't remember.

"Let's not play games," he said. "I'm in charge of this cruise, and I really need to know what everyone's doing. It's a team effort, even you."

"I'm calling it 'Fire and Ice,'" she said.

"Well, I trust you're not going to be lighting anything on fire,"

Ray said. "Fire on ships is a pretty big no-no."

"Oh," she said.

He leaned in closer. "What exactly did you have in mind?"

"Maybe we should go into the hallway," she said.

Even then, she was sure everyone in the galley heard his explosion. It was something like, "Fuck no! You can't light paper on fire! And you can't put anything in or on the ocean! That's completely prohibited by MARPOL!"

(Like she was supposed to know who or what MARPOL was.)

And then: "I don't give a fuck if it's organic and biodegradable! I don't give a fuck about neutral pH."

She had never guessed that the man who loved copepods could project quite so much negative energy. Something was seriously out of alignment.

They went up to the wheelhouse to talk to Captain Billy. He was picking on his guitar, but he stopped to hear her out. If his eyebrows went up, at least he didn't yell. Potentially this was because Ray had already led with, "I told her absolutely no, but she wants to explain to you herself what she was going to come up here and tell you anyway. It's about *art*."

And so she had to defend the whole effort again. The paper she used was made from plant fibers and had not killed any trees or been bleached or chemically treated in any way; it was acid-free. The ice was made from freshwater and was not significantly different from sea ice, which loses its salt when it freezes. (She knew they must both know all about sea ice, but she felt it important to show that *she* knew.) There was a little soy-based ink on some of the sculptures, very organic. And she would be using very small dabs of an organic clay as adhesive. She would not light the sculptures until they were in the water, and she would use a pole to immediately steer them away from the ship. The weather was as calm as could be, a good omen.

Captain Billy looked amused.

"It's out of the question," Ray said.

"I've been seeing a lot of pomarine jaegers," Captain Billy said, pointing through the window. "More than usual."

Annabel said, "I'll wear a float coat and will also tie into a line that someone can hold. I'm always very safety-conscious."

Captain Billy turned to her. "You won't throw any stones into the sea, will you?"

"No, of course not. I don't have any stones. It's just paper and ice, and they'll both disappear."

Ray started to say something, but Captain Billy cut him off. "Because throwing stones into the sea causes huge waves and storms."

Annabel couldn't tell from his face if she was meant to believe him.

"And no flowers?"

"I don't have any flowers. Where would I get flowers?" She didn't say that perhaps some of her sculptures might *look* like flowers.

"That's good, because flowers on a ship are very bad luck. You know why?"

"Why?"

"Because they can be made into a funeral wreath."

Ray said, "I thought it was because flowers would draw it to earth and other flowers. The same reason it's no good to paint a vessel green. That's just asking for it to go aground."

Annabel looked from one to the other. Surely they didn't believe that crap?

Captain Billy glanced down at her sandals. "I have to ask. You don't have flat feet, do you?"

"No, I do not have flat feet."

"Because flat feet are very bad luck on any boat." He adjusted something with the steering. "Well, then," he said. "We've done worse things on this ship. Haven't we, Ray? That time two years ago, the spring cruise?"

Ray pressed his lips together.

"But what I don't get," Captain Billy said, "is, how is that art, if there's nothing left to see? Sorry for my ignorance."

"Exactly my point," Ray said. "How does that meet the objective of bringing our work to the public, of helping to interpret oceanography so that the public will have a deeper appreciation of what we do out here?"

They both looked at Annabel, like sharks that thought they had her trapped. But this was a question that she had heard before. "With art," she said, "you don't look for results. It operates in ways we can't anticipate and in ways that might not be obvious. This project is about healing the ocean. That's the best work I can do, putting my energy and my skills into that." She paused before adding, "This is what I do. I don't question what *you* do. I figure you know your business, and I trust that it has value even when I don't understand what the measurements are or how to read these screens." She nodded toward the electronics, with their green lines and pulsing points.

They were apparently stunned by her logic. Neither of them said anything. Captain Billy was steering his ship, and Ray picked up binoculars to look at something in the distance. When he put them down, he said, "You do understand that burning things puts carbon dioxide into the atmosphere, and the ocean absorbs much of that?"

"Compared to the fuel this boat is burning?"

"Ship," Captain Billy said. "Maybe that's the point. We're all a bunch of fucking hypocrites, crying about what we're doing to the earth and ocean while we make it all worse. Like fucking recycling, sorting out cans and cardboard. Like it makes a difference. I hate that shit."

"It does make a difference," Annabel said. She didn't really mean to, but she did stamp her foot a little on the carpet, and she did have an issue with her arches although she was never going to admit it on *this* boat. "Every little bit makes a difference. Intention makes a difference."

Ray put back the binoculars. "I'm going now. You two can discuss art and hypocrisy all you like. I'm not involved."

When he was gone, Captain Billy said, "I've done more than I want of memorials at sea. Ashes blowing in the wind. Laying wreathes. I'm not opposed to doing something now and then that's a bit more fun."

Thus it was that, when the sky was dark and the smile of a moon hung over them, they gathered on the back deck. Captain Billy was standing by the closed gate, having turned the pilothouse over to the first mate and put himself in charge of operation safety. Annabel's eleven ice platforms formed an aesthetically pleasing line across the deck and reflected the light in an interesting, fractured way. She was busy making final adjustments, adhering the sculptures to the ice with her bits of clay. She was aware that the second mate, the engineer, and the cook were all standing by the back door, looking moderately interested, and that students from both shifts were gathered around, leaning in to see what she was doing, chattering away about what they imagined the sculptures to be. "Moon jelly," she heard. And "Irish Lord." "This look like lemming in hospital gown," said Nastiya, who had crouched beside Annabel and was poking a finger into one. "Nudibranch," Marybeth said. Annabel didn't know what a nudibranch was, but she liked the sound of it, and she liked that the girls were deploying their imaginations.

When everything was ready, Annabel gave her little speech, her invocation. She praised Sedna, the sea goddess, and asked her to forgive their boat upon the water, and all their transgressions. She specifically mentioned ocean acidification and called it, familiarly, OA. "We know not what we've done," she said. She pressed her hands in the prayer position and made her bow. *"Namaste.* The light in me greets the light in all of you."

The ship was now idling, just the thrum of the engines like blood coursing through all living beings. Captain Billy opened the gate and took the first sculpture on its ice base from her mittened hands into his gloved hands. He had come equipped with a sling for lowering the sculpture to the water and a trident for holding it away. The second mate stepped forward with another pole with a butane torch attached to its end and, like clockwork, the three of them passed, lowered, and lit her magnum opus. One flaming beauty after another sailed off into the darkness.

The ship throttled forward, and the lights grouped and strung out, flaring and reflecting just as she'd seen them in her mind, those bright centers of hope spreading their warmth over the surrounding sea and then dwindling, fading, dissolving into the other elements. The messages of sacred love and healing, soy-inked inside the paper folds, were released to the universe.

Tears streamed down her face, and the scene blurred before her, the tiny lights like fireflies now, blinking and wavering, and then turning off. Behind her there was a great silence and then, when the last light disappeared into the darkness, a cheer went up from the crowd. "That was so cool!" Tina was shouting in her ear. Alex had his arms thrown up over his head. Marybeth was trying to hug her. Captain Billy announced, "It never happened," but he was smiling and posing with the trident like King Neptune. She heard someone else say, "I have no clue, but I liked it." Helen crept up and took ahold of her sleeve. "I suppose you know that in the mythology, Sedna's father cut off her fingers, and her fingers became the seals, walrus, and the whales."

It was right then—at that perfect and preordained minute— that the porpoises appeared. They were suddenly all around the ship, their splashes catching the ship's light and making their own fire.

The sound of them, breaking the water and blowing their quick and bubbled breaths, rose above the ship's rumble.

It was in that same moment that Annabel became aware of Ray and his daughter at the side rail. Aurora stood in front, Ray behind her with his arms wrapped around her shoulders. "Stood" was not the right word. The girl was leaping, springing from her toes, and singing out, "I see them! I see them! I *see* you!" and her father was trying to hold her, however awkwardly, down to earth.

CHAPTER FOUR

On Friday, when they were back in port, they unloaded most of their gear and crates of samples into the warehouse and the vans, and then the whole group walked uptown to the Poopdeck, a notorious fishermen's bar. They swayed up the street like drunken sailors, their weeklong sea legs stumbling over the unmoving earth, the concrete sidewalk. Their newly awakened phones held to their ears, they shouted to friends and family. "I'm back!" "It was great!" "Tomorrow!" "He said *what?*" They may or may not have noticed the sun lowering behind the mountains, the colors—the vegetative greens, the roses and golds of summer's late flowers—popping. Emboldened crows loitered along the roadside. Other people—other people!—passed them, pushing baby strollers, walking a dog the size of a small moose, in rattling pickups with open windows and music blasting.

At the Poopdeck, they leaned on the bar, tipsy even before the first pitchers were poured, and crowded around a couple of tables to wolf burgers and fries. Aurora waved breadsticks.

The bar was famous for its sawdust floor smelling of sour beer, its low ceilings, and the probably-thousands of dollar bills tacked all over the walls and signed with names and hometowns. There were, in addition, decorative flourishes consisting of women's underwear.

There was the inevitable explanation. "Dude, it has nothing to do with poop," Tina bellowed. "It's the back part of the ship, the deck over the cabins in the back. It's from some French word."

Ray went right for a double whiskey, his purification over. He started with the good Jameson and was quickly softening into a soporific repose. The barmaid had just shouted at a very drunk person lighting a cigarette, and Ray observed to Colin beside him, "Only in Alaska. They can serve you 'til you're falling down drunk, but you betcha we're gonna keep the air all fresh and healthy for you." Only in Alaska, too, were you encouraged to bring guns, concealed and otherwise, into bars—because you never knew when you might need to defend your fellow tavern-mates from a mass murderer.

Ray watched his crew with benign amusement. There was pool playing and music, and then there was dancing. There was drinking and more drinking, beer and tequila shots and some fancy flavored vodkas. The students had worked hard and earned their revelry. They would be hungover tomorrow, but it was a long drive back to Fairbanks and Ray already knew who would share the driving. The others could sleep. They could stop for coffee as often as anyone wanted, at any roadhouse or wilderness espresso stand, and they could stop for roadside barfing. Aurora was the only one he needed to supervise tonight, and he didn't even care if she, for once, filled up on junk food.

In most respects, the cruise had been a success. The calm weather had made it all easy. They'd reached all the stations and got what they needed—another CTD data set, the prod, the nutrients, his beloved zooplankton, the OA samples. He'd taken umpteen zooplankton photos, some of which were very good indeed and all of which would occupy him for weeks of early mornings as he reviewed and sorted them. No one had been hurt, or even gotten seriously seasick. There'd been no real drama, not after Mr. Acidification had left. That Annabel woman, he could have done without her. The stuff with the ice and the mashed-up paper she called sculpture—he wouldn't need to think of it again, beyond putting some bullshit statement in his reports. He had made it through Seahab and met his reward.

Still, all was not well with the ocean. The surface temperatures had been alarmingly hot—more than a degree warmer than they'd ever found in September, in places up to five degrees above the average. In sixty-degree water, phytoplankton had been spurred to a late bloom. Even with that extra food, zooplankton numbers were low, the usual species seeking deeper, cooler water. The tows were sometimes jammed with jellyfish. Of course, as he was always impressing upon the students, considerable fluctuation in the abundance of different species was expected year to year.

Some results they'd have to wait for. All those samples to be tested for alkalinity and carbon. Then they'd learn more of the acidification story. He hadn't seen any obvious damage, but that didn't mean that the animals weren't working harder to build their calcium carbonate structures.

Ray ordered another drink and leaned back against the wall. Compared to the Earth's destruction and the many mysteries it was his obligation to confront, his personal issues should feel like bug bites on a bear. Still, it was *his* life. When he'd checked his phone, there was nothing from his wife except a businesslike reminder that she'd be away for the weekend and he should make sure that Sam had what he needed for a school project. He vaguely remembered something about a triathlon Nelda had been training for—this might have been the weekend. There'd also been three increasingly hostile calls from someone in the vast university bureaucracy demanding that he immediately print, sign, scan, and e-mail something called an effort certification statement. There was a garbled message from someone wanting a pteropod photograph. Everyone always wanted to use his photos; no one was ever interested in paying for them.

Ray didn't need praise or monetary reward, but he wouldn't have minded some acknowledgment, from someone, somewhere, of the essential work his team had just performed. Even a simple voice mail or text along the way: *thinking of you, hope it's all going well.* He imagined Jackson Oakley wishing him well, apologizing for his absence. *That* would never happen.

Annabel, in slingback shoes and a low-cut, thigh-high dress, had found her groove swing dancing. She danced with Tina and Cinda and then with Alex, Robert, and Marybeth in turn, and then back to Robert. Robert turned out to be an excellent swing dancer, capable of lifting, spinning, and flipping her, and the two of them flew around the floor with abandon, only sometimes clobbering someone with an elbow or a heel.

When they took a break, Robert launched into a long and nostalgic story about a former dance partner in California, a married Latina with two small children. He'd met her at a dance club, and they'd danced so perfectly together, so completely in sync. All the other dancers admired them. They won contests. "Totally innocent," Robert said. "It was all about the dance."

The hot-blooded Latino husband, in any case, had busted Robert's car's headlights, and Robert had never gone back to the dance club or attempted to see the woman again. Then he'd moved to Fairbanks.

Annabel listened to the great unwinding of details about the woman's body, her outfits, and the gold teeth that glittered when she laughed, and she partially revised her assumption about Robert's gayness. It seemed to her that Robert had either loved the woman or wanted to *be* her.

They danced again, and Annabel shouted above the music, "I'm a cuckoo coccolithophore!" She imagined herself covered in shifting calcium plates, and with extra swings of her hips, she willed crunchy good health toward the Gulf, to all the precious coccolithophores and their brethren.

Aurora had wanted to come to the bar, of course. She could have stayed on the ship, watching a movie or texting her friends. She had felt in exile during the long week on the ship. She had thought it would be more exciting. Her father had oversold it. There was a lot of water out there, a lot of nothing.

She hadn't complained, though, because it was better than school and all she had to do now was write a report about what she learned, which would be half a page. She had learned that even women snore, and a little bit about playing the guitar, and how to operate the can crusher in the galley. She was kidding about half a page. Her father would help her, and they would put in things about the ocean and looking in the microscope, birds' names, and the size of a whale's eye equaling an orange. The porpoises were cool, the way they swam around the ship. The artist was cool. And she had gotten to watch movies she was not allowed to see at home, with sexy parts and bad language.

She was also having a secret crush on Alex, who had very long eyelashes you could appreciate when he took off his glasses. He was always doing that—taking off his glasses to clean them with a handkerchief. She had spent much of the week thinking about him in non-boat circumstances as a way of entertaining herself.

At the table they were all clowning around, saying things like "That was a flaming good time" and "He is a flaming idiot" and "I am so flaming thirsty." This was because she was there and they were not supposed to swear in her presence, as though when they said "flaming" or "frigging" or "effing" it wasn't just the same as saying "fucking," which is what she heard. But that was only part of it. "Flaming" was the new word because they weren't supposed to talk about setting stuff on fire when they were on the ship, so it was a kind of joke.

Her father was singing along now, words about setting the night on fire. It was some old song from the hippie times. At home, her father liked to play records and sing when he was having drinks. Sometimes then he liked to have long, serious talks with her or her brother, but they were always depressing, about how terrible everything was and how there was no real point in life except propagation and evolution-shit. She usually stopped listening when he got to the pointlessness part.

Aurora saw her father exchange glances with the artist, who was dancing with Cinda or maybe just by herself and came now to the table to peel her father's hand away from his glass. She practically dragged him onto the dance floor, where he looked sheepish and then stupid as he danced a stupid dance like a washing machine, sliding his feet and twisting his arms back and forth. She loved her father, but he was a science nerd and was never going to be as cool as he wanted to be.

Helen sat with her glass of wine at the table with the others, who hopped up and down for dancing or lining up quarters at the pool and foosball tables. For some time she'd been half-watching an older Native woman who was hunched on a stool at the end of the bar. The woman was small and thin and her feet didn't reach the footrest part of the stool. She was by herself, just sitting and, now and then tipping back a beer bottle.

Helen did not frequent bars on a regular basis. She knew all too well the role that alcohol played in the destruction of so many Native families. In Igalik, ostensibly a "dry" village, she'd seen men she knew to be kind get blind-drunk on bootleg and beat their wives and children. Boys she'd known had killed themselves after drinking. Her own aunt, her mother's youngest sister, had fallen from a boat and was never found; the boyfriend had been so drunk he couldn't remember when she'd fallen out or where the boat had been or much of anything about that summer day, now years ago. Later, he put a bullet in his head.

She felt sorry for the woman at the bar, and was embarrassed by her, too.

The others came and went and shouted into their cell phones, and another pitcher arrived at the table. Clothes came off, revealing tank tops and shapely biceps, and Colin's T-shirt with a scientific equation. Helen's eyes kept returning to the woman at the bar. She seemed to be talking to the bartender, the bartender nodding neutrally as he went on filling pints and squirting soda. When the woman rotated on her seat and looked into the room behind her, Helen saw the familiar features that might have been Iñupiat or might belong to this southern coast—Alutiiq or Sugpiaq, even Eyak. It was a face that had seen some hard living. She turned her own gaze to the cover of Aurora's paperback lying on the table: two fair-haired girls in white dresses running through a green field. Clearly, the pretty girls were running *toward* something, not away.

When her phone vibrated she checked the number and felt her heart give a little lurch. She got up and hurried outside to the curb. The last light was leaving the sky, and the streetlamps had come on.

Jackson's voice boomed. How was she? Had it been a good trip? No problems with equipment? His slightly Southern accent melted through her like a sip of warmed seal oil. Whatever had been awkward for him seemed to be over. He was the mentor checking in. He was showing that he did care, that things between them were back to what they had been.

She gave him a short report: the weather, the number of sample jars, how hard all the students had worked. (This might have been her slight dig, a reference to being short one participant.) No, no problems. Everything had gone smoothly. (This might have been her second small dig; he hadn't been needed after all.)

She wanted to hear him say something about his leaving. An apology? His regret for abandoning her and the team? A further justification for his decision?

But she also wanted him to be proud of her.

"Now the work begins," he said with a laugh.

They spoke for just a few minutes, confirming the group's return schedule and that they'd see each other soon. It was a good thing that he'd stayed behind, he finally said, because he'd had to make a sudden trip south. To Las Vegas. A meeting with funders. He'd gotten back himself just the night before. Yes, it had been really hot there—he'd much rather have been in Alaska.

When Helen turned back to the bar, Aurora was standing just outside the door, watching her.

Half-panicked, Helen ran through her side of the conversation. Had she mentioned any names, said anything she wouldn't want overheard? Anything too personal? She'd asked about the desert heat, said "interesting," "sounds good," "see you soon."

All very professional. Except that she didn't feel very professional—the blood in her cheeks, the tightness in her chest, her general confusion about how she should feel. Others might disapprove of the relationship she and Jackson had, but why shouldn't she, in the current circumstance, check in with her advisor about the work he'd assigned her?

"Hey, girl," she said to Aurora. "Needing some fresh air?"

Aurora only nodded, solemnly.

Annabel ordered another grapefruit and soda. The bartender, she thought, had been flirting with her. He wore a greased-point mustache he was way too proud of and had tats on his knuckles that, if she'd been interested, she would have tried to read.

Colin, the boy wonder, was at her elbow. "Ever heard of a flaming Dr. Pepper? It's amaretto and something else, in a shot glass you light on fire and drop into beer."

"Lovely," Annabel said. She might have been getting a little tired of all the fire puns, the references to flaming and fire-lighting, "Jumping Jack Flash" and the ridiculous song about a candle, a sexually charged reference to an electric eel. It was all in good fun, of course, a kind of code or special handshake, a language that had bonded the lot of them together. They had made an effort to include her.

She bought Colin a beer, which seemed the generous thing to do. All evening she'd been indulging her new young friends—and herself—in the myth that an artist could be financially successful in a world where no one would ever buy what she made. The truth was that her work—too large, too conceptual, lacking iconic mountains and wildlife—would always have a limited audience. It was easier now to do ephemeral work and not worry about trying to have shows or store the work when a show was over. Her friends' homes—and their garages, basements, and outbuildings—had about reached their capacities.

With loosened tongue, Colin felt it necessary to tell her that he couldn't believe that she was way older than his parents, maybe as old as his grandmother. "I would normally never call an older woman by their first name. And your dancing is awesome."

"By her first name," Annabel corrected.

"Whose?" Colin only looked confused.

"Never mind. You're not an English major."

The shaded light over the pool table was swaying from someone having bumped it, creating a wave effect with the shadows it cast.

"You're the wave guy," Annabel said. "Give me a word, something from physics, something with a great sound." A new idea, bringing together the rhythms of movement and language, was stirring in her head.

"You mean like 'sinusoidal?'"

She borrowed a pen from the bartender and had Colin write the word on a napkin. "I'm old, you know. I have to write things down or I forget them."

Colin was well into an explanation of wavelengths and nodes.

"Please." She put a finger to her lips. "TMI. I'll look it up later, *mon petit.*"

Swing music was playing again, and the sweaty guy she'd been dancing with, the one with the "Spawn Till You Die" T-shirt by a commercial artist she could not dislike because he had a great sense of humor, was approaching and about to bow to her.

Aurora pretended she was Jane Goodall studying monkeys. She had recently learned that people had almost the same DNA as chimpanzees, and she had been noticing that their behaviors were not so different. They fought, they mated, they protected their babies.

She watched as a bearded man in an oil-stained shirt approached their table and sat down beside Nastiya. She could tell he was a monkey with mating on his mind. He asked Nastiya, "Are you from that research ship?"

"Yes." Nastiya pointed a finger at several of the others, including Aurora. "Many of us." Aurora could see that if Nastiya had fur, some of it would be fluffed out in a guarding kind of way. Goodall would call it a defensive posture. She saw Nastiya look at the man's hands, which had oil worked into their cracks, and thought that Nastiya might be thinking they belonged to someone who could do useful work. In the monkey world, skill equaled a good provider and protector and that equaled a good mate. It was not the same as being dirty in a disgusting way. Now Nastiya was relaxing her fur.

"What were you looking at out there?" the man asked.

"Oh, about the ocean. Oceanography. Biology, chemistry."

The man was hearing her Russianness, and he smiled at this.

A second man, wearing an Icicle Seafoods ball cap, pulled up a chair. He leaned in and asked, "Is it true the ocean's turning to acid?"

Nastiya had fur again. "Not acid," she said. "More acid. There is difference."

Oily Hands turned to Ball Cap and said something very scientific, all about the pH scale and how it was logarithmic. "So what is it now?" he asked Nastiya. "The ocean surface out here"—he waved an arm—"is eight-something?"

The female monkey's fur was smoothed again. "Depend," she said. "Depend on day and season, mixing. Sometimes less than eight. The important is aragonite undersaturation." Aurora could tell that Nastiya was using the big words to show her value, also as a test to see if Oily Hands was equal to her value. Oily Hands nodded and scratched his beard. "I don't pretend to understand it all," he said, "but I'm a fisherman—we're fishermen—and it seems like we'd better start learning what this means for our fisheries."

After that, Aurora read her book again, but mostly she listened to the conversation, because it was more interesting than the part of the book she had come to, which was blah-blah—too much about a farm and chickens. Oily Hands, it turned out, had a name, Brad, and a fishing boat named Silver Star. Ball Cap had a name, too, but he was clearly not the top ape, and almost right away he jumped into another tree. Nastiya told Brad about her work, and then he talked about catching fish, and then they talked about him not being a greenie but how he was against bottom trawling and so was she. Brad quoted someone famous about everything in the universe being hitched together, and Nastiya got excited about that and clinked her beer glass against his beer bottle, which was almost like touching, almost like they might be getting ready to pick lice out of one another's fur.

Helen played foosball and lost. In all sports, she lacked competitiveness. Back at the table, she listened to Alex talk about permafrost and methane. He had an idea for drawing methane from Arctic lakes to provide villages with energy. She was challenging his sense of practicality when she felt a tap on her shoulder.

The Native woman who'd been sitting at the bar was even less attractive close up. Her face was pitted like a piece of pumice, her eyes rheumy. When she opened her mouth, Helen saw that she was missing most of her teeth.

"Got a smoke?" she said to Helen and made a gesture of holding a cigarette and darting it toward her mouth.

Helen smiled politely. "No, I'm sorry, I don't smoke. I don't think any of my friends here do, either."

The woman did not seem disappointed, or she seemed used to disappointment on a grander scale. "You and me," she said to Helen, leaning closer, "we the only real people here." She turned to Alex and studied his Asian face. "You almost real people." She was laughing as she shuffled off.

Alex shook his head as though he didn't get the joke and thought the woman was just insanely blabbering. It was possible that he didn't know that Iñupiat and Yup'ik and Sugpiaq and most of the other names that Alaska Natives called themselves translate to "the real people," to distinguish themselves from other people who were not real but foreign, not the genuine articles.

Helen didn't want to have to explain. There was too much to explain, too much history, too much of feeling bad for what happened to Native people, her own complicated feelings about living "white." She couldn't say that she was better than that woman, or better than her aunt who drowned drunk or her mother or other aunts or any of her cousins. Luckier, in so many ways. But also less real.

"That's just sad," Alex said.

Ray had danced like a fool and hurt his wrist playing foosball too vigorously and talked, until he could escape, with two tourist ladies who were very admiring of Sarah Palin and assumed that he would know if her unwed daughter with the children was collecting child support. He had had several drinks but was excellent, as usual, at not "showing it." He merely felt soft around his edges and a little sorrowful. It was clearer than ever to him that, despite their challenges, the research cruises were the highlights of his years. The cruises were the singular times in his life when the importance of his work and his place in that work were uncontested and central. Now it was back to normal life for eight months. Back to students who were only going through the motions, back to his windowless office in a soulless university, back to mundane household chores and the usual criticisms.

Aurora had left for the ship with the first exodus. He missed her already. He regretted the missed opportunities on the ship, when he might have spent more time with her, might have done a better job of exciting her mind with scientific discovery. She'd been a good soldier.

Others might have called Ray a morose drunk, or a depressive, but Ray preferred to think of himself as introspective, philosophical, realistically insightful. If he sunk into his thoughts, and his thoughts were about a troubled world, whose fault was that? It was his right, even, to feel sorry for himself. It was his right to feel depressed by his country's failure of leadership—the Law of the Sea, global warming, POPS, education, research funding; he could go on and on and probably would have had he been home, sunk into his recliner with budget spreadsheets lying like leaf litter around him, the patience-stretched Nelda pretending to listen.

He thought about a time on the ship when he'd been clearing his head up on the flying bridge. The ship had been stopped at a station, and out of the sky a small, feverishly flapping bird appeared, heading for the ship as though it were a spot of land, a necessary refuge. It was close enough to recognize—a fox sparrow, that terrestrial fun-fellow with the cheeriest of forest calls. Just then the ship started up, pulling away from the bird. He watched as it fell into the sea, exhausted. And then it was up again, chasing the ship, making another desperate attempt to reach safety. And falling back, and then falling again into the ocean. He didn't see it again. It had not even occurred to him, when the bird first appeared in its race, to climb down the ladder and ask Captain Billy to ease up. He was not a person to interfere with nature, which is not cruel but indifferent. But it occurred to him now that he might have at least mourned a small death, and that he was and would always be an asshole.

Marybeth came and sat beside him. "So I called my boy-friend," she said, "and he was like, 'Are you back already?' That was the first thing he said. 'Are you back already?'"

"Ouch."

Ray was sure she was going to cry, and then where would he be? —comforting a drunk female student in a bar, having to walk her back to the ship, having to say something that would make her feel better without being an outright fraud. He could not defend his sex— or gender, or whatever it was called these days. Men were incredibly selfish and insensitive; get used to it.

Mercifully, his phone beeped. "Excuse me," he said. "I better check this."

It was an incoming text from a science news service he sub-scribed to. "Swedish Nuclear Plant Shut Down by Jellyfish." To ward off more boyfriend talk, he followed the link to the news item. There'd been such a large *Aurelia* bloom in the Baltic Sea's near-shore waters that the facility's intake pipes had clogged, again. He read excerpts to Marybeth: "The moon jelly is a species that blooms in extreme areas that are overfished or have bad conditions." "The fish leave and the moon jelly takes over the ecosystem." "The biggest problem is that there's no monitoring in the Baltic Sea to produce the data that scientists need to tackle the issue."

"There you go," Ray said. "We've got the same species. And increased blooms. And limited data. A good project for some grad student."

Marybeth said, "It took jellyfish to shut down a nuclear plant? Yay, jellyfish!"

That was not quite the response Ray would have wished for. "Not exactly," he said, as teacherly as he could. "First, it's just a temporary shutdown. Second, a lot of people rely on that power, and we wouldn't want to see it replaced with coal. And third, blooms like that are a real concern."

Now the girl looked rejected, her brilliant antinuke campaign dashed.

"Remember what I said on the ship, about reverse evolution? Were you there when we looked at the big lion's mane?"

She nodded.

The students had gotten to see plenty of jellyfish, blob-like as the ship cruised past and then, at station stops, undulating in their great beauty. They were mostly moon jellyfish, of all sizes, delicate tentacles waving below their pulsing bells. There were, of course, all those juveniles in the plankton tows. There had also been the large orange lion's mane jelly that Ray netted for the students to examine. On the deck, where it collapsed into a gelatinous heap, he'd pointed with his pencil at the eight lobes of the bell and the arrangement of tangled tentacles (with their stinging nematocysts) that gave the animal its name. When they dumped it back to the sea, its soft body had been cut by the net's web, leaving it less perfect than it had come to them. Another sacrifice for science.

He'd given his talk about reverse evolution, about how jellyfish were ancient creatures that had evolved in earlier ocean conditions and were generally capable of tolerating CO_2-rich waters. As the oceans warmed and became more acidic, and as other species faded into extinction, jellies might survive and prosper.

"Durable," Marybeth said. "You called them durable." She fished the maraschino cherry out of whatever concoction she was drinking and held it by its stem. "I don't really like these. Would you like to eat my cherry?"

There she was, innocently holding out a fruit.

"No thank you," he said quickly, hoping that his face didn't give anything away. *Eat my cherry?* Did she really have no idea? Was she that young? Had language perhaps changed that much, lost its meaning?

She set the cherry on a napkin, where it stared at him obscenely.

Ray closed his eyes and leaned back, banishing the unbidden image. Some Janis Joplin wannabe was wailing one more sad song.

An abrupt punch to his shoulder jerked him upright.

It was that woman.

"Don't get too comfortable." Annabel pulled a chair close and straddled it backwards, her arms folded across its back. She turned to Marybeth. "Hey, angel. I'm going to miss you."

Calamity Jane, Ray was thinking, *reeking of patchouli oil instead of gunpowder.*

"Hey," she said to Ray, "before we all go our separate ways, I wanted to say thank you for letting me come on your cruise."

"Of course," he said. "It was a delight." Not for the first time, he was trying to recall exactly who in the art department was going to receive his wrath. Although maybe it was his own fault for not vetting these other people the way he vetted the students. His track record was not good. There'd been the third-grade teacher who spent the whole time reading Victorian novels and taking showers. There'd been the writer who filled a notebook with notes but never published anything that he knew of. There was someone else who made cartoons of a stick figure named Zoe Plankton, a humorless imitation of a SpongeBob character. He couldn't, of course, forget that other artist, the one who had made quite nice drawings and tried to help with the sampling, generally getting in the way; that poor fellow had collected some interesting brown specimens and was pulling them apart, staring into them, trying to figure out what kind of egg cases they were, and no one wanted to tell him he'd gathered up shit from the flushing of the tanks. Where were the Ernst Haeckels of the twenty-first century?

And now the Annabel art was ash in the sea. He wished he could believe that, like a magic powder, the burned-up paper could heal what ailed them all. He would have to make up something for his report—something about the benefits of art—and he was not a creative writer. He would rather stick his bare arm into a swarm of *Cubozoa*.

Annabel was looking at him intently. Maybe she really was psychic. Maybe she could see right into his unappreciative and damaged soul. He tried to banish all thought. He sat up a little straighter.

"A delight?" she said. She broke into a smile that took up half her face.

His phone binged again, another timely rescue.

"Dance with me," Annabel said to Marybeth, flinging out an arm. The two of them teetered off while he checked his message.

It was another bulletin from the same news service. "University of the North Leading Ocean Research." That *was* news. Maybe he'd been at sea a lot longer than he thought and was returning as Rip Van Winkle. He scanned the article, picked up from some publication he'd never heard of, something called *Environment Today*. There were several quotes from Dr. Jackson Oakley, about money being spent, international collaboration, Alaska as a crossroads, how "precedent-setting" the work of the university's new Office of Ocean Acidification Science was. "Just this month our leading scientists have been investigating the ocean's chemical components for a better understanding of the carbon cycle."

Ray felt himself doing a not-so-slow burn. Really? Oakley was publicly touting a version of their university that Ray didn't even recognize, and an activity that bore little resemblance to the who and what of his team's last week? What bullshit!

Oakley, the article said, was "marshaling the efforts" on ocean research.

Ray turned off his phone and finished his drink. He could not even be flattered by being called an (unnamed) "leading scientist."

That lying prick.

PART 2

Chapter Five

B ack home, the birch and aspen leaves had flipped to yellow. Ray returned to teaching classes and supervising his grad students, started writing up the cruise report, sorted through his new photos and posted the best to his online gallery, performed as the husband and the father, split and stacked firewood without harming himself, walked the old dog around the neighborhood. Aside from his immediate and bitter complaint to his wife about Oakley's dereliction of duties and self-promotion, he let that anger go. (It might be more accurate to say that Nelda threatened to serve his dinner in the garage, with the dog, if he didn't shut up about it.) It didn't seem that anyone else had seen the article in the obscure publication, in any case. No one mentioned it.

The students from the cruise continued to hang out together and to be easy with one another and with him. He could imagine them, years later, calling across the country for each other's advice and collaboration. He would be the one, *emeritus,* that they would come back to for affirmation, the elder they would thank when they accepted their various prizes. This was his generous view of the future, and of himself.

He was trying to be more optimistic these days, imagining a different future than the one that was always suggesting itself.

In the biology lab he monitored the zooplankton work, the ongoing identification and counts from the cruise tows, those samples preserved from the Multinet.

"Is usual suspect," he heard Nastiya say one afternoon, as she looked through an undergrad's scope, the girl waiting patiently at her side. It was funny how readily she adopted his own expressions, even the idioms beyond her reference. It was not unlike raising a child and hearing your own words come out of its mouth. One of his son's first words had been "jelly," not in a context that went with peanut butter but in wonder at the tiny sea creatures they captured together in jars and the larger ones washed up on beaches and carefully poked at. That private language acquisition had not, however, survived *Sesame Street* and then every kind of commercial advertising.

On his way to the whiteboard at the end of the room, Ray passed his Keeling Curve poster and did his usual internal salute. For students, there was no better example than the famous curve, with its seasonal jags steepening up the wall, to demonstrate the necessity of a time series, to impress upon them the importance of collecting basic ocean data season after season, year after year. His standard lectures always emphasized that what Charles David Keeling learned about the steady rise in atmospheric CO_2 from his first measurements in the 1950s was fundamental to the study and understanding of global warming.

Ray had long ago forgiven Keeling for his skepticism about measuring ocean pH. The man had knocked himself out to refine his atmospheric measuring tools and to establish that CO_2 was distributed evenly in the atmosphere. The ocean was a different story, less uniform and far more complicated in its processes and exchanges. Keeling had asked the tough questions and pushed for proofs, standards, impeccable study. He'd been a knowledgeable, if somewhat rigid, skeptic—before the word "skeptic" was hijacked to mean someone who attacked on the basis of ideology.

At the whiteboard, Ray wrote out the Latin names of common copepod species: *Acartia longiremis, Neocalanus cristatus, Neocalanus flemingeri, Oithona similis, Pseudocalandus minutus*. He liked the students to get in the habit of using the scientific names. He also liked them to think about Linnaean taxonomy and the relationships between species and within genera, to be able to classify a new species they might not have seen before. In the current age of illiteracy, he also wanted them to learn to spell. Computer dictionaries and spell-check did not help with *chaetognatha*. At one time he'd corrected spellings on student papers, and then for a short time written snide comments, but now he just circled misspellings and not even all of them.

Scientific nomenclature was where all languages and cultures neutralized, where everyone had a common language and reference. It was not by accident that the University of the North enrolled a large number of foreign students and that they were concentrated in the sciences. In the lab right now, among five students, two were Russian, one German, one South African (but raised in the United States), and the last was what he would have called "white bread American" if that wasn't so offensive. This was the student Nastiya was helping, a girl from Ketchikan. All of them happened to be women.

Where was Marybeth? She had been devoting herself to marine cladocerans to an obsessive degree, but now, according to Nastiya, she had a new boyfriend, one with pierced eyebrows, and was more absent than not. Nastiya too had a new boyfriend, a fisherman. These girls changed boyfriends the way he changed socks. He hoped that Marybeth, not the brightest bulb but far from the dullest, wouldn't slack on her studies. On the other hand, he always felt a little embarrassed when he saw her. He would always think of that damn maraschino cherry.

"You see gill?" Nastiya was saying. "That tell you . . . ?" The Ketchikan girl mumbled something Ray couldn't hear.

Ray was mildly annoyed because Nastiya was supposed to get him a draft of the paper she was supposedly writing about temporal changes in the growth and development of *Metridia pacifica*. He would, of course, have to add the English. When she was done instructing, he stopped at her station and was opening his mouth to say he-was-not-sure-what when her arm suddenly jerked sideways, knocking into her microscope. "You scare me," she accused him.

He ended up apologizing and never asked about the paper, which would have been pointless anyway. Nastiya did great work but seemed to live in a different time zone, one that differed not by hours but by days and sometimes weeks. She had a unique capacity to focus on temporal developments in the ocean without any awareness of the time that flew by her every day.

He was the one at fault, as usual, around women.

On his way home for the day, he passed the enlarged wing and bright signage for the new Office of Ocean Acidification Science. "Oakley," he growled under his breath. So what if the man had a talent for raising money for his department, his section, his very individual work? Ocean chemistry was getting all the money, and marine biology and all the rest were starving. My God, was that new carpet? And a receptionist? Was it not enough that Oakley had all the shiny new equipment—the second VINDTA and all that other stuff for measuring CO_2 molecules? Ray didn't have the funds to buy an extra box of glass slides.

People often said that Ray and Nelda were a perfect match. These were usually people who didn't know them well. They meant that Ray could be dour and steadfast, and Nelda was lighthearted and more fun, more socially at ease. They balanced one another.

"Put on a clean shirt and a sports jacket," Nelda said when he got home that evening. "We're going to the flute concert." Nelda was also bossy, a quality less apparent to those who didn't live with her. In most matters, this wasn't something Ray objected to, since it meant she took care of things like knowing what was appropriate attire and making sure that said attire was hanging, clean, in the closet. Ray would not have gone to a flute concert on his own. He was not sure why they were going, though he noted that it was *the* flute concert, not *a* flute concert. He made himself a drink.

"We're leaving in half an hour," Nelda said. She had already showered and was pinkly aglow from the hot water and the run he assumed she'd made before the shower. Lately she had a new circle of women friends who gathered at the end of the road and ran on the trail through the woods. She generally came back with gossip about breakups and liaisons, kids caught with pot, university politics he knew nothing about, as well as bird sightings; yesterday they'd seen a merlin chasing a raven.

"Any good birds today?" he asked.

She looked at him like she didn't know what he was talking about. "Oh, birds. Lots of juncos." She was going through the day's mail, pitching most of it into the trash. "How was school today?" She always asked this, the same words she used with Sam and Aurora. It was her way of being light about his work, not to downplay its importance but to encourage him to have a good attitude, to not feel discouraged by the many things that were discouraging today in higher education. At least this was how he chose to interpret her question. He watched her drink from a glass of ice water, the cubes clinking together, her long bare throat as smooth as a girl's.

"My day was OK," he said. "Another journal wants one of my pteropod photos. I'm the pteropod photo king." He sank into the couch and wished he didn't have to go anywhere, least of all to a flute concert. How could you have a concert of all flutes? Even one was too high-pitched for him. He much preferred an oboe, or a cello—

anything in a lower register. Some kind of quartet, or quintet, prefer-
ably strings. A bass guitar would be a good idea. He was not that
much for music overall, unless he had had several drinks and could
feel the rhythm in his bones. Like that night in the bar after the last
cruise. Already he was nostalgic for that time, the whole thing: the
cruise, the students, the ocean, the throb of the ship, the sense of
exploration, the joy of learning, the company of his daughter.

"Where are the kids?" he asked.

"Sam's with a friend, at his house. Aurora's feeding the Jacobsons' cat. They're away for a week. They're paying her to feed and
play with the cat and to water plants."

Ray didn't know many of Sam's friends, not well. He didn't
know the Jacobsons either, although apparently they were neighbors, and apparently Aurora was responsible enough to be trusted at
their house. Ray and his family were confirmed dog people and had
never had a cat; he wondered if he should worry about Aurora getting too fond of one. He couldn't abide cats that wrapped themselves
around his legs or jumped onto his lap—something they seemed
driven to do whenever he and they ended up in a room together.

"Pteropods are everywhere now," his wife said. "A few years
ago no one had even heard of them. No one except you and your
plankton people. Now they're popping up all over. It's like that time
I asked you what ontology was, and then we both started to see the
word everywhere, in everything we read."

Ray had already forgotten what ontology was, except that it
was not his kind of "ology." He would continue to do his part on
behalf of the little snails, though. If he could make pteropods the
poster creatures of ocean acidification, the way that polar bears were
the poster creatures of global warming, that would be no small
achievement. His drink was almost empty, and he wondered if he
had time for a second. He started to get up.

"Clean shirt," Nelda said.

NANCY LORD

"When the ocean's dead, no one's going to care if I'm wearing a clean shirt." *Or about flute concerts,* he almost added.

"Please, tonight, do not talk about a dead ocean," she said. "Please don't depress everyone. No one wants to hear bad news all the time. If anyone asks, just say you're continuing to document zooplankton species."

"Don't ask, don't tell," he said.

"Please," she said.

Who were these *everyone, no one, anyone?* Who else went to flute concerts, and what did they talk about while they mingled in the lobby? An image of Jackson Oakley came into his head: the man pimping his program all the way through the halls of the university, to the politicians and the media, among concertgoers. That's what it took—the charmer face, the handshake, happy talk. Could a person be honest about what was happening and leave people feeling good? That was a trick he'd like to learn.

The following week, a colleague in the fisheries department brought Ray some live pteropods from the Arctic. This was the same species, *Limacina helicina,* that his cruise group was familiar with from the Gulf of Alaska. The shelled pteropods were notoriously hard to transport and to maintain in captivity, and Ray was grateful for their delivery in bottles of cold seawater within a very few hours of capture, jetted straight down from Barrow.

Not for the first time, Ray wondered why Alaska's marine sciences program was located at the campus in Fairbanks, about as far as you could get in Alaska from any actual marine habitat. His department had no capacity for holding marine creatures or working in any way with seawater or ocean conditions. Routinely, he had to send grad students off to other institutions in other states and countries to conduct their research with living systems.

"Wonder" was not the right word for his thought. He knew

why things were where they were. The university had been established in Fairbanks to create a reason for people to live in forty-below temperatures—to populate Alaska's interior, much the way the Russians established factories in Siberia to force people to live there and lay claim to the resource wealth. Once the buildings and people were set in Fairbanks, they simply stayed. That was the definition of inertia, after all.

Ray already had numerous photos of *Limacina helicina* from the Gulf, but if someone wanted an illustration for an article about the Arctic, he wanted to be able to provide what was unquestionably an Arctic specimen. The received batch were juveniles—what were referred to as "pre-winter"; he knew they would be smallish and sluggish, their processes slowed to coast through the Arctic cold and darkness in a state requiring little metabolic effort.

He stayed in the lab late that night, toiling like a fashion photographer to capture his tiny subjects from different sides, in different poses: "wings" extended, "wings" curled, dark bodies tight in their translucent shells, the magnificent spirals of the shells. The earthbound science building, unlike a rocking ship, allowed him good long looks and carefully arranged shots.

Not every shell was perfect. In fact, nine out of the twenty he looked at verged on opaque and bore tiny, almost imperceptible pittings.

He sat with a tightened stomach under the buzzing fluorescent lights and went through all the reasons that this group of pteropods could be compromised. During this time of year in the Arctic, that amount of wear and tear on juveniles might be natural, expected. Nor could he vouch for the conditions of their capture and transport; they were fragile creatures. And he'd been handling them himself, perhaps not carefully enough.

Perhaps he was only seeing imperfections because he was looking for them? He knew well enough that a person—no matter how "scientific"—tended to find what he expected, if not what he wanted.

Still, he couldn't avoid the possibility—was it a probability?—that what he was looking at was shell dissolution from acidification. It was happening elsewhere; upwellings along the West Coast had carried corrosive water over the shelf to wreak havoc on Washington's commercial oyster farms. It was happening decades sooner than had been thought possible just a few years ago. Was it already that bad in the Arctic?

His undergrad students in the Intro to Marine Biology class already knew the story of Victoria Fabry, the oceanographer who discovered pteropod response to increased CO_2 way back in 1985. When she'd collected too many live study specimens in a glass jar and they respired, their shells began to turn from transparent to opaque and chalky. At the time, the fact that shells could dissolve like that was merely interesting, and inconvenient for her study of shell growth. No one back then, or even for years later, dreamed that the chemistry of an entire ocean could be altered enough to make a difference to its creatures.

The next morning, the class was excited to have live pteropods to examine. Although the animals had slowed down, the students could still see some of their swimming motion and, in many cases, the beating hearts that showed through their shells.

He quizzed them: "Why are pteropods hard to keep in captivity?"

"They eat one another?"

"They make too much CO_2?"

"They starve to death?"

He gave the nod to the young man with the last answer. "And why do they starve to death?"

The kid shrugged.

"How do these pteropods eat?"

Most of them knew this. "Mucous nets!"

"That's right. They put out their feet to help them drift, and then float a mucous net that acts like a parachute to trap food. Then they eat the net and its food. What happens to their mucous nets in captivity?"

"The CO_2 corrodes them."

"They fall apart."

The rest looked at him expectantly, waiting for the correct answer.

"How would we test this?"

He kept questioning until they understood what delicate creatures pteropods were and that removal from their natural environments disturbed them in ways that kept them from floating their nets. "They're very sensitive," he said. "Like me."

No response. Why did students never get his jokes?

"So here's what we're going to do. To understand the biology of these animals, we need to know some chemistry, right? Chemistry affects biology, as biology affects chemistry. We're going to replicate Victoria Fabry's accidental experiment—sort of—and see what happens."

It was very crude, what he had them do. They measured pH and set up the jars so they could bubble in additional CO_2. They developed a hypothesis: the higher the CO_2 the sooner the pteropod shells would show obvious corrosion and the greater that corrosion would be.

Some of the shells, yes, were already showing signs of dissolution. He was careful to explain why this might be the case. And, no—to the girl who asked, accusingly—they were not *torturing* animals. Yes, he had called the snails "animals," but he didn't think that animal rights were applicable.

After class, Ray returned a titration kit to the chemistry lab in the OA office. Helen was there, running samples through the two

VINDTA machines. She was wearing stylish glasses—purple—that he didn't remember from the cruise, and a white lab coat. "Ours?" he asked, pointing to crates of jars.

"Yes," she said. "With the new machine, we're able to run the samples through much faster. We had a backlog before." She was looking at tubing as though there was something interesting about it, or as a way of avoiding looking at him. After all that time together on the ship, he thought she could be a little friendlier.

"Results?"

"Just data," she said. "Preliminary. You know—it needs to all be compiled, checked and rechecked, analyzed. It takes time. You should ask Professor Oakley about it."

Professor Oakley?

"You mean our friend Jackson?" He recalled that the university president, Dr. (as in Medieval Literature) Petterson, had become very big on emphasizing titles and credentials.

She turned even colder. "Professor Oakley says if people are going to take OA seriously, they have to take *him* seriously, and he doesn't want anyone calling him Jack. In the media he's Dr. Oakley."

"I never call him Jack." Ray was thinking, *Jackson's not pretentious enough?*

A silence fell between them while she scrutinized the equipment. A student who had been writing at a desk in the back of the lab packed up and left the room.

"You should ask him." She turned and faced him. "He's got some interesting results from NOAA's Arctic cruise and this one, and the Bering Sea. There's some consistency."

"Interesting how?"

She hesitated. "He's being careful. He doesn't want us speculating. If you talk to him, don't say I said anything. I don't even know what he might share with you. I know he's concerned."

Ray fisted his hands in the pocket of his vest. "We're all in this together," he lied. "We're all colleagues here. It's good to see you again."

He went straight to the new receptionist and asked for Oakley. By his first name. The narrowing of the young woman's eyes suggested annoyance, perhaps questioning whether he was important enough to be bothering *her*, never mind the boss he had just insufficiently respected, but she took his name and went down the hall, leaving him to sit in a corner and breathe new-carpet chemicals. He thumbed through an old *National Wildlife* magazine, feeling as though he was at the dentist's office. A radio on the receptionist's desk was tuned low, but he recognized the angry voice from clips sometimes shown on the late-night comedy news shows. Really? Did anyone still listen to that crap? The yelling was, coincidentally enough, about the evils of the "liberal" American education system. "These young people, they talk about global warming like it's some big issue, because that's what they've been taught! They don't know what you and I know is true—that it's all a big hoax! They believe what they've been told by the liberals!"

My God.

But the receptionist was back, motioning him toward the inner sanctum. He fumbled for a kindly explanation: she could be a student, she could be studying media, she could be doing an assignment to examine the way propagandists manipulate language. Was that a notebook on her desk?

And then he was stumbling over more plush carpet into a spacious, brightly lit corner office with a view of birch forest dusted with the season's first snow, a desk with multiple computer monitors, a smallish conference table surrounded by three chairs, a couch, and an ornate antique floor lamp. There was far too much order to the room: bookshelves where the books were all upright, papers in neat piles, a large and soothing mountain-and-river landscape perfectly centered over the couch. Ray took this all in before shaking Oakley's hand and sitting down in perhaps the nicest office chair he'd ever experienced. Oakley was unreasonably tanned.

"I was just returning something," Ray said, "and wondered if you might be in. I thought maybe we should have coffee sometime and go over the fall cruise results, start thinking about spring and the projects and personnel for that."

"Pretty busy," Oakley drawled. "Didn't I give you what you needed for the cruise report?"

"I want to keep current with the data, keep sharing what we learn so we can grow the program and put together the next research plan." Why did he feel like a child begging for some indulgence? *Please, just give me the candy!* Why was there a power dynamic here? Was it the chairs, the view? (His own office not only lacked windows but smelled of formaldehyde.) When Oakley leaned forward Ray saw that *his* chair, squeaking, was black leather and chrome—a chair with a designer name, incredibly expensive, the kind you only saw (or imagined, in his case) in oil company boardrooms, with a padded headrest.

Oakley picked up a tablet. "Give me a deadline. I can keep track better if I use this."

"Ah, I haven't really thought in terms of a deadline. I was thinking more like, let's keep talking. Let's make sure everyone knows what's happening related to ocean conditions, how to talk about it, how to integrate the research."

Oakley tapped on his tablet, appeared to be reading something. "The people I need to talk to right now are funders. Senators, congressmen, the NOAA folks. I'm leaving for D.C. in the morning. Maybe when I get back. I've got to secure the funding first, got to make this university *the* place for OA research." He stood up and shrugged his way into a navy blue sports jacket. A small American flag pin was attached to the lapel. Ray tried not to recoil from the Republicanism of it: my country right or wrong, and science be damned.

"I thought you might have some preliminary data," Ray said, getting to his feet. "Or could tell me when you will. I'd like to put your measurements together with our biology, look for relationships."

"Nothing in science is ever so simple." The flag pin—its gold outline—twinkled.

"I didn't say 'simple,'" Ray said, a bit more forcefully than he intended. "It's because it's not simple that we need all the disciplines to work together, to find the larger patterns, to share information and hypotheses." He stopped himself. Why was he explaining a basic scientific principle to a chemical oceanographer who, if you believed his bio, had won prestigious awards and published dozens of papers?

Oakley chuckled. "Timing," he said. "It's the timing that's all-important. Trust me on this." He held out his arm to indicate the door, and Ray shuffled through just in front of him. They shook hands again, and then Oakley strode away.

Timing? Trust me? Trust this guy to do the "messaging," as they called it these days? Not if that hyperbolic piece of shit—that "environment" news item he'd seen—was any example. On the other hand, maybe it was useful to have a person on your team who could speak to Republicans and talk-radio listeners, could play their game. Maybe. That was not part of his skill set—or of the other scientists he knew.

On his way past the receptionist—who seemed to be Googling something he doubted was either work- or school-related—he noticed framed photos on the wall: Alaska's two senators and one congressman, Republicans all. He stopped to study the flawless, touched-up faces and the inscriptions—*To Jackson Oakley, best wishes.* When he was again through the open double-doors that seemed like a portal between worlds, he looked up at the wide blue and green banner that announced the Office of Ocean Acidification

Science. The much smaller text on the bottom indicated that the banner had come from the graphics department at DKI. DKI was a partnership between a Native corporation and the largest oil company prospecting in Arctic waters.

Ray was quite sure that the university had its own graphics department for making banners and signs. DKI? Was that necessary?

Chapter Six

A nnabel was selective about the schools in which she would teach, ever since the one in Delta Junction had complained about her clothes. She felt terrible, still, about having to abandon those most in need of what she had to offer; the children in repressive communities had so few options for keeping their little souls alive. It was pathetic what she'd found the regular teachers doing as "art." Tracing hands and coloring in the outlines to look like turkeys! "Collages" made of magazine advertising, where the children had simply glued together pictures of the consumer culture they coveted. Nothing she saw in what the teachers were pushing as art had anything to do with composition, line or color, or irony. Never mind actual creativity.

"Do not get me going," she'd said to the principal at the Fairbanks school, explaining why she'd walked away from Delta Junction and left the teachers there in the lurch, without a week of their own lesson plans. "I really wanted to work with those students. But I could not have the school dictating my personal clothing." That awful time, when she'd been called to the principal's office like a truant, flooded back over her. Nylons? Were they kidding her? They wanted her to wear nylons, and nothing with a heel over one inch high? They wanted a bra under the camisole? It was the children who had missed out, who would go through life joylessly, thinking that art was either macaroni glued to a juice can or something old and cracked, beyond their understanding, in a museum.

Fairbanks, fortunately, was a more enlightened place, for Alaska. The presence of the university meant that at least some of the adult population was educated, read books, was interested in more than driving four-wheelers through salmon streams and shooting up road signs. They did not freak out over dreadlocks.

The principal at the middle school, a lovely woman with her hair in a long graying braid, seemed amused by her Delta Junction story. Annabel had worked in her school before, several times, and there'd never been a problem. The students loved her. The wild animal mural, with its foot-long mosquito and only slightly larger trumpeting mammoth, had been a particular success. Those students, several years ago now, had learned about proportions, and they knew when to fuck with proportions and to be playful.

Annabel, of course, did not say "fuck" to any students, or teachers, or even the most enlightened principal. Proportion and distortion, she said. What do we perceive as large and small? What role does physical distance play? Time? Emotional distance? What did Picasso do? Look at this. Look again. She wanted them to understand that so much of art, of life, was about learning to see.

And so she began her two-week school residency, which coincidentally corresponded with the sixth grade's study of the ocean. Perfect karma. Here, far from the actual ocean, she would draw upon what she'd learned from the Gulf of Alaska. There were those linear thinkers—she formed a picture in her mind of one of Ray's confused looks—who could not have foreseen this dynamic, who might never understand the way every single thing enters the universe of thought and intuition and bubbles back up in unexpected ways and places. She herself could not have anticipated that she'd be conversing, right now, with another person who loved jellyfish— and not just to eat, although the principal had talked a lot to Annabel about her trip to Japan and the jellyfish strips she'd eaten with soy and chili sauce. How often did she get to say *Medusozoa* in an ordinary conversation?

So of course it was also karma when Annabel walked into the sixth-grade classroom and saw Aurora staring back at her. Not with hostility, although Annabel now regretted not making more of an effort to befriend her on the boat. The look was maybe that of preteen indifference, the kind that such girls cultivate. And a little bit of narrowed eye, as though she either was nearsighted and trying to bring Annabel into focus or recalling some unkind thing her father had undoubtedly said about her.

Annabel looked past her at the other round faces and the ADHD squirmings and jigglings and hair twirlings and the one kid with his head on his desk, and she went into circus mode, which meant that she whipped around some scarves while introducing herself, and then recited part of "The Rime of the Ancient Mariner," and then had them all on their feet with arms extended like an albatross's soaring wings. She explained what they'd be doing together for the next two weeks. In her proposal she'd called it "integrated art," but now she called it "exploration," "play," "expression." They would be working with balloons that they could twist into shapes or tape together, and with papier-mâché, and recycled materials like newspapers and paper towel tubes and lint they would collect from their clothes dryers at home. They were welcome to incorporate poetry and song; they could compose original music. They could work by themselves and in teams. Yes, they would also be using paints.

Annabel hated to be prescriptive, but she'd learned in working with students that they needed some parameters, a structure suitable to their age. Some of these kids would not know how to begin, would not think they were capable of "art." Others would automatically turn to what they already knew; they would produce drawings of their favorite fighter jets. She paused her talk and stretched her arms in a variation of the yogic star pose. "What we want to explore with our art is the sea and what lives in the sea. This can be sea creatures—especially creatures you might have just learned about. Like, I just learned about lantern fish that glow in the dark depths of the ocean." She'd found an awesome Internet photo and tapped the computer now to project the lit fish onto the classroom screen.

"Like halibut?" a boy shouted. "I caught one in Homer."

"Maybe like halibut," she said. "Maybe something smaller, like a parasite that attaches itself to a halibut."

They were all shouting now, and Annabel turned to the whiteboard and wrote down their ideas as fast as she could hear them. Killer whales and seals and starfish, guppies and king crab and tuna fish. Corals and sponges. Sharks. Many specific kinds of sharks. Salmon. King salmon. "Let's go smaller," she said.

"Minnows," someone said.

"Smaller."

Yes, they knew about plankton. They told her that plankton are responsible for half the world's oxygen. Really? She was dubious, but she was, once again, not a scientist or even a sixth-grader, and she just nodded. (Later, diligently, she looked it up. How had she never known something that important? Good old photosynthesis: plants on land do half the work, and phytoplankton do the other half.) The students told her, authoritatively, that plankton were at the base of the ocean's food chain and without plankton there'd be no fish or whales.

She showed more images—humpback whales breaching, sea otters, weird puffy fish, bloodless icefish from Antarctica, different kinds of plankton as seen under a microscope. A pteropod in its beautiful shell. At least one of the plankton images she'd lifted from the Internet, she realized, was Ray's. His name was right there, swimming in its corner. She hesitated, unsure whether it was better to pass over it without acknowledgment and risk offending his daughter, or to call attention to it and risk embarrassing her. She lingered too long on the cute little amphipod while trying to make up her mind, then went on to the lumpsucker.

From there, she laid out more of her plan: the next day, two-dimensional drawing to get some ideas going, then 3D with paper, tissue, found materials. She wanted everyone to think about the overhead space in the commons: what if the air space was the water column and the water column was full of plankton and fish and the other things that lived there? How would they populate it? Their assignment was to think about this, and to bring in any images or ideas they might like to work with. Yes, they could use their imaginations. They *should* use their imaginations. Art wasn't about making replicas; it was about interpretation. Yes, see you tomorrow.

Through all this, she had not made eye contact with Aurora. Aurora had not been among the shouting and arm-thrusting children. Annabel had only a dim sense of the girl sitting quietly, maybe slouching, at her desk. Now, as two boys crowded around Annabel to expand on their knowledge of sharks, shark teeth, and shark attacks, she looked over and saw Aurora, standing, looking back. Aurora rolled her eyes to the ceiling.

What that meant, Annabel didn't know. It might have been: *those boys are so immature and ridiculous with their sharks.* Or it might have been: *you're so ridiculous. Your plagiarized images, your ideas about a water column in the school, I'm not playing this game.*

She was gone from the room before Annabel could extricate herself from the shark enthusiasts.

———

NANCY LORD

At the beginning of each session, Annabel tried to introduce a particular concept. On the second day she wanted them to think about *seeing*, how essential it was for both scientists and artists to see both clearly and imaginatively. She had them look at more pictures of marine creatures, and then she took away the images and had them draw what they'd seen. She told them the story of Georg Steller, the naturalist who had come to Alaska from Russia with Vitus Bering.

"Almost all of what we know about the animal known as the Steller's sea cow is from what he recorded." This was before photography, she had to remind them; no, no video either. She showed them a drawing of the extinct animal: big, lumpy body, little head, a tail like a whale's, forelimbs and bristled feet for pulling itself through shallow waters. "That expedition discovered the sea cow around an island near the Russian coast, and within a very few years, hunters who stopped at that island killed the last one." She ignored the boy who pretended to be shooting at the projected image.

"Why did they kill them all?" a girl asked, almost in tears.

She had lost control of her narrative; she hated when that happened. She tried to explain about the hunters being hungry, the sea cows being slow and fearless. "Back then, no one worried about extinction, because they thought the world was so large and plentiful there would always be more of everything." She thought, but did not say, that ignorant people then, as now, assumed someone else—God—was directing their actions. Dominion and all that.

"My point is," Annabel said, bouncing up onto her toes, "that there's still a great deal to be discovered in our fabulous world. Every day someone's identifying some new sea creature, some new little bryozoan." She wasn't exactly sure what a bryozoan was, but the word had come to her. From the boat, she thought. She was pretty sure no one in present company would ask.

"What's a bryozoan?" A girl with bangs in her eyes stumbled over the pronunciation.

97

Thank God for Wikipedia. Annabel tapped into Google, and there it was: bryozoa, moss animals, filter feeders, colonial.

"But let me finish with Steller," she said, and brought up another image. "This is another creature that Steller described, that he thought he saw in Alaska. He called it a 'sea ape' and described it as having a head like a dog, no feet or arms or fins in the front, and a tail like a shark. It had thick gray hair and was playing with a piece of seaweed. The problem is that no one's ever seen an animal like this again, and there are no primate species that live in the ocean. If it wasn't an ape, what was it? Do you think he saw a new and very rare species, or do you think he might have seen something else but not really *seen* it?"

They liked the idea of a sea monkey, no problem with that part of their imaginations. They wanted to believe. But they could hypothesize, too: maybe some of the animal was hidden by the water, or maybe Steller was woozy from seasickness or he drank too much brandy, or he was trying too hard to find new animals and get famous. "Maybe he was a jerk," one of the it-takes-one-to-know-one boys said. They were, as a class, getting restless, and it was time to bring on the balloons.

She showed one last image, an immature fur seal that many scientists had concluded was most likely Steller's "sea ape."

"But it's a mystery," Annabel concluded, "and we like it like that. We get to appreciate the mystery, the wonder of it. We don't always need answers, do we?"

Aurora was nodding, or rocking in her seat—in any case, moving her head up and down. She didn't look displeased.

In the evenings, after she'd prepared for the next day with the students, Annabel worked on her art. She lived alone, except for daddy longlegs, the inoffensive arachnids that appeared with the first cold and eventually folded up as bent-kneed corpses in her cabin's corners, and for the occasional mouse or vole or shrew—she was embarrassed that she didn't know the difference—that would dash across the floor and, once, left a nest of pink babies among her scarves.

Her cabin was "dry," which meant that she hauled her water and took showers at the university when she went there for lap swimming. She maintained a Zen-like simplicity in her home—a few carefully placed bleached bones and river-washed stones, a few copies of *Artforum,* her futon. Her outhouse was more extravagant; adorned with suns, moons, and a ringed Saturn, it sheltered her collection of action figures in unusual physical positions. Her outhouse was, in fact, somewhat famous; it had once been featured in a book about Alaska outhouses, with a close-up of her George Bush doll squatting and waving.

This evening, almost halfway through her residency with the sixth grade, she sat in the light of her floor lamp, making lace and fretting about the girl who kept crumpling up or trashing all of her efforts because, she claimed, they "weren't good enough." Tatting was something her grandmother had taught her when she was a girl, certainly as imperfect as any, and she'd recently returned to it with the idea of tatting up the holes in a chain-link fence. She sat cross-legged on her Navajo rug and meditated on patterns—the ones in the rug; the ones in the Bach cantata she was listening to; the ones in her knotted lace; the ones in the cosmos. What was it they said about Persian rugs? The best ones were perfectly imperfect and precisely imprecise, because only God was perfect.

She watched her hands, the magnificent construction of bones and tendons and skin; muscle memory alone led them through the series of hitches and rings. How amazing was that?

Patterns and waves. *Sinusoidal,* the word young Colin had given her.

She had not had intention, but there it was: thread knot by thread loop, what was accruing looked very much like a coccolithophore. There were ovals and openings and intricate connectors, overlays and recesses, a complex geometry. Everything these days, it seemed, was starting to look to her like one or another kind of ornate plankton.

Or some kind of damaged plankton. Plates corroding, shells flaking and breaking, all the possibilities of negative space. It seemed that her jaunt on the sea, and the sad story developing there, was taking her into new dimensions.

By the second week, they were in full production. The class had great fun with balloons of multiple shapes, twisting them into sea mammal and fish forms before covering them with papier-mâché. (Inevitably, there'd been some boy-mischief with the phallus-shaped balloons, holding them in front of their crotches and all that.) Some students were at the painting stage. Others were working in teams to construct body-sized puppets of sea anemones (with wavy tentacles), giant squids (with monster eyeballs), and lots of sharks (with, of course, snapping jaws). The regular teacher had even joined them to help tear up newspaper and tie balloons.

On Tuesday afternoon, after beginning with a passage from Gertrude Stein ("Art isn't everything. It's just *about* everything."), Annabel circulated through the room, lending technical assistance. The girl who had been so unhappy with her first attempts was now building an exquisite tube worm. A boy with a sea turtle needed help with its cardboard legs.

"What about fins?" she asked another boy, whose fish was very much balloon-shaped—a poisonous blowfish, he'd told her. "How does this fish propel itself through the water?"

He shrugged, shoulders tight against his ears.

"She has an awesome caudal fin," Annabel said, careful to balance her pronoun use. She fingered the fish's meager tail, the one she had previously helped build from torn and gluey newspaper strips.

"What can we do with felt and glue? What about pieces of pipe cleaner?" She put her hands on the boy's thin shoulders and squeezed them, just a little, just for three seconds. Teachers—even visiting art teachers— weren't supposed to touch students.

At a girls' table, Aurora was working on a large, balloon-filled jellyfish. She showed Annabel how she was going to finish off the bell part and build the long, flowy, curtainy part from more papier-mâché. "These are called oral arms," Aurora told her. She pointed at the colored photograph she was using as her reference. "There are four, but I can't see them very well. They're all bunched up." Then she would add the tentacles, which would be orange string. "Twenty-four to thirty-two is typical for a sea nettle," she explained. "So maybe twenty-eight."

"That's terrific," Annabel said. She was a little concerned about how literal the girl was. She was not making a scientific model. Or maybe, in her case, she was.

The boys in the corner were getting too loud again, and Annabel circled back. Literal was not a problem here. Imagination was not a problem. The boys had built a clumsy mermaid with balloon breasts.

Annabel stood with her hands on her hips. "At the very least you're going to cover this creature with fish scales." She showed them how to layer metallic paper over the papier-mâché so that it looked like armor, right up to the neckline. "And then you can use a marker to draw a few thousand scales."

They looked back at her with anguished eyes. *A few thousand?*

"Attention, class!" Annabel called. "When you start painting, I want you to know we have lots of white paint. I want you to use a lot of *white paint!*"

In the end, Annabel was almost entirely happy with the whole process and the sea creatures that were its result. They had plenty of lovely creatures—including multiple jellyfish, several cylindrical shapes that could be plankton, and one comely pteropod with a rainbow-colored shell and very long antennae topped with plastic eyeballs—to hang in the commons. A few larger, heavier creatures would be paraded. Two girls had collaborated on a poem written on a circular paper shell, and one boy had made computer music he called "marine snow," that sounded just like one would expect—that is, a lot of plinking.

The presentation to the school would be on Friday, and on Thursday afternoon she got the custodian to help her hang the show. She laid out the work on the commons floor so that once it was in the air, there'd be a pleasing mix of shapes, sizes, and colors hanging from fishing line at a variety of levels.

The show was about two-thirds hung when a voice called out, "That's wrong."

Annabel was holding the ladder for the custodian and gave a quick glance. Aurora, in puffy coat and elfin cap, stood in the doorway, bent under a full backpack. *"What's wrong?"*

"You've got the rockfish up high and the jellyfish low. And that other one's too high—that flatfish, whatever it is."

"There's another jellyfish up high," Annabel said. Aurora's own anatomically perfect jellyfish was still on the floor, waiting to be hung where it could be easily admired.

"My dad's coming to get me," Aurora said. "He'll help. I told him we were hanging things and he said, 'At least they'll still exist.'"

Annabel said, "I don't know that we need any help."

"But he knows more than you about the water column."

"I'm sure he does." Annabel gave her attention to a star-shaped diatom slowly twisting on its line. "You do understand, don't you, that this project isn't meant to represent the actual ocean or the actual creatures in the ocean? It's an artistic expression?"

But Aurora was gone. A few minutes later she was back, and

she and her father were both craning their necks, looking up at Annabel's unscientific ocean. Ray was wearing a ridiculous tasseled ski cap.

"It's art," Annabel said, her spine stiffening.

The custodian finished with the hammerhead shark and reached for her to hand him the next piece, the weak-finned blowfish.

"I like it," Ray said.

Annabel nearly dropped her fish.

He walked around to the side, and then he saw the mermaid/ sea ape. It had been the bosomy mermaid, and then, for reasons not shared with Annabel but that she suspected might have had something to do with the difficulty of constructing arms, it had become a sea ape. The face was now furry. Alas, it still had bulgy breasts, though they were well covered with layers of paper and feathery fronds meant to look like seaweed. "It's a girl sea ape," the boys had explained.

"What is *that*?" Ray asked.

"A sea ape."

He didn't say anything for a minute, and then he breathed, "Of course."

It was then that the principal, that lovely woman, arrived from her office. "What's this about blacklights?"

Annabel indicated the blacklights in the corner, the ones she'd brought from storage, from a project she'd done years before. "Let's try them," she said. "We need the other lights off."

"I don't understand," the principal said.

"It's just for the final presentation," Annabel explained. "We'll get everyone in here, we'll turn off the regular lights, turn on the blacklights, the creatures will be all bioluminescence-y."

The principal crossed her arms over her chest. "I think not. Lights off, with this age group? They'll be all over one another."

"No we won't," Aurora said.

"Why not just try it?" Ray said. He'd taken off his cap and looked mildly authoritative. "I mean, just now, and see what happens?" He turned to Annabel and pulled in his chin, a look of skepticism. "What makes you think the ultraviolet light is going to make the artwork *bioluminescence-y?*" He exaggerated the word as though he was trying to spit it between his teeth. Without waiting for an answer, he extended his hand to the principal. "I'm Aurora's father," he said. "And Sam's, if you remember him. I teach marine biology at the university."

The principal shook her head, but she said to the custodian, "Mr. Preston, you can go turn off the lights."

As it turned out, with the lit exit sign, the purple glow of the blacklights, and the doorway open to the hall, the commons wasn't completely dark. It was, however, dark enough for every splash and drip of Annabel's white paint to glow. Of course Annabel knew about paint with phosphors! Of course she'd used a good part of her budget on the right white, and nontoxic paint! Of course she'd encouraged liberal white painting, and had done this without telling the students anything about why the paint was special or what they might expect.

A chorus of "wows" came from the doorway, where a handful of students had gathered. One, wearing a white shirt that had clearly been washed with a phosphate detergent, glowed like his own bulb. Annabel looked down at her ballet slippers—glowing—and then her fingernails—glowing.

"That is so cool," Aurora said, gazing upward.

Ray nudged Annabel's slipper with his big boot. "You'll have to teach them the difference between phosphorescence and bioluminescence. They're not the same thing, as I'm sure you know."

"Well, isn't this very hippie-dippy," the principal said. "Groovy psychedelic. All we need now is a strobe light."

"I have one," Annabel said.

The principal looked at her sharply. "Don't push your luck." But then she was smiling, and her teeth were white, too.

And so, the next day, the other classes came into the commons one by one and were treated to the blacklight show. The sixth graders, in a wonderfully choreographed presentation, paraded the puppets with flashlight eyes and pointed out the various species swimming and drifting overhead. They described bioluminescence and its role in the marine world. They gave little speeches about how dark the deep ocean is, and how the animals there communicate. The marine snow music played, and the boy who made it explained in a reasonably coherent if excitable manner about marine snow being "little pieces of dead things that float down and look like snow." The girls with the poem read it together and rhymed plankton with Langdon, the name of a basketball player they liked. The boys with the sea ape shared Steller's story and provided their own theory that Steller needed glasses but was otherwise a pretty good scientist. Although, one added, if he really had thought he had seen a rare animal, he should not have tried to shoot it.

The show was so good that they put it on one evening for parents, and the newspaper sent a reporter who wrote an enthusiastic article about the value of art in schools. In identifying some of the planktonic species, the reporter wrote "terrapod" instead of "pteropod." Reading this made Annabel smack herself in the forehead.

The only negative about the evening with the parents came at the end. When Ray and his wife were leaving, he nodded nicely to Annabel but then couldn't seem to help himself. He said, "Next time, you could ask me about diatoms. There seems to be some confusion. Oh, and"—his wife was tugging on his sleeve—"pteropods do not have eyeballs. Or eyes. They have nerve cells on the end of their antennae, but they can't see."

Chapter Seven

For Thanksgiving, Helen went "home" for the first time in a year. She'd been born in Barrow and raised mostly in Anchorage, but Igalik was where her mother's people were from. "From time immemorial," they liked to say. Her grandmother and aunts and uncles and most of her cousins still lived there. In fact, Helen could say that she was related to almost everyone in the village, by birth or marriage or adoption.

As a little girl she'd stayed most summers with her *aana*. Those had been crazy-wonderful times: the constant daylight, children running loose as baby foxes, every face familiar. Her cousins became the siblings she lacked. When her mother was between husbands, Helen had stayed one whole school year.

Now, Thanksgiving. All morning she and her *aana* had spent with pots of hot Crisco, making the famous fry bread with raisins that everyone loved. Other relatives and friends had run in and out, borrowing a soup pot, looking for Jell-O mix. Now, boots crunching on the hard-packed snow, Helen carried a last tray down the street to the community center. For once, the wind was still; the zero-degree air on her face felt good, especially after the kitchen's greasy heat.

The day was turning toward dusk, the sky softening to the south where the distant mountains folded into blue ribbons and the sun rested somewhere below them. In the other direction, blocked in part by the hulking school building and the clinic, the frozen Arctic Ocean stretched to the thin gray line of horizon. Towering snowdrifts between houses were sculpted into the shapes of playground slides and giant, feathery bird wings, and more snow, blasted by the wind, furred the sides of houses and sheds and the Conex shipping containers that people used for storage. Helen's heart swelled to the whiteness of the snow, the clean air, the good smells of her childhood. *Ai-ee,* how could she not love this place?

She had a lot to think about, and perhaps here, where she'd once felt so solidly grounded, was the place to do it.

Across the street, two tiny older women, sisters, shuffled along in their knee-length parkas, pulling their wheeled plastic coolers behind them. Helen knew them well—knew their children and grandchildren, had known their now-dead husbands. *"Unnusatkun!"* she greeted them. "Where are those boys to help you?"

"They play basketball," the older one answered. "They come soon."

A truck rumbled past, faces smearing against the windows, many hands waving. A group of children with their father hurried up, shouting, "Helen! Helen!"

"Look at you," Helen said, trying to remember all their names.

"Happy Thanksgiving!" they all shouted. The father—Freddy, the one she'd heard now led his father's whaling crew—held a baby against his chest. "How is Fairbanks?" he said, and then offered his own answer. "Too many people."

"Yes," Helen agreed. "Too many people. But I like the university."

"You always the smartest girl," Freddy said. He smiled his jagged-tooth smile.

They were converging on the community center from every

direction: more elders in their best clothes, children carrying smaller children, flush-faced cooks with steaming pots and pans, men with another folding table. Helen, like a fish in a school, followed them through the doorway.

Inside, the smells were of delicious foods, warm bodies, and—distinctly and spectacularly—whale. Indeed, the whole front of the room was filled with rubber totes and bags of bowhead whale—black and white maktak, marbled meat, frozen chunks with their oily, nutty fragrance.

Helen maneuvered her tray to an empty spot on a table already crowded with *niqipiaq,* their Eskimo food. She piled her parka with others in a corner and found her *aana* seated in one of the folding chairs, visiting with other elders. "Happy Thanksgiving! Happy Thanksgiving!" Helen made her way around the room, shaking hands as she went, greeting her friends, her neighbors, the elders who had watched over her as she grew up, the uncle who had taught her to fish and the other uncle, who taught her checkers, her Aunt Susie, the teachers she had met before and the new teachers, the *tanik* clerk at the post office, her cousin who was going to get married and the cousin's husband-to-be, the little cousins, the new babies. She had to hold the new babies and praise each one. Children danced all around her: girls with fancy barrettes in their hair, boys with buttoned vests over white shirts.

"We fatten you up," her grandmother's friend Bernice said, pinching her arm. She watched Bernice examine her clothing through her thick and dusty glasses—the calico *atikluk* worn over leggings. Helen had chosen the material—a deep purple with lighter purple flowers—and Aunt Susie had sewn it for her, with all the rickrack trimming. Helen blushed. At her age she should not only be sewing her own *atikluks* but making them for others. Her fancy *kamiks,* too—she'd paid a woman in Fairbanks, a stranger, to make her sealskin boots.

After everyone had gathered and the minister had given the Thanksgiving prayer in both languages, Helen joined with other young people to take the food around the room. She and her cousin Elton, a high school junior, carried between them a huge pot of goose soup, ladling first into the elders' bowls and then circling the room. Before and behind them, other teams carried equally large pots of sheep soup, duck soup, and caribou stew. Other servers followed with trays of fry bread and Eskimo donuts. Then they switched to the dry fish, and the turkey and ham the village corporation had supplied. The giant bowl of crowberries. Pasta and Jell-O salads. The servers went around again with seconds and thirds, and the women opened their coolers and filled their Tupperware containers with soup and fish and turkey.

In this way, Helen leaned into every face, heard about who was away, who was sick, who had had all his teeth taken out. She answered the questions about how her mother was (well, with a new job in a billing office) and where her boyfriend was (too busy for one, can't find a man as handsome as you, a smile—depending on who was asking). She fetched napkins and cans of soda. All the elders said how glad they were that she had come. You take care of your *aana,* they said. You don't forget us. You make us proud.

She blushed to hear that. She had come back, she loved these people, but was she not drawing further from them all the time? Was she not measuring herself against the white world and its definitions of success? She couldn't tell them about Jackson, couldn't have brought him here even if their relationship wasn't a secret. His polished shoes and "good" haircut—they were foreign to this place. He would not have known what to do with his hands without his phones and tablets, and he would not have tolerated sitting on a metal folding chair for hours. Although he would be charming, and the villagers would be impressed, in the way they could be, by what they thought was better than all they were.

Perhaps, despite all the advantages she'd had, she was a girl from Igalik after all, conditioned to admire what she was not.

This was a new thought, one that was just settling, like a flock of ducks on a pond. She had been flying with it all the way from Fairbanks, from her last meeting with Jackson, unable or unwilling to find it a calm landing spot.

Her uncle's friend Amos turned to her. "You should come earlier, for whaling. And polar bears. Twenty-eight at one time this year." Amos had started his own tourism business, driving people who flew in from Fairbanks to the boneyard past the airport. This was where the whale carcasses were left after whaling for the bears to scavenge. Helen couldn't remember bears coming so close to town when she was a child. Things were different now, with the summer sea ice gone. Everyone had been telling her how early the ice had gone out in spring, how it was still gone during whaling, how late it had returned. The bears waited on shore for the ice.

"I'd like to see the bears," Helen said. "Maybe next year."

"Before they're gone," Amos said.

He meant, Helen knew, not gone as in "gone from town, out on the ice" but gone as in "extinct."

Amos took a drink of his soda. "They say pretty soon all the ice will be melted, and no more bears."

"Yes," Helen said. "They say that. But the ice will last longer north of Canada, and some bears will survive there." She was very aware of the studies that showed Alaska's polar bears losing weight and having fewer cubs—clear signs of food stress. Some were swimming very long distances from the ice edge. After storms, others were spotted from the air—white lumps floating, motionless, drowned.

"I say they'll adapt," Amos said. "Just like us. *Nanuuq* is very smart."

Elton was giving her a look. Too much talk, not enough ham. This was not the time and place to elaborate on the disastrous effects of global warming. Or to tell Amos that her scientist colleagues routinely said, with no word-mincing, "Polar bears are toast." If only bears could change how they lived as easily as Amos could change from hunter to tour guide.

A poster on the wall, beside the list of Iñupiat values, bore a picture of a polar bear's face and the words: *Beware! Do not leave children unattended or food in the open!*

"You see polar bear tracks behind the school this morning?" the next woman asked her. "One skinny one still hanging around."

But it was time, now that everyone had filled up on so many good foods, for the next event. The servers, still in their pairs, lifted and dragged the heavy totes and bags of whale delicacies around the room, starting again with the elders and circling through. The prized maktak, the dark meat, the slices of tongue and flipper and fluke. Helen bent to ask each waiting person the size of his or her household, then set one or two or several hunks of gleaming maktak into the cooler or the black garbage bag the person held open. This sharing by the whaling captains—to all according to need—was as it had always been and would be, the Iñupiat way.

Women took out their *ulus* and, on cardboard laid on tops of coolers or on their plastic plates, cut maktak into thin slices, and everyone began eating again. Elders' eyes lit up, little boys smacked their lips and dipped pieces into pools of mustard, the smallest children held their mouths open like begging baby birds.

Back at the tables, the servers now filled their own plates.

Sophie, the cousin who was being married, was six months pregnant and had dark circles under her eyes but was otherwise the same smiling girl Helen had carted around on her hip and woven wildflower bracelets with. The day after Thanksgiving, which was also the day before Sophie's wedding, Helen crossed the street from her *aana*'s to visit with her cousins and help with the wedding preparations.

Everyone had slept late that morning, after all that food and then an evening return to the community center for hours and hours of dancing. She loved to see how fiercely Eskimo dance had returned to Igalik and how generational it was: the old men with their drums, the teenagers crouched and leaping as imagined hunters, tiny children in their tiny boots imitating it all.

"Do you like it?" Sophie asked, opening a box she'd pulled from under the bed so Helen could see the wedding dress, blue chiffon with an empire waist.

"It's beautiful. You'll look fabulous."

In the next room, a game show was on the TV, and various children including Sophie's younger siblings and her toddler were playing around it. Someone had a toy helicopter powered with a rubber band, and they were taking turns winding and releasing it. Sophie's mother, Helen's Aunt Clare, was in the kitchen making pancakes.

Some of the older cousins came in from outdoors, bringing with them the mixed smells of freezing air, cigarettes, and marijuana. Elton, with earbuds and saggy pants, was nodding to a beat. They all sat around the Formica table and ate pancakes with berries and syrup. The boys talked about taking the snowmachines into the mountains to look for caribou. Thomas, the husband-to-be, got out his knife and went looking through a drawer for a sharpening stone. A loud laugh track now came from the TV.

It was all so familiar—familial—to Helen. She loved the closeness, the ease with which everyone flowed through the small rooms and in and out of conversation, the moist warmth of them all. Aunt Clare brought a pot of tea to the table. Her cousin Nina was cracking eggs for the wedding cake. Helen looked around at the faces that were so like her own. The anxiety she'd brought north with her was dissolving.

And yet. This wasn't her life and would never be in her future.

She couldn't imagine waking each morning in the same small house, always among the same known faces, and then filling each day with cutting meat and making tea and caring for babies. Even if she could be a teacher or an administrator, this would not be enough. She looked around again at the others, who were arguing, playfully, about who did the best cover of a Lady Gaga song.

Did she feel superior? If she was smart in school-ways, she also knew that there were many ways of being smart, and many sources of education. She'd be helpless before a broken-down snowmachine. She barely knew how to pluck a goose. But she had ambition, and that should not be a bad thing, in any culture. She wanted to make a difference in the world.

Jackson had said this to her: "You've got the temperament to be an amazing scientist." She had thought, then, that he meant to be encouraging.

"Helen brought pastries," Sophie said. "And baby oranges."

And she had, brought a box of frosted pastries from the best Fairbanks bakery, a big box of clementines, and a pineapple. No one traveled to any village without filling up her baggage with the maximum allowed weight—and that usually meant food. The pastries were not the healthiest—but heck, she only visited once a year, and this was a wedding!

Thomas, at a computer in the corner, offered to show her his pictures of the big storm in July—the one that had pounded the coastline, undercutting the bluff and flooding the airport. He said, almost as though he were boasting, "Three days no planes could land, and then only a Cessna."

Helen had monitored the situation from afar. Without the airport, there was no way in or out of the village, no lifeline. Fortunately, there hadn't been any medical emergencies, and everyone came together to care for one another and the community's needs. At the university this was called "resilience." The Iñupiat had their own word for it—*inuuniaq*—the business of staying alive. Always, they'd been good at that.

Now, though, they needed to move the airport farther from the ocean, and it wasn't clear where it could move to or who would pay. It was only clear that it would be very expensive.

Thomas showed her a few photos of polar bears and an *ukpiq*—snowy owl—and then left with Sophie's older brother to see about gas for a snowmachine.

Sophie said, "He complains all the time about the Internet. How slow it is. If it was faster, and cell phones, he would have a business selling posters and calendars he makes with his photos. He wants to make videos." Thomas's job now was running the village recreation program, which, as far as Helen understood, meant opening and closing the gym for basketball. Sophie deposited an armload of ribbon spools and tissue papers on the table and started cutting ribbons for Helen to tie and curl.

Elton had sprawled on the couch. "One more year of high school," Helen said. "Are you thinking of college? Will you come to Fairbanks?" Some of her cousins, including Sophie, had tried the university, but none had "stuck." They got homesick, or they weren't academically prepared by a high school where the science teacher also taught math and shop classes, in all four grades.

Elton shrugged.

Aunt Clare said, "She gets to take cruises."

"That's part of what I do," Helen said. "Oceanography involves getting out there and taking samples, looking at change. But there's every kind of program at the university. Engineering, computers, nursing."

Nina, who was just a freshman, was leaning against the electric oven, gathering its heat. "You study the ocean?"

"I study the chemistry of the ocean and especially the cycling of carbon. There's a pretty big concern right now about the way the ocean's absorbing so much carbon dioxide."

The lowered eyes stopped her. She told Nina a little more about what she did at the university, trying to make it sound attractive. The cruises, the lab machinery, teaching younger students. "Not everyone loves data," she apologized, "but I do."

Sophie was frowning at her ribbons, or maybe just frowning in general.

The conversation shifted back to the wedding. Sophie wanted to make sure the teachers knew they were invited. Would Helen do her hair in a French braid?

Helen tried to stay in the moment, but her mind was elsewhere. There was no getting around that it had not gone well just before she left Fairbanks. How much of it was about the data and how much was something else, she wasn't sure. None of it felt right.

She'd checked and rechecked her data. She'd gone over it with Jackson. He'd studied the printouts, shuffled pages, pursed his lips.

They of course knew that acidification was occurring in Alaska's cold waters and that, as she'd explained to Annabel on the ship, much of the water along the continental shelves was already—way ahead of predictions—seasonally undersaturated with aragonite, a threat to shell-building. On their cruise, the waters where so much lived were already affected. One of her tasks had been to separate out the amount of carbon dioxide absorption attributed to human activities—the anthropogenic "signal"—from their samples. When she did that, the undersaturation went away. Cause and effect.

But there was more. When she took into account the biological productivity of the sampled areas, the acidity was higher where there was more life. Productivity was pulling in carbon dioxide from the atmosphere, acting as a "pump." This suggested to her that the most biologically rich areas would be the most vulnerable to acidification.

The results from the Gulf cruise—preliminary as they might be—were supported by data from the Bering Sea and the Arctic. In the Arctic, the reduction in sea ice correlated to increasing acidification. There was modeling involved—not her field—but a Japanese paper she'd read projected that, of all the oceans, the Arctic would suffer the most rapid and sharpest decline in pH.

"So how are we going to present this?" Helen had asked Jackson when she finally got time with him. He'd been traveling again and otherwise occupied with administrative work, and she'd had trouble getting him to sit down at the computer. "A cross-school meeting? Bring in the biologists for the productivity aspects?"

There were protocols, Helen knew. You shared your data and theories with your colleagues—in this case Ray Berringer and the other biologists, but also those working in physics, geography, modeling. They asked tough questions to force you to defend the work, and they helped you identify any aspects or possibilities that might need additional scrutiny. They contributed from their own fields. Papers would be written, reviewed, published. Even before that, with preliminary findings of any significance, it was necessary to work with the university's communications people to inform the larger community.

"Screw Ray Berringer," Jackson had said. "Him and his bugs."

It had taken Helen a minute to respond, and she'd said very quietly, deferentially, "It's not really about Professor Berringer. It's about sharing the data and letting people know how serious this is."

"Sorry," Jackson said. He covered her small hand with his large knuckly one. His gold Oxford ring, with the image of an open book surrounded by crowns, was hard against her skin. "It's just that some people will jump to conclusions. We're not going to put this out there right now."

"We're not going to put what out? None of it?"

"I don't want to be alarmist. This is the kind of information that isn't easy to interpret. People get excited, think it's the end of the world. One year's numbers do not a crisis make."

"What about the anthropogenic signal?"

He looked at her sternly. "What we've got right now is very limited data, and I want to take an appropriate amount of time to review that. There's really nothing yet to share. So please, it stays in-house." He rose from his chair with a half-smile. "Good work, though. Woods Hole is going to be lucky to get you."

That had been it. He'd left the room, and then she'd gathered her papers and left. They'd talked on the phone a couple of times before she came to Igalik, briefly. Nothing really. Just "have a good vacation." She flew north; he flew south—something work-related and something about selling a house he'd owned with his former wife. He'd complained about an incompetent real estate agent.

He had no patience with people who couldn't perform their jobs.

He was recommending her for a fellowship at Woods Hole, a dream position.

He was reminding her of the influence he could exert.

Not so long ago, there was a system that worked. You sought the advice of elders, and then followed it. Helen, eating leftover turkey and pie with her grandmother that evening, watched the old woman's head bend over her plate. Her *aana's* experience in life, with the wisdom passed down to her from *her* elders, could not be relevant to Helen's current dilemma. Their worlds had spun too far from one another.

Instead, they spoke of the old days. Her *aana*, more and more, liked to live in memories of that time—the sod houses, camping every summer on the barrier islands, the time her brother had a pet baby polar bear that lived in the house with them. This was a story Helen had heard dozens of times, but she had never asked what became of the bear. Now she did.

"It got bigger and they take it away."

"Who took it away?"

"I don't know. Its name is *Qannik*."

"The bear's name."

"Yes. Now there are more polar bears."

"Around the village, you mean."

"The hunters say there are more bears now."

This was not the first time Helen had heard this argument—that because hunters were seeing more bears, that must mean there *were* more bears. If there were more bears, it was OK to shoot more. She explained a little about the ice and the data transmitted to satellites from bears wearing research collars, but her grandmother only shook her head and pushed out her lower lip. *Aana* was very firm about one thing: it was wrong to put collars on bears.

There were popping noises from outside. Helen guessed they were the cracker shells used to haze bears from town, or maybe someone was finishing the holiday with a few firecrackers. Her grandmother didn't seem to hear the noise, and Helen didn't say anything. A short while later, though, Elton came to give them the news. The skinny bear that had been hanging around was dead. "It came on Henry's porch, trying to get some scraps." Now they were taking it to the shop behind the school to skin it. Did Helen want to see it?

She went. When she got there, the bear was laid out on its back, legs splayed, its vulva exposed. Helen could only think how like a woman it looked—a woman waiting on an exam table for a cold speculum to split her. The bear was small and angular, its emaciated body covered with fur as dirty as an old mophead. Children were taking turns lifting and holding its large paws, examining the rough pads and the claws. They were excited: a bear they could touch!

She left before the men cut into it.

Outside, the streetlights hovered over the village with enough sickly yellow pall to obscure the night sky. She stood in the quiet and the cold for a few minutes, trying to restore her equilibrium, her objective and unsentimental self. She'd seen plenty of dead animals in her life, had helped with butchering, cleaning intestines, boiling hearts. Why did she suddenly feel so emotional about a single dead bear? It was a *good* thing that someone had shot it. It could have been dangerous, so desperately hungry it might have snatched a child from the playground. It couldn't have survived the winter, in any case; it would have died a miserable, starving death.

She turned off the main road and walked to the end of the street where the lights gave out and the eroding bluff fell away to the frozen ocean. Some of the older houses on the end weren't connected to the utilidor for water and sewer, and slabs of lake ice were lined up like big mirror shards in their yards, to be taken indoors and melted as needed. Some of the old ways continued. Beyond that, past the steel barrier that kept drivers from driving off the edge, the jumbles of sea ice were awash in starlight. There, between what remained of beach and what formed horizon, lay her Arctic Ocean, *Tabiuq*. She pictured the globe that was Earth from above its shrinking ice cap, a view that had only been possible for a little longer than her lifetime. She knew, as her elders had not, that their ocean flowed from and into all other oceans and acted as a singular circulatory system and heat engine for the planet.

It was not, she realized, the fact of a dead bear that had unmoored her. It was the unnaturalness, the wrongness. A female bear of that age should have been a fattened and denned-up bear ready to give birth. Perhaps this one was sick; perhaps there was something else wrong with it, something that had nothing to do with the loss of summer sea ice, seals, a place to stand, the breakdown of its world. In the old days, a shaman would have had an explanation: someone had not behaved properly, had not respected the land or the sea or what they provided. In the old days, the bear would have brought a warning, and the warning would have been heard.

There was little room, anymore, for supernatural belief.

Someone should measure the fat on that bear. Someone should check its ovaries. For a few moments she thought of going back, asking to cut and bag samples to send to people with the tools of science. They were getting used to that in the village—used to experts coming in, shooting darts into bears and pulling their teeth, cutting testicles from dead whales, scraping scales off fish. Most of the people found this distasteful, disrespectful. It was not the way they were raised to live.

Every child learned Iñupiat values, the ones painted on the community center wall. *Sharing. Respect for others. Cooperation. Respect for nature. Responsibility to tribe.*

Helen stayed at the edge of the frozen, starlit sea until the cold pressed knowing into her bones.

CHAPTER EIGHT

December was always a difficult month in Fairbanks. Not as cold as January, usually, but depression-dark. The sun was never much more than a heatless pale ball crossing the sky, usually behind trees, for a couple of hours in the middle of the day. You had to pay attention; you had to make yourself leave the building and walk to your car or the library while there was a chance to catch some natural light. You had to take vitamin D pills. Aside from that, it was the end of the semester. Papers were due, tests needed to be given and graded, everything had to come together in a crescendo of achievement. If students (or faculty, or the breakfast cook in the cafeteria) were going to have nervous breakdowns, this was the inevitable and inconvenient time.

Ray had his ways of coping, not all of which involved alcohol. Nelda had bought him a lightbox a few Christmases before, and he dutifully sat before it each morning with his coffee and his laptop, on which he read *Science Daily* and *The Onion*. On this morning he read that the military was studying the camouflage abilities of cephalopods before turning to "Man in Coma Enters GOP Race, Already Topping Polls."

As he'd known would happen, the group from the September cruise had stayed in touch, with each other and with him. The students went out together for pizza and beer and to brain-blasting concerts. They stopped by his office, not always for an apparent reason. Nastiya and Marybeth were two of his students, and he supervised their work. Nastiya had finally, sort of, finished a draft of her paper on *Metridia pacifica,* despite the long weekends with her fisherman-boyfriend. Tina and Cinda were also completing their degrees, and he'd allowed Cinda, who had told him more than he needed to know about her wayward husband, to sometimes bring her two young children to the lab, where they sat at a corner table and drew pictures that scared Ray; there was a lot of black and deep purple crayon and sometimes a figure that looked like a dad-man exploding. Colin, of course, never tired of talking about his wave vectors but was also now in a band called Angular Frequency and was raising money to make a CD; Ray gave him twenty dollars. Alex conferred about his nutrient work and Ray tried to appear smart enough to understand him. Robert had come out as gay, or bi, or trans—Ray was not sure which.

They were all good kids. They would all get the grades and honors they expected, their scholastic entitlements.

Helen he'd seen less of. Since that time in October when he'd chatted with her in the chemistry lab, they'd crossed paths maybe two or three more times in the building, once at the snack bar where she was eating a plate of nachos. She'd looked a little embarrassed, perhaps about being seen eating plasticized orange cheese, and they'd only exchanged pleasantries. She might have thought he blamed her for the lack of cooperation he'd gotten from Oakley. That fucker still had never gotten back to him.

Soon enough, everything student-related would empty, like water down a drain, from his mind. For Christmas break, Ray and his family were headed to Belize. The tropical corals and the outrageous *Cnidarian planulae* were calling him—not to mention the sun, the warm water, and the piña coladas.

But first, Ray needed to file his year-end report for the National Science Foundation grant that had largely funded the fall cruise. Most of this was easy—who had participated, what work was accomplished, how many samples were collected. There was the usual boilerplate about the value of developing the next generation of ocean scientists and the importance of the work given all the changes, including the anthropogenic ones, that the oceans were experiencing. He cut and pasted from previous reports that he doubted anyone at the NSF had even read. He'd written up the status summary: the overly warm temperatures, phytoplankton bloom, zooplankton species and abundance. He referenced the data about zooplankton growth and reproduction rates and the nutrient chemistry and chlorophyll measurements. He folded in the couple of sentences Oakley had given him when he first asked, which amounted to the facts that they had taken hundreds of samples to measure for dissolved inorganic carbon and total alkalinity, and that ocean acidification was something essential to monitor.

Ray had the report up on his computer screen. It was the same old dilemma: the NSF wanted to know (and to be able to convince the politicians) that public funds had been well spent. The data themselves were meaningless to most people, and there was no point in sharing raw numbers. The data only made meaning, only became essential, when they were collected long term and analyzed for trends. But the funding came year by year, and year by year all he had was more data and some mushy language about variation, the time series, and the influence of El Niño and La Niña. Nothing dramatic. Nothing sexy.

He spruced up the report by tying his zooplankton results into practical purposes—that is, hypothesizing a bit about the relation to salmon populations. No one—not even the NSF—really cared about plankton by themselves. He read through what he had and felt again the deficiency regarding ocean acidification. OA was the hot topic. OA was driving ocean research these days. He had to have those preliminary results. He had to create at least a spark of interest in what they had found and what it might mean for his zooplankton and all the rest.

He typed up an e-mail to Jackson Oakley:

> *Jackson, deadline time. I need something more, something current, on OA work for the final GOA cruise report. Please send results however prelim ASAP. I know I don't need to tell you how important this is so we continue to get funding.*

Before he sent it off, he deleted the last sentence and typed in *Thanks* instead.

Two days later, there was no answer from Oakley. Ray walked over to the OA office wing.

"Dr. Oakley is away," the nice secretary told him, smiling like she was somehow delivering good news. "Oh, yes, he checks his e-mail regularly. He texts constantly. I'm sure he'll get right back to you."

Ray, sweating in the wool layers he was used to wearing in his underheated part of the building, tried not to scowl. "Do you talk to him?"

She stiffened. "Of course."

"When you do, would you please tell him that Ray Berringer needs to hear from him?"

"I'll do that." She penciled a note and then turned away and began to gather some papers that Ray suspected didn't need gathering.

On his way out, he looked for Helen and found her clattering a keyboard in an office next to the lab. He stood in the open doorway. "Working on your thesis?"

She looked startled to see him. "In part. Yes. You know how it goes."

"Remind me what your title is."

She didn't answer right away. Pauses were something Ray was familiar with, working with Native students. You had to learn to wait, if you wanted to be culturally sensitive. He counted *one, two.*

She said very softly, "Seasonal Aragonite Undersaturation Rates."

Ray nodded. "Where's your professor these days?"

Helen motioned him closer. Professor Oakley, she told him, was somewhere in Texas, she didn't know where or when he'd be back—sometime the next week. She had tried—twice now—to get him to call a meeting with everyone involved with OA. She'd gone home for Thanksgiving. She'd given it a lot of thought. She didn't know what to do.

Ray wasn't sure he was following.

She looked nervously past him, into the hall. "He doesn't want to share the data or talk about what it means. He asked me not to. He says it's about timing. Waiting for what? Why would you not share your data with your colleagues?"

Ray leaned against the doorjamb. "I don't know. Why would you not share your data with your colleagues?"

They stared at one another.

She said, "He's the chair of my thesis committee."

"Of course he is."

"I don't know what to do," she said again.

Ray thought of asking her to trust him, although as soon as the thought came to him he pictured Oakley, that time in his office, using those same, drenched-in-insincerity, trust-me words. Instead he said, flatly, "I've been waiting for him to answer my e-mail. I asked him for something for the cruise report, something to justify our work so we can get more funding for next year."

"He seems to find funding for OA."

"I've noticed. But not the integrated work."

Helen took a scrap of paper from her desk and wrote something down. She handed it to Ray. "Please don't tell anyone I gave this to you. *Please*. But look it up. Google around. There's a link."

Ray looked at the scrap. *Council for Science Integrity*. He looked back at Helen, chewing on her lip. He understood that she didn't mean solely a URL link. "Very cloak and dagger," he said, forcing a grin. He folded the paper into a square no bigger than a thumbtack and shoved it deep into his pocket, then made as if to crouch like the cartoon Pink Panther, shoulders to his ears, before hopping into the open.

Back at this desk, Ray immediately Googled. The first thing he saw on the Council for Science Integrity website was the opportunity to order a book called *Climate Change Debunked*. At the bottom of the page, the Council was described as "a clearinghouse of scientific information on environmental solutions for a healthy future." The Council had sponsored a conference several months earlier called "Climate Change: Overheated Rhetoric" that featured "distinguished scientists and think tank scholars" who spoke, apparently as one voice, about abandoning "the failed hypothesis of man-made climate change" and embracing "true science and economics to understand our ever-changing climate and its cycles."

Ray's vision blurred as he felt the black pressure behind his eyeballs build. Those fuckers? Surely Jackson Oakley didn't have anything to do with deniers! He looked away, to his wall poster from the last scientific conference, with maps of temperature regimes and copepod distributions. He breathed until he could see again, could read more. He looked at a list of conference speakers: no actual climate scientists, of course. He recognized the name of a physicist who had once been quite famous for developing artificial satellites but was now elderly and demented; he had famously said that warming, should it come, would be good for humanity because then wine grapes could be grown in England. He saw the name of the equally repellent but less sympathetic (by virtue of still being in possession of most of his mind) US senator who did his best to threaten and defund federal agencies that had anything to do with protecting the environment.

In large letters at the bottom of the conference page: federal and state elected officials had been invited to attend at no cost.

There was more: conjured-up news articles about the expense of wind technology and "evidence" that the ice caps were fine, policy papers, podcasts, speaker events, and a legislative forum (prominently encouraging legislators to oppose "costly and unnecessary" actions to address "fraudulent" global warming).

Ray Googled again. According to various bloggers, funding for the bogus group came from the oil, gas, and coal industries.

He almost didn't hear the knock on his door. Colin. Ray waved him in. "I'm kind of on a mission here," he told him. "What do you know about the Council for Science Integrity? They might be getting involved with OA."

Colin wrinkled his nose and pulled his phone from a pocket. He had something in about two seconds: a policy paper produced by the Council, attacking "biased" newspaper reportage about "alleged ocean acidification." The sin of a North Carolina newspaper had been to report that a documentary film had presented ocean acidification as a danger. According to a senior fellow at the Council for Science Integrity, a fact-checker would have found that the ocean was not acidic but alkaline, and that ocean acidification could not have increased by 30 percent since the pH had only dropped by 0.1. The newspaper, the fellow claimed, shared the film's liberal bias instead of questioning its alarmism.

"That's just plain wrong," Colin said, indignant. "I doubt very much that either the film or the reporter said the ocean was acidic. Didn't that guy bother to find out what OA means, what acidification involves? Look, every single thing he criticizes here as being bad information is factual. It's *science.* He's screwing with the numbers. This guy is *bullshit!"*

Ray was feeling the pressure behind his eyes again. "Colin," he said, "think about it. What's the guy's purpose here? Is he really trying to discredit the science, or the film or newspaper? No. This is a classic campaign to confuse the public. If people think there's controversy surrounding the subject, industry wins. They get to keep building their coal plants and fracking for oil. It's the same shit they've been doing for years with global warming."

At that moment, Ray would have given almost anything to quit the computer and go home and have a drink. A major part of him, the part that just wanted to go on counting copepods and photographing larval fish and admiring the innocence of students, wanted to leave what he knew right there.

"What?" Colin said.

"What?"

"You were going to say something else."

Ray nodded slowly. "Yes. Google 'Council for Science Integrity' and 'Oakley.'"

And there it was. Dr. Jackson Oakley had attended a Council seminar at the CSI headquarters, which were, of course, in Houston. Dr. Jackson Oakley, of the University of the North's Office of Ocean Acidification Science. The Council for Science Integrity was pleased to have Dr. Jackson Oakley as an advisor.

"Huh?" Colin squirmed like he was trying to hold in a fart. "Why would he be advising those guys?"

Ray was already typing furiously, with true, raging fury. And then he hit "send."

Two days later, Ray still did not have any data from Oakley. He did, however, have a "rather urgent" message from the dean.

"This is rather unfortunate," Dean Morris said when Ray took a seat in his office, the big uncluttered desk between them. Ray could not help noticing that the dean had the same kind of designer chair as Jackson Oakley, a chair that squeaked when the dean leaned back as if to put extra distance between them. "First of all, I assume you know the university code of conduct?" Ray nodded. "The part about professional standards and civility?" Ray nodded again. "Well, that's not the most unfortunate part. Unfortunately, your intemperate e-mail ended up with the local newspaper. I'm sure they'll be calling you for additional comment. They've already asked me what the heck is going on."

"My e-mail was leaked to the newspaper?"

"Leaked, hacked, given, I don't know—or really care. The point is that they're doing a story about a professor—that would be you—attacking another professor. I am *not* a happy man." He looked over his glasses at Ray. Actually, he looked *comically* over his glasses, like the clichéd school principal trying to put the fear of God into a boy who had thrown one too many spitballs. Ray knew he should be acting both respectful and contrite, but the fact that the dean was an ineffectual ass was getting in his way, as was the knowledge that the only way newspaper people would have his e-mail was if Oakley had given it to them. He was trying to remember just what he'd written and how rude it might sound to someone who didn't know the situation. And he was beginning to seethe again that Oakley could not be bothered to respond to any of his e-mails, even to acknowledge receiving them and offer some excuse about his data, but he obviously had time to forward Ray's e-mail. And why would he even do that? Why would he want to draw attention to the fact that he was receiving the ire of a colleague? The motive part of it was puzzling Ray. But the dean was waiting for him to say something.

"Professionalism?" Ray said. "Is it professional to associate with an industry-paid propaganda group dedicated to denying and misrepresenting science?"

"Are you suggesting that Dr. Oakley has behaved unprofessionally?"

"Yes, I am."

"And if you have such a suspicion, do you know what the proper channels are for that concern? Do they involve sending obscene e-mails?"

Probably not, Ray had to admit. Or probably, yes, he should have brought his concerns to the dean and he probably should not have sent an e-mail when he was upset. Ray tried to explain about needing OA data, and then about the Council for Science Integrity.

"Were you drunk?" the dean interrupted him.

Ray could feel himself sinking. Clearly, this whole meeting was about *him, his* inappropriate behavior, the need for *him* to be called on the carpet. "No, I was not," he said. "I was angry."

"Perhaps you need some anger management training?"

Oh, God no. Not that. Not some therapy group where he'd have to sit in a circle and practice saying nice things.

The dean squeaked his chair again and shook his head slowly. There was a big silence while he stared at Ray with an expression that looked to Ray like loathing. "I haven't talked to that reporter yet. I said I'd call him back. What I'm going to tell him is that you've been reprimanded for unprofessional behavior and I'm sure it won't happen again. If he calls you, I suggest you have the same story. You're sorry, you have only the greatest respect for Dr. Oakley. You were out of line and it won't happen again. And believe me, it won't happen again or you'll be out of here. If you're asked what you were upset about or meant by the word 'shill,' your answer is that you were under personal stress and chose your words imprudently. You have only the greatest respect for Dr. Oakley. Now get the fuck out of here."

Ray swallowed hard. "You don't want to know about the Council for Science Integrity?"

The dean started out of his chair, like a leopard seal going after a penguin. "Do you think I don't know anything, that you need to educate me? I'm going to say it one more time: 'sorry,' 'respect,' 'won't happen again.' There's no Council for Science Integrity in there. I hear or read that name anywhere, you are finished."

It was only later that Ray thought of all the better answers he should have had, all the comebacks he should have made. Freedom of speech, for one. Academic freedom. *Actual* integrity. Had the dean threatened him? Yes. Did the threat work? Well, yes. The dean was never going to forgive him for that time at the university president's house when he tripped over a riser, spilling red wine on white carpet. Who puts steps in the middle of living space? And white carpet in Alaska? Anyone might have tripped, but it had to be him, and he had to complain about the step, and the dean hadn't hesitated to issue him a formal warning about his "alcohol problem."

The newspaper, of course, botched the reporting. Ray had thought they might discover the true story all on their own, without him having to spell it out. Instead, they merely reported that he had called an esteemed colleague a shill, for reasons unknown, and then had refused to tell the paper why he had used that word. The relevant quote from him was, "I regret making such an unprofessional outburst, which I believed was between me and Dr. Oakley, whose work on ocean acidification is extremely important. I hold the highest regard for that work." Not exactly the script, but hopefully close enough. The dean had his own quote about Professor Berringer being reminded of the university code of conduct and that all university employees and students should be familiar with the code and, in addition, exhibit proper respect for one another, whether in person or through electronic means. "We have zero tolerance for bullying and harassment of any kind on this campus," the dean said. "The offender in this case has been reprimanded and assured me that such behavior will not be repeated." Dr. Oakley had been unavailable for comment. The reporter didn't say how the newspaper had obtained a private e-mail, except to note that all university e-mail was considered public since the university was a state entity and the records of all state entities were a matter of public record.

Colin was the first to show up at Ray's door, outraged. Not at Oakley and the fake organization or the dean and university or the newspaper, but at Ray. "You refused to say why Oakley is a shill? He *is* a shill! And worse! That guy needs to be exposed!"

Ray was only able to talk him down by convincing him that they needed a greater strategy, that they should make a strategic retreat. "If I lose my job, then I not only lose my credibility, I also lose my access to information, right? We've got to hang low for a bit here. And be *strategic.*" He liked that word; it played well with the gaming set. "I already acted impulsively once. Don't you make the same mistake."

Nastiya and her fisherman-boyfriend came by. "I am so sorry," she said with a long face. "You are losing your job."

Ray said, "I don't think I'm losing my job."

"Oh, yes, I think you lose your job."

The boyfriend said, "The ocean's going to hell, and all they're worried about is whether you're calling someone a name? What am I supposed to do when the fish are all dead?"

Tina brought him a pink blooming Christmas cactus and set it in a corner of his office. "Solidarity," she said.

Cinda and her two kids brought him cookies and black drawings, and she shared with him that her husband had not only moved out of their house but had moved in with another woman, and therefore she wasn't going to be able to finish the semester's work on time and she appreciated his understanding. She needed an A to keep her student funding, which was even more critical now than before, and she'd catch up during spring semester, absolutely.

He saw Alex in the hall, and Alex punched him in the arm and said, obscurely, "I'm on the team."

Marybeth wanted to know what was happening and why everyone was talking about a cover-up. Was it true that he'd been forbidden to talk about zooplankton production? Was it true that Big Oil had funded a university position to promote the economic benefits of oil and gas development, and that there was no money for the spring research cruise?

Robert had shaved his head. He sat in Ray's office and said, "I'd volunteer to go to Texas, but I'm afraid I'd get beat up. Texas is, like, the most racist and homophobic place in the whole country, plus they put people to death on a daily basis. They love the death penalty and waving flags."

It seemed to Ray that the situation was rapidly taking on a life of its own, mutating perhaps. He didn't always know what the students were referring to, and he tried, to a degree, to quell what might be rumors. No, fish weren't exactly dying yet from acidification. Yes, we'll have cruise funding for the next year. Texas? Who suggested that anyone go to Texas? Robert had given him a conspiratorial look and then turned away.

At home, the comments were somewhat less supportive. Nelda said, "Are you an idiot? Yes, you are an idiot," and left for a run. She looked great in spandex and a fetching wool balaclava.

His son, Sam, asked, "You wrote 'fuck' in an e-mail?" It was clear from the question that he too thought his father was an idiot.

Aurora cried. "I'm so embarrassed. How could you do this to me?"

Ray didn't answer his phone. When he listened to his voice mail, it contained the usual student excuses, a couple expressions of sympathy and/or concern for his stress level, and a loud buzzing like a table saw going through metal.

Ray did not see or hear from Helen. He went over and over the two simple sentences he'd written in his e-mail—the *what the fuck do you think you're doing* one and the *you're a goddamn shill* one—searching for any possible way he might have implicated her. There were dozens of ways that he might have learned about Oakley's involvement with the bogus organization, and he hadn't even mentioned the place specifically. Oakley might be a shill in more ways than one. Who knew how he'd interpreted the message?

No, what was frightening Ray was what he'd disclosed to the dean, and what the dean had said in reply. The dean knew about the Council for Science Integrity. The dean knew now, if he didn't before, that Oakley was involved there. And he didn't care. Or he thought it was a good thing. The dean might be involved himself. The dean might be working with Oakley on all this, might be soliciting funds in exchange for—what? Ray hesitated to use the word "corruption." He didn't hesitate very much to himself, but it wasn't a word he was going to go public with.

Could he be wrong? Could there be an innocent explanation for everything? Maybe Oakley was infiltrating the bogus group, just pretending to align himself with them? Maybe Oakley hadn't understood what they were all about, and maybe he thought he could legitimately advise them, educate them about OA and its dangers? Occam's razor: go with the simplest theory first. He was no longer sure what the simplest one was.

Ray sat in his office with his head in his hands and was terrified that he might have put Helen's career in jeopardy.

When he looked up, his pteropod photos were swimming across his screensaver in an accusatory frenzy. They were the very face of jeopardy—regardless of the dramatics on one university campus. Regardless of everything that was already too late to correct.

What happened in the next moment belonged, in both timing and flair, to a movie script that Ray would have found laughably unbelievable. But there it was: the premonitory knock on the door, and then *that woman,* that *artist,* flinging herself into Ray's space like a superhero character. She was wearing black neoprene, skintight, with some kind of red emblem painted on her front, and she was draped in what looked like part of a moth-eaten parachute, the cloud-colored kind used by pilots in World War II. The parachute flowed behind her like a wedding train. In what might have been a ninja move, she gripped in both hands a cardboard sword wrapped in silver duct tape. Ray was still taking in the outfit, including the combat boots, the sword, the glittery spangles and—yes—tiny green frogs adhered to the sword, and he was trying to not fall out of his chair from shock and laughter, when Annabel sang out, "I'm here to defend your honor and the planktonic world! Pteropods unite!"

Only later did it come to him that the emblem on her chest represented a whorled shell, and that the parachute might have looked, to someone with an imaginative eye, like a pteropod's mucous net.

PART 3

CHAPTER NINE

This is the month when most people kill themselves," Brad was saying. Brad, the fisherman they'd met in the bar in September —now Nastiya's boyfriend—was an expert on most things, Helen had learned, in the more than two hours since they'd left Fairbanks. Perhaps not really an expert, but more like an opinionator. He liked to pontificate on every subject, from the making of birch syrup to the history of Aleut enslavement to the diet of sea lions to the hazards of those jet contrails in the sky to politics and the harebrained (all of them) people in Congress. From what Helen could tell, he got just enough right to sound like he knew something.

Now he went on, "They tell themselves, 'things will get better after the holidays, things will get better when the light starts to return,' and then of course things don't get better."

Helen, who had been to more than one suicide prevention workshop, knew for a fact that May, closely followed by April, was the peak month for depression and suicides in Alaska. December had the fewest suicides, and she wasn't sure where January fit in. Brad was partially right; when there was more light and the general population was active and upbeat, that's when those who were still feeling hopeless were most likely to give up. Village people in those workshops used "suicide" as a verb: "my nephew suicide."

She said nothing, only pulled the blanket closer around her. The passenger-side door of Brad's truck didn't seal well, and her right side was freezing. Nastiya, squeezed between Brad and Helen, was altogether too warm and kept complaining of it.

"Road trip! Road trip!" Nastiya was chanting now. She was a sponge for American culture.

Helen focused her attention on the white, sunlit world beyond their windows. She seldom made the daylong drive to Anchorage and had never seen Denali with such ice-water clarity. As they approached the mountain, the few clouds cleared away, leaving Denali to tower brilliantly over the foothills. The nearer landscape was equally gorgeous: all that feathery frost sparkling from every twig of every shrub, and then the deep green of the spruce. And there, flying low across a drifted hillside, a ptarmigan, only distinguished from the white background by its motion and the light catching on its wings. She pointed but already it was gone. "Ptarmigan," she said.

"You know why they call the town of Chicken 'Chicken?'" Brad asked. "Because they couldn't spell 'ptarmigan.'"

Helen nodded. She'd heard that one before.

She was, she admitted, nervous about her presentation. Brad and Nastiya had gotten her invited to a fishermen's gathering to talk about ocean acidification. She'd spoken about it before, but only to science students and once at a science conference as part of a panel. This was the first time she was "going public." She was not at all sure how much information was going to be enough for her audience, how much would be too much. Fishermen had a lot of direct knowledge of their environment, and a significant number had earned biology or fisheries degrees before deciding that catching fish was more satisfying than studying or managing them. According to Brad, most of them already knew about OA and had a lot of questions.

She hadn't told Jackson that she'd be giving a presentation, and she hadn't sought his permission. What was that old saying? It's easier to ask for forgiveness than for permission?

What had happened to poor Ray Berringer before the Christmas break was deeply unsettling to her. She hadn't thought through the possible consequences of giving him that slip of paper. And then she'd kept her distance, sick with guilt about the harm that had come to him and about her own silence and her liaison—if that's what it was—with Jackson. She was still seeing him—and still, of course, working with him—but it was as though they'd come to some understanding, without either one saying so, that certain subjects, once dismissed, weren't spoken of again.

When the first newspaper article had appeared, he'd called her immediately to warn her about a "messiness." He'd made it clear it had nothing to do with her but was about a professional and perhaps personal jealousy over his other affiliations. She should not let it upset her.

Then, a couple of days later, when the Council for Science Integrity had been briefly, and blandly, mentioned in a follow-up article, he'd caught her leaving a class and pulled her aside. "Just so you know," he'd said, "I consult and advise on OA wherever I'm asked. This is part of my university service and fully approved by the dean. If we only talk to the people who agree with us, what's the point?"

She had given him a look she hoped betrayed nothing. She wanted to think the best of him, wanted there to be an easy reconciliation between her desires and her doubts. If she felt the distance between them growing, she wanted it to be only that she was gaining confidence in who she was, not losing respect for the man to whom she'd given a piece of her heart—and to whom she owed so much.

It was after that that some of the students had caused an uproar, had talked about a walkout. But they lacked a critical mass and they weren't willing to walk out on exams—to forfeit a semester's credit, even for a worthy (if ill-defined) cause—and then they departed for the holidays. By the time the new semester started, things had settled down. There seemed to be a general confusion about what had actually happened. No one had been fired, after all. *Personality clash, byzantine intra-university politics, overreaction:* she heard these phrases, and then nothing. The community did a great shrugging of shoulders and went on to protest, mildly enough, the announced hikes in tuition.

If she was feeling bad about what had happened to Ray, she was also angry with him. Why had he acted so impulsively? Was that pit bull attack the best he could do? And then he'd immediately backed off. He went to his office and sorted zooplankton photos; at least that's what she'd heard from Nastiya and the others. The Council for Science Integrity had gotten a free pass.

It was not, she insisted to herself, that anything related to OA was actually being censored or misrepresented. It was just that no one was connecting the dots; no one was interpreting the work or giving meaning to the data. Jackson's favorite word was "ongoing." "The work is ongoing." Everything was "preliminary." Sometimes "speculative." There were many unknowns. No conclusions could be drawn. It was important to exhibit caution (another of his favorite words) when discussing the work.

Jackson was, mostly, not even present on campus. The semester had barely started and he was off on another trip, this time to China.

Nastiya sat up straighter in the truck. "So much mean."

Brad said, "What so much mean?"

"University. What they do to Ray."

"Meanness," Brad said. "It's the American way. Competition. Capitalism." He spit out the word. "You step on everyone else to advance yourself."

"I don't," Nastiya said. "Helen don't. Helen,"—she turned her head to face Helen—"is true what they say, your Oakley is working for criminals? He takes money to give bad information? I thought Mafia is only in Russia."

Brad laughed. "Mafia! The goddamned Mafia! An American institution if I ever heard of one."

Apparently, Helen thought, the outrage and rumors hadn't disappeared altogether. "That's not true, Nastiya. Professor Oakley isn't doing anything criminal." She hated that she had to sound so defensive. "He raises money from many sources. One source is a very conservative think tank that questions the science around climate change and OA."

"That's so fucking corrupt!" Brad shouted over the heater's roar. "Just like the whole corporate-controlled political system! Just like giving money to members of Congress! It's called 'buying influence!'"

"Who told you there was something criminal?" Helen wondered if this was recent, or just an old rumor still occupying Nastiya's steel-trap mind. Certainly she'd heard this at the time: Ray had uncovered a serious wrongdoing, variously interpreted. Of course she'd also heard that Ray was jealous, that Ray was drunk.

"I hear that. I hear the name of that place that makes bad science."

"It's not a secret," Helen said. "It was in the paper. Professor Oakley said he attended something at the Council for Science Integrity, to learn what they were doing, and then agreed to give them some advice. We don't have to like it. We can think it's better to stay far away from that kind of group and not lend it credibility. But it's not criminal. The dean approved it."

"Oh, the dean," Nastiya said. "He is a blowjob."

"Blowhard," Helen corrected.

"He is a blowjob!" Brad repeated this with fresh glee.

Helen was wishing she'd been quicker, or braver, or less taken aback by the way Jackson had caught her in the hall, publicly, to defend his questionable connection. She should have said to him, "People who agree with us? What is there about science to agree or not agree about? It's *science.*" Now she said to Nastiya, "Sometimes it's hard to separate science and policy."

"Like those guys have any ethics!" Brad beat his steering wheel.

Nastiya said, "Colin tells us Oakley lights a backfire. He protects himself, like in a forest on fire."

This time Nastiya had it right, both the idiom and the truth. Colin had bitterly complained that Oakley had spun his own story in the newspaper and no one had challenged him.

"I am with Ray," Nastiya said. "Why southern species are in our nets? Why there is more or less eggs? Depends on temperature, chemistry, storms, primary production." Nastiya began expounding on her thesis work, copepods this and copepods that.

Brad interrupted. "No copepods, no salmon."

"Ray say we need the data sets, over years and years and different seasons. Every set is better to understand what is happen."

Helen said, "You're lucky to be working with him."

"He is a little mad with me." Nastiya bit her lip. "I am still late with my paper. And because I say, why not let Annabel do some art? Remember Annabel, from ship? She came to university with sword and wants to defend Ray. She is a little crazy."

Yes, Helen had heard about that. Everyone in that wing at the time had heard him shouting. He was apparently more afraid of being supported by an experimental artist than of being torn down by the people who were supposed to have his back.

Nastiya said, "She spoke Russian words to me. She only know *dasvidaniya* and *borshch.*"

Brad pushed a CD into the player and turned it up loud. Midnight Oil: a lot of harmonica and then something about food on the table, a blue-sky mine, hole in the ground.

They drove without talking after that, as Denali filled more of the sky. At last Brad turned off the highway, drove a short way down a snow-packed road, and stopped next to a chain-link fence surrounding a big, white, blocky, windowless building. He turned off the music. "Just wanted to see this white elephant for myself."

"What it is?" Nastiya asked.

"This is the famous 'clean coal' power plant that our government spent a gazillion dollars on, and it's never operated because it doesn't work." Brad looked pleased about this.

Helen wasn't sure that it had never worked. From what she'd read, there had been technological difficulties and cost overruns when it was built in the '90s as a demonstration project, and then no one had wanted to buy the power. It had run for a testing period—using a process that reduced the worst emissions—and then had been mothballed. Here it sat, completely silent and still, a monument in the wilderness. A small steam plume—Helen assumed it was from whatever heating system was keeping the whole thing from freezing —floated up from a vent on one side. The boxy facility didn't look anything like a coal plant to her; it didn't have a single smokestack.

"There's no such thing as clean coal," Brad announced. "All it means is they put extra scrubbers on to take out more sulfur and particulate crap. Burning coal spews way more carbon dioxide than oil. It needs to be shut down. All of it."

For added emphasis, Brad stomped the gas pedal and spun the truck around on the ice, then fishtailed back to the highway.

Helen said nothing. She could envy people like Brad, if not Brad himself, who were so sure about everything.

There was a good crowd at the fishermen's meeting—commercial fishing men and women, too, from all over the state. They were salmon fishermen, and halibut and black cod longliners, crabbers, herring seiners, sea cucumber divers. They listened to presentations about run projections and techniques for measuring biomass, about new strategies for avoiding bycatch, and about the hazards of fish farming. Politicians already campaigning for the next election took turns saying how important the commercial fisheries were and why they were the best men (and one woman) to represent those interests.

When it was her turn, Helen pretended that there wasn't a room full of burly men and women staring at her in her silk blouse and powder-blue scarf, but that there were just two people—Nastiya and Brad—waiting to hear what she had to say. She saw them sitting upright in their folding chairs—Nastiya biting into a sweet roll— and then was glad when the lights were lowered.

Her first slide went up on the screen. It was the now-classic graph showing the increase in carbon dioxide in the atmosphere matched against the increase in global temperature. Then the newer one showing the ocean's CO_2 absorption tracking atmospheric CO_2, and pH falling off. Then the carbon cycle illustration with all its arrows and, to make a point, the cartoony humans sailing away in a little boat. "How will changes in ocean chemistry affect marine life?" she read from the next slide. She showed the pictures of the molecules with their red, white, and black atoms—the CO_2 and the H_2O and the carbonate ion combining to make two bicarbonate ions. "Calcification—the building of shells and skeletons with calcium carbonate—depends on carbonate ions. When the seawater loses those carbonate ions, calcification is impeded." She listed some of the marine organisms that rely on shells during at least one stage of their development. "Calcifiers are among the most abundant forms of marine life and an essential part of our marine ecosystems."

The room was utterly quiet.

"This is just one example of how the food web might be affected," she said, advancing to "Diet of Juvenile Pink Salmon." The bar graph showed the main food sources for salmon across several study years. "You see here that juvenile salmon have a varied diet— copepods, amphipods, euphasiids, larval forms of crab and shrimp, even insects. But most years they depend on this critter"—she used the laser pointer to circle a photo of *Limacina helicina*—"to a very great degree. As you can see, upwards of 60 percent of their diet by weight. Pteropods are marine snails, with shells, and they are already being affected by acidification."

She let that statement sit with them for a moment. "How do we know this? Because studies have found that the waters along our coasts are already undersaturated with aragonite, a form of calcium carbonate. That means calcifiers like pteropods need to work harder to gather their building materials. Keep in mind that cold water absorbs more carbon dioxide than warmer water."

She showed a sequence of pteropod shells dissolving in a controlled study. "This is not happening yet in the ocean, not as dramatically as this, but if present trends continue, the corrosive water off our coasts will reach this level of pH within decades." Her voice quaked. She'd never seen the images—so clearly progressing from jewellike perfection to grotesque, nightmarish blob—projected onto a screen, as large as planets. Her words suddenly felt terribly measured, terribly inadequate to represent the disastrous truth.

Next slide—other biological processes affected by acidification. She was worried about time and ran over these quickly.

She went to her last slide. "This is preliminary data, but it's clearly a warning sign. You can see the trend." Her voice continued to shake as she explained the graphs she'd prepared for the Gulf of Alaska, where so many of the fishermen fished. She had stepped out, yes she had. There it all was. The undersaturation levels. The steep increases, the line representing the point where nothing with a carbonate shell would be expected to survive. She tried to dismiss a vision of a frowning Jackson and his words of restraint. He had once praised her for being egoless. If she didn't have an ego, where was the emotion coming from? Iñupiat people do not bring attention to themselves. Did she like the attention? Did it make her feel important?

Or was it the work, and the results, that were important?

Nastiya was giving her a thumbs-up. Helen's eyes moved across the dim room and took in the men and women leaning forward in their seats. They were studying her charts and rubbing their jaws. They were standing in the back, whispering. These were the people who needed to know, to plan their lives. She looked back to Nastiya, and to Brad beside her. Brad was holding his clenched fist over his head as the lights went up.

There was time for questions. Her stomach tightened. Now she would embarrass herself with what she didn't know! But no, she knew the answer about the upwellings at the oyster farms in the Northwest, and she knew the next one about plankton blooms. She apologized that her background wasn't in biology or fisheries, but mostly she knew enough and she had—oh, yes—one more slide with websites they could visit for more information. More hands were shooting up all over the room.

She spoke about adaptation, and what experiments were being done with monitoring buoys, and, as simply as she could, about the difference in shell-building mechanisms between mollusks and crabs. She emphasized that different species would respond to acidification in different ways—all presumably with some cost to growth, reproduction, or general health—and that those studies were just starting and not easy to conduct. "What we do know," she said, "is that ocean acidification is real, it's happening, and anyone who makes a living from the sea should be concerned."

"So what you're saying," a man in the back called out, "is we should tell our kids not to go into the fishing business. There's no future in it."

She shook her head. "I'm saying take this knowledge into account for career decisions. You might want to diversify."

"Jellyfish," someone said.

A rumbling went around the room.

"My question is then—" a man in the middle rose to his feet—"if it's all going to hell and we can't do anything to stop it, then why don't we forget all the regulations and quotas and just fish like hell while we still can, before there's nothing left?"

Helen pictured Amos, up in Igalik, saying with such encouragement, "Come see them before they're gone." She looked back at Nastiya, who sat now with a stone face. "That's not really the message I hoped to convey. We need to manage fisheries for resilience, and we need to learn a lot more about, like I said, species-specific responses." She decided not to say anything about the need to reduce fishing pressure on vulnerable species. "Of course, we need to address the issue of carbon emissions. If we can limit global carbon emissions and bring down the amount in the atmosphere, there will be less absorption by the ocean and over time things will stabilize. But the ocean will be absorbing carbon dioxide for a long time yet, just from what's already in the atmosphere, so things will get worse before they can get better."

"And now," the facilitator said, "on that cheerful note, let's take a break and come back for our next speakers, who're going to tell us about warming salmon streams and salmon viruses!"

Helen's mother and stepfather had gone to Mexico for a couple of weeks, so Helen stayed in Anchorage with her old college roommate, Jean. Jean was Tlingit on her mother's side, and Helen—although she regretted the stereotype—associated her with Tlingit fierceness. Back in college Jean had been outraged by every slight to her culture, to women, to the less privileged, to a clean bathroom. She stood tall and proud and wore on every important occasion her red and black vest with her clan's killer whale on its back. Now she worked for a social service agency on a housing program for chronic inebriates, and she was a warrior for that cause and the unfortunate souls battling both addiction and discrimination.

That evening after the fishermen's meeting, Helen and Jean sat at Jean's kitchen table with takeout Thai and caught up.

"So that was the way it ended," Helen said. "That one guy saying let's catch them all while we can, and when I looked around it was like everyone was registering the same thought—basically that the situation is hopeless. You know, I kind of have to agree. I mean, what can any of them do to fix the problem? Nothing. It's too late. They can put more efficient engines in their boats or even convert to sails, but it won't matter."

"They're screwed," Jean agreed. Her silver bracelets with the Tlingit designs clunked against the tabletop.

Helen's shoulders sagged. "I felt like the doomsday messenger. And then, right after me was this woman who's been studying water temperatures in salmon streams. A lot of them are so warm they already exceed water quality standards, and in some cases salmon are dying before they can spawn. Then there was the guy from the Yukon River with a report on the ich virus. You know about ich? It's in the king salmon there and makes the meat all mealy and gross, so it's only fit for dogs. The warmer the water, the worse it is."

Jean refilled their water glasses. "Let's talk about—I don't know—men who are not fishermen. You got someone?"

Helen sank farther. The weight of things. "No time. Work, study, advise some Native students, hope the car runs, deal with the car not running. I joined a dance group." She felt bad about lying to Jean. Or semi-lying. Her feelings for Jackson were getting more complicated all the time, more compartmentalized, awkwardly jammed into her several ways of knowing. She recognized that beyond her usual divided self, she was many things—loyal, dependent, doubting, both softening and steadying. He might have been distancing himself, too—perhaps a natural cooling, perhaps something else. She could not have explained any of it.

"Native dance?" Jean repeated. "They include men. Drummers

might have good hands. Although I've found car mechanics to be very practical. Then you'd have less trouble with your car."

"I'm sure. Yes, Native dance. The core group is from Point Hope."

This discussion was not unlike ones they'd been having since their undergrad days. There was a saying about men in Alaska, and they both accepted its clichéd truth: the odds are good, but the goods are odd. If you were hoping to find someone who shared your cultural background, the odds were much less good and the goods were still frustratingly odd. Educated Native women most often ended up with non-Native men. It would not be unusual, or thought inappropriate, for Helen to settle down with a man like Jackson Oakley. A man *like* him.

Jean put on some fusion music they both enjoyed. The artists were Yup'ik, African American, and Greenlandic, and they mixed African and Caribbean sound with Yup'ik drumming and chanting.

"So, other than that, it was a success," Jean said.

"My presentation? Other than that, and other than speaking out of school."

"Depends on what school."

Jean's words sat between them. Helen knew exactly what she meant. She'd been schooled by elders, and now she was being schooled by fishermen.

"And no time to waste," Jean said. "Ring the alarms. Yell 'fire.'"

"Scientists don't usually go around yelling 'fire.'"

"Even when their pants are burning?"

Now Helen had to smile. *Liar, liar, pants on fire.*

Jean waved a spoon. "I'm glad I've got such a simple job. I just go to community council meetings and argue that having a bunch of drunks living in their neighborhoods is charitable and won't hurt property values. And then I go and pick one of those drunks off the sidewalk and read him the riot act about screwing it all up. Problem,

151

action, result. Not that we'll ever solve the real problem of alcoholism. But what I need to do every day is straightforward, and I see the results right away."

Helen would not have wanted Jean's job. Still, she got her point. Science was frustratingly slow to add up to anything you could call a result, and then what do you do with *that*? She tried again to grip a tiny piece of pork with her chopsticks. "You know how to advocate for a cause. Most scientists aren't even any good at explaining how they work and what they know, or the value of the work, the reason for it."

"Remember when we took that TEK class together?"

That was back when traditional ecological knowledge was just beginning to get some respect, and a series of Native elders had spoken to their class about what had been passed down to them about the natural world. The elders understood the connections between winds and sea ice, what seabirds were eating, when seals would be fat or thin, where the whales traveled.

"Remember," Jean said, "how the speakers complained about the scientists messing around, dropping in to measure ice or dig up a seal den. They were like, 'Just ask the elders! What you want to know, the elders already know these things. They can tell you!'"

"We're better now," Helen said, defensively. "Most researchers are respectful, better with two-way communication, asking people what they know and think. It's still hard to incorporate traditional knowledge into studies." She told Jean about the conversation with her grandmother: more polar bear sightings must equal more bears. "Sometimes what people think they know is just wrong—or maybe wishful."

Jean popped up again to heat tea water. "You can't blame her for that. What's happening now—all this change—is unlike anything they have any experience with. I hear that a lot—'I used to be able to predict the weather, but now I can't.' Or the sea ice. Or when the caribou will come through. Still, with all the combined knowledge, don't we have enough information to start *doing* something? When can you stop studying and start fixing? Enough already about global warming and poisoning the air and water and species going extinct! We *know* enough. It's time to just *do* it! Start cleaning things up!" Jean marched into the next room and yanked the curtains closed.

"I don't disagree." Helen raised her voice to be heard through the doorway. "I don't know why we let people insist on absolute proof before we do anything."

"Here's an analogy," Jean said, returning to the table. "What if I said I won't help alcoholics until we understand why they're alcoholics and how to cure alcoholism?" She reached across the table to grasp Helen's wrist. "If I have to bring all my alcoholics to Fairbanks and turn them loose in the president's office with 'It's our ocean too' signs, I'll do that."

Helen pictured a Tlingit warrior charging into battle in a blur of red and black, a wave of followers, like a towering tsunami, behind her. Lead or follow, she thought. But don't stand still. And you sure as hell can't retreat. There was no retreating now.

Jean slowly loosened her grip on her wrist. The regular, steady beat of a Yup'ik drum drove her words. "We gotta ... shake ... that ... place ... up."

Later, the drumbeat stayed with Helen. There was a reason the Yup'ik and Iñupiat—and most indigenous peoples she knew of— had used drums to concentrate their minds, to power them with spirit. There was a reason the early missionaries had put a stop to such "pagan," unruly, hypnotic music. At dance practices, the older men rapped their hoop drums and chanted, *Aye-ah, aye-ah,* sometimes throating the hollow-bone sounds of *oogruk*. They reminded her of her Igalik elders and the ghost of her grandfather who'd once sat among them, although he most often wanted people to know he was related to a Boston whaler and was more than Eskimo. As she danced with the women—feet planted, knees bending and straightening, arms motioning to one side and then the other—she felt as graceful and strong as a swan.

After practice, her beating heart carried her to Jackson's office, where she placed a revised draft of her thesis on his desk.

"What's this?"

"I worked the conclusion section some more."

His eyes narrowed.

"But, really, the reason I came"—she took a deep breath—"is to say that I made a mistake to get personally involved with you. I hope you understand. I need to not see you—that way—anymore."

He cleared his throat. "It's that pteropod gang, isn't it?" He smiled, the smile that had so recently weakened her knees and now seemed somehow calculating, cloying, even sinister. "Your choice. Why you'd want to throw your lot in with Berringer and his parasites, I don't know, but that's up to you."

Helen was both relieved that he'd taken her pronouncement so calmly and dismayed that he seemed to have so little reaction, as though he'd never placed that much value on her or their relationship to begin with. And that distancing: he'd turned the subject so that it wasn't even about the two of them, it was all about her taking another side. Or not even that. Perhaps, for him, it was only about him—about feeling "ganged up on."

"OK then," she said and turned to leave.

"I had higher expectations for you," he called after her. "And I'm fond enough of you to warn you. You really should stay clear of Berringer. He's got some odd appetites."

It took her several steps to reach the doorway. When she crossed through and took a last look back, it was to see a hunch-shouldered man swiveled in his chair, tossing her thesis paper onto a stack behind him.

CHAPTER TEN

It was killing Ray, to be silenced. Silenced and shamed. The vacation to Belize, with his unhappy family, had hardly been a respite. They'd all acted as though Alaska and his job didn't exist, that the only world they knew was made of hot sand and warm water, barefooted living. Still, pretending could only take them so far.

Both before and after Belize, he did indeed close himself into his office and work on his zooplankton photos, sorting and selecting and posting them on the website. He granted multiple permissions for their use in journals, textbooks, and magazine articles. Pteropods were much in demand. Ray reasoned that he was subtly advancing his cause by spreading pteropod love around the world. He wanted every single person to see how beautiful the tiny creatures were and to want to care for them as they cared for the largest whales. *Focus,* he said to himself. Do one thing right and admirably, and the rest . . .

OK, he was kidding himself. No one was going to love marine snails, no matter that he enlarged them to the size of kittens and showed off their beautiful curves and floaty "wings." It would scarcely help to call them "sea butterflies" and "sea angels." But a guy had to have his fantasies.

And then he got a phone call. "Stacy Foster here," the husky woman's voice announced, as though there was no doubt that he would know who Stacy Foster was. He did, in fact, know. Stacy Foster hosted, in Anchorage, the only "liberal" radio talk show in the state. She loved to stick it to politicians and to support lost causes of all kinds. She was always being counterattacked in the right-wing media, which is why everyone in Alaska, miles beyond her radio waves, either admired or (mostly) detested her.

Was Ray paranoid?

If not, why did he immediately assume that the caller was not the notorious Stacy Foster but someone posing as her, someone who would prove beyond all doubt what an ass he was or, at a minimum, make him a laughingstock, the way those two Canadians had pranked Sarah Palin by pretending to be the French president discussing his hot wife and praising Palin's knowledge of foreign policy.

"I'd love to have you on my show," the voice said. "I'd like to shed a little light on what's going on there at the university, the academic freedom aspect and the gag order."

Ray hung up.

Minutes later he had an e-mail from her—or the prankster with a fake e-mail address. The message—*Let's talk, just on background if that's most comfortable*—sounded real enough, but he was not going to fall for it. If he said no, he'd look like he was hiding something, and if he said yes he'd risk finding himself trapped. It was a classic case of lose-lose. His only choice was to ignore the message, refrain from replying—which meant that she'd find someone else to speak about what might have happened. There was that high school history teacher down in Anchorage who was always going off about how his academic freedom was interfered with whenever he was called out for teaching that Alaska was a colony being raped by multinational corporations. He really did not want that prima donna speaking about his case. Lose, lose, and lose.

He headed for the snack bar to drown himself in reindeer stew.

He was bent over his bowl when he heard the voice. "Hello there, friend." He turned to look into Oakley's over-tanned and smiling face.

Friend? *Friend?*

"So sorry about that mix-up," Oakley said.

Ray had not laid eyes on Oakley since the time he'd gone to his office and practically begged him for his data. Which he'd never gotten.

"I don't believe I'm your friend," Ray said around the reindeer and carrot in his mouth. "What mix-up would that be?"

"When I meant to reply to you and somehow it went haywire and went to someone who gave it to the paper. Another Ray, I guess. I need to clean out my address book."

"Somehow," Ray said, after swallowing, "I don't think that's how it works."

Oakley shrugged as though the whole thing was inconsequential.

Ray turned back to his stew. "Please leave me alone."

"It's for the best," Oakley said. "You'll see. You just need to learn to rise above principle."

"Excuse me?" Now Ray was getting hot. "I need to learn from you? I need to rise above principle?" What the fuck did that mean, "rise above principle?"

"Oh-oh," Oakley said. "I see you're having trouble with anger management again."

In a previous life, Ray would have risen to his feet and belted the guy. Which, of course, would have proved Oakley's point. But now, the neocortex of his brain talked to the reptilian part and said: *the behavior that will serve you at this moment is not fight but flight.* He picked up his bowl of stew and walked away.

Like the calanoid species making vertical migrations to avoid predation, he thought, once he was back in his dungeon of an office.

Flagellate away. Live. Live to be the predator. That had been a successful evolutionary strategy for so many. It was about positioning.

He looked up Anchorage phone numbers and found the one for the radio station where Stacy Foster had her show. He called and had a rather long conversation with a young man who could not confirm that she'd called him. Neither would he confirm that the phone number e-mailed to him was hers. Apparently Stacy Foster got a lot of hate calls and e-mails, and the station did not give out or confirm any of her contact information. Eventually Ray left a message that if she was trying to reach him she should call again and should ask for "Mr. Ctenophore." He'd spelled it out, carefully, for the young man.

Within an hour they were talking. Background only, Ray insisted. Off the record, not to be taped or quoted or attributed. But then, it quickly turned out that she already knew way more than he did.

She knew all about the Council for Science Integrity, the corporations and people associated with it, and its mission of distorting science. She knew that Jackson Oakley was linked up and had spent considerable time in the last year at the headquarters and had visited a number of industry groups and corporate offices. He had gone rabbit hunting with the president of a major coal company. He had been quoted in a trade group journal saying, "The jury is still out on ocean acidification," and "We all know that carbon dioxide is vital to life on earth." She even had some university records showing that gifts had been made to the OA office from an organization called Global Health, which appeared to be another front group for polluting industries, and the "philanthropic" arms of several oil companies. "And some government entity from China," she told him. "I'm trying to find out more about it. What do you know?"

"Nothing compared to you," he admitted. "Where'd you get all that?"

She chuckled. "I've got multiple anonymous sources and no

one I can put on the air. What would it take to have you agree to be a guest?"

"A new job?"

Now she laughed out loud. "What if we just totally stick to the science? I ask you about what you see happening in the oceans and we take a few calls, and then I let you go and I do my own thing about how I tried to get Jackson Oakley to speak with us but he declined."

"You did? He did?"

"Yes, and then I say some things about his affiliations and so on, but you're gone from the call and not associated with any of that."

Ray was remembering his conversation with Colin about being strategic. He'd never really understood the difference between strategy and tactics.

"You're a *scientist,*" Stacy reminded him.

A few days later, Ray was on the air via his home phone line, discussing the interdisciplinary nature of ocean science and the implications of ocean acidification.

Stacy asked him, "Is there one place at the university where all this information is brought together?"

Ray said, carefully, "We have within the university a school of ocean sciences."

"And isn't there a new office or center specifically to study ocean acidification?"

"Yes." Ray was sweating in his—appropriate—sweatpants and sweatshirt, hoping she remembered the part of their agreement about sticking to the science.

"Do you see much of that office's director, Jackson Oakley?"

"Not very much."

"I'm not going to put you on the spot here, Professor Berringer. I know you can't comment on the behavior of colleagues or on university protocols. Let's stick to this very disturbing science and take a couple of calls."

Perhaps it was inevitable, but the first caller asked, "Aren't you that professor who got in trouble for calling that other guy a swindler?" Ray wished he was in the radio studio and could make eye contact with Stacy. He'd be doing more than making eye contact, more like drawing his finger across his throat.

But she was on it. "Caller," she said, "I believe the word was 'shill,' and I promised Professor Berringer we'd be sticking to the science here. He has to leave us shortly, and we want to fit in as much science as we can. But stay with us for the second half of the show, because I have some independent information and a few thoughts to share during that portion."

Whew!

He answered a fisherman's question about how salmon and halibut might be affected, one about the difference between acidity and pH, and then one about volcanoes, which he said were not a significant contributor to global warming or ocean acidification because the yearly emissions of carbon dioxide from volcanoes were matched by human contributions in just a few days. And then Stacy, very adroitly, was thanking him and saying good-bye, although she left him on a listening line so he could hear the rest of the show.

"I have independently researched the university's new Office of Ocean Acidification Science," she said, "and I'm alarmed at what I've discovered. Ocean acidification is a very serious threat, likely eclipsing the dangers of global warming, and our university should be in the forefront of research. But something funny—and I don't mean ha-ha—is going on there." And then she laid it out. She put in some good words for "the real and ethical scientists like Professor Berringer" and took on—like a hailstorm—Oakley, the bogus Council for Science Integrity, rule by corporation, and the university establishment "that will do anything for the next building paid for by some lobbying group, and shame on our legislature for starving our educational system and abetting this outrageous and corrupt practice." His speakerphone was practically melting from the heat of her words.

And then—the calls. Her regular audience loved this stuff and was all over it. "Throw the bums out!" "Everything's for sale!" "Corporations are not people!" "I'll never send my kid to that university!" "We're all going down, and those people are feathering their own nests!"

Ray's heart was hurting. He loved the university! Now it—like Congress and the presidency, like government in general, Wal-Mart, religions, all institutions, everything we used to believe in—was being crapped on. Everyone was a cynic. He wished he could call up, wished he could say, "No, hold on, let's take positive action." What would that positive action be? Get back on track. Do the science, do the policy, educate our students and all our citizens, save the planet.

Oh, but wait. Wasn't it already too late?

The next caller said, "Well, there's one hero in all this. That Roy Harringer guy. I admire that guy for standing up and telling it like it is."

Ray literally stood up. He was trying not to be flattered, and he was hoping that by getting his name wrong the man might not be implicating him. *No, it wasn't me—it was someone named Roy Harringer.* What had he told "like it is?" More than likely, all those nitwits listening with half an ear thought that he—Roy or Ray—had told Stacy all the dirt that she'd just dished.

Stacy was signing off, thanking the callers, promoting an upcoming spay-your-animals event, and then his line went to music. He ended his connection, then thrust his hands into his sweatshirt pockets and landed one hand on the paper napkin he'd detained from his flight back from Belize. Apparently the airlines couldn't afford their own napkins anymore, and this red and white one was advertising Coca-Cola with a cartoony picture of three terribly cute polar bears and the slogan "Together we can help protect their home." He was not sure how consuming flavored water—with all the energy that went into making those aluminum cans and plastic bottles and transporting them around the world—could possibly help protect polar bears, but, then, he was confirmedly the half-empty-glass guy. He hoped the soft drink industry wasn't trying to suggest that fizzing sodas with carbon dioxide helped fight global warming.

A drink, though—that might be a good idea. Since he was already standing, and since he had the napkin in hand, and since it had been a very trying morning in which he'd conducted himself quite well indeed, he continued into the kitchen to pour himself a drink. He was not sure whether he was celebrating or whether the drink was more like enjoying a last meal before your execution, but, in either case, no Coca-Cola was involved.

This time it was the president who wanted to see him.

Dr. Richard Petterson, the medieval lit scholar, loved soccer matches, hagiographies, and quoting *Beowulf.* He was known as an innocuous administrator given to hosting visiting dignitaries at his house, where he would sometimes recite his own medieval-sounding poems involving courtly love and alliteration. Except for that one time when he'd apologized for spilling red wine on his white carpet, Ray had never exchanged more than a polite nod with the man.

The first thing that Ray noticed on entering the president's office was that he had the same kind of expensive desk chair as the dean and Oakley did *and* a full-length leather couch. A print—or maybe it was the original—of a Fred Machetanz polar bear covered one wall. The president indicated that they should sit at a large, round, tropical-wood table—a nicely democratic gesture, Ray thought.

The president clasped his hands on an unopened file folder and frowned at Ray. "Your behavior has not reflected well on this institution," he said.

When Ray realized, after several seconds, that he was expected to say something, he decided the thing to say was "I'm sorry."

"Let's see here." The president opened the file and peered into it. "You are a marine biologist specializing in zooplankton," he stated as though it was an accusation on the order of "You are a felon in possession of a firearm."

"That's correct."

"You are not a chemist."

"Correct."

"You are not a volcanologist."

Ray was beginning to see where this was going. "No, I am not a volcanologist."

"Or an expert in salmon and salmon management."

"Not an expert, no."

"Then I'm not sure why you feel you should speak for those disciplines." The president again stared at him as though he was expecting some kind of answer.

Ray stared back. He noticed that the president's eyebrows pretty much ran together over the top of his nose, not as dramatically as that Mexican artist his wife liked—the woman they'd made a movie about, a movie he'd watched with Nelda and pretended to like for household harmony—but thick and hairy enough. Beyond him, out the window and down in the quad, some students were flinging handfuls of dry snow at one another.

"There's a danger," the president said, "when faculty members speak publicly about areas outside their disciplines. When they get facts wrong, they discredit themselves, not to mention this institution, and cause confusion in the fields."

"Did I get something wrong?"

"Apparently."

Then, silence, except for the ticking of an antique clock Ray had just noticed. Apparently the president wasn't going to tell him what was apparent enough to him.

Ray had to ask. "What?"

The president looked at his notes again. "You're not qualified to speak about how possible changes to ocean chemistry will affect commercial fisheries."

"What did I say that was wrong? That commercial species depend on the lower trophic species, some of which are calcifiers, and calcifiers will be affected by ocean acidification?"

"Listen," the president said. The room's lighting was not flattering to his chin whiskers. "I'm not an expert on this either, but I did consult the experts and they tell me that alarmist talk, not based on sound science, is a problem. You've been reprimanded once about this already, so this time I'm putting you on probation. You may not continue to harass your colleagues or otherwise display unprofessional behavior. If you do, we'll have to terminate your contract."

"Uh," Ray said, "academic freedom?" *Experts? Sound science?* He was pretty sure where Petterson was getting his experts, and everyone knew that "sound science," had been co-opted by the anti-science people to describe their version of what they wanted the science to be. He was also thinking that Petterson had not gotten over the red-wine incident.

"I'm sure you'll avail yourself of the faculty handbook, which includes definitions as well as the grievance procedure. You might note who's at the top of the grievance process, after all the appeals." The president tucked his chin so that Ray would get his point.

"The apex species," Ray said.

"Biology is not my field," Petterson said in a way that sounded boastful.

Ray thought that was probably his cue to get up and leave. But Petterson opened his mouth again, and what came out was, "A little knowledge can be a dangerous thing."

Ray waited.

"Trust me on this. Appearances may not be what they seem. Believe me, we have bigger fish to fry here."

Ray could not believe the medieval president had just strung together four clichés in a row.

Petterson stood up. "So I'm asking your indulgence. Please refrain from shooting your mouth off. Try to understand that there's a bigger picture here, something that may not be clear to you right now but that's in good hands."

Eight clichés.

"As clear as mud," Ray said, taking the president's outstretched hand and shaking it like it was a shark's fin.

What was clear to him was that whatever was going on—and it couldn't be good—went right to the top.

The very next day, while Ray pondered whether or not he lived in the equivalent of a hypoxic dead zone, one of the students in his Intro class showed up during his office hours. He could not remember her name, but he was pretty sure she was the one who had objected to injecting CO_2 into the jars with the pteropods and "torturing" them. His impression was that she had missed quite a few classes and when she was there, she sat in the back or on the side near the door and frequently checked her phone. While she flopped down in the wooden chair and began with a litany of excuses he pretended he was continuing a search for something while he was in fact trying to locate his grade book so he could sneak a look and find her name. Kelsey, Chelsea, Ashley—one of those names. Because he was trying to both disguise his search and wrack his brain, he couldn't fully hear and appreciate what she was saying, which was something like *wah-wah my brother got his toes frozen* and something about missing class because she—or maybe it was her brother or mother—needed a CAT scan, or maybe there was an actual cat involved. He nodded and found the brown grade book and turned away to stick it inside a copy of *Conservation Biology*.

"Excuse me just a moment," he said. "I just need to get this citation." He turned grade book pages inside journal pages until he got to the current class.

"OK, Jessica," he said. "Now I can give you my full attention."

"Megan," she said. "Oh, my God, you don't even know my name!" She burst into tears, and her hair, brown streaked with green, fell over her face.

"Megan, of course," he said. "I meant Megan. I misspoke. Forgive me, Megan. Now, what can I do for you?"

She sniffled, and he looked around his office for something like a Kleenex, a roll of toilet paper, a napkin not overly stained with ketchup. Nothing. She would have to use the sleeve on that very expensive (white, baffled, down past her ass, goose-down) parka with the faux fur collar.

What she wanted, of course, was to be excused from missing not just past classes and labs but also future ones that conflicted with her need to accompany her mother to the hospital for chemo treatments. And the paper that was due—well, that would have to wait, too. She wanted to be assured that she wouldn't be penalized for absences that were beyond her control. She needed to maintain her grade point average.

She unzipped her parka and laid it over the chair back. Underneath she was wearing a low-cut top that pretty much exposed her breasts, and low-rise jeans above which rose a well-fed belly with a protruding and jeweled belly button. Ray was standing by his file cabinet and couldn't help getting a full view. He also could not, in the small room, move any farther away nor put his desk between them without squeezing past her and the chair.

He was noncommittal. As long as he'd been teaching, Ray had never figured out just how far he was required to go to accommodate health issues and family emergencies or obligations. Several times in the past he'd tried to get some guidance from student services or his colleagues, and the response was always the same: versions of *do what you think is best but, fuck—just give him (or her) what he (or she) wants, sure, the A, and be done with it. Because otherwise the student will appeal a bad grade, and then you'll have to explain why you were such a prick when his (or her) mother was dying, etc.* This offended his ethics, but he understood the practicality of it, and so he usually clenched his teeth and passed those students along, hoping always that karma—not that he believed in karma—would catch up with the worst offenders.

"I'm so sorry about your mother," Ray weaseled. "I'll take that into account of course, but do what you can. Try to do the reading, and then maybe, I don't know, you can do some makeup work when things settle down."

"When do I have time to read?" She looked like she was ready to cry again.

"Well," Ray tried. "Reading is usually a big part of a college education."

He was quite used to seeing inappropriately dressed female students, but he thought that if this one thought she looked attractive she had quite the opposite of an anorexia problem. But still a body image issue. This was something Nelda had done women's studies work in, back in the day, and still frequently noted for him. The girl leaned even closer, and he couldn't help seeing the strain of her breasts against and over her top, the large whiteness etched with tiny blue lines, a frightening glacier capable of a mighty surge.

And then she leapt up and grabbed her coat and was out the door, cursing under her breath and pushing past another student waiting in the hall.

"That could have gone better," Ray said aloud, returning to his desk.

Of all people, his next visitor was Helen, in her studious purple glasses. She was looking behind her. "What's *she* so upset about?"

Ray held his tongue. Mindy, Mandy, Amelia—he'd forgotten the girl's name again. An emotional wreck. He noticed that Helen was holding a file folder. "At least you're not here to badger me about a grade. But I should warn you, you ought to be steering clear of me."

"That's what Jackson told me." She sat in the same chair so recently vacated.

"Seriously," he said. "I've been scolded by President Petterson himself. I'm not to mingle with those outside my discipline. I wouldn't want to get you in trouble."

She smiled. "I think I do quite well getting myself in trouble. I wanted to tell you I thought you did a great job on the radio."

"You heard it?"

She gave him a look like, *Who didn't?* "Internet, you know. Podcasts?"

Oh, right. Podcasts. Listen anywhere, any time, forever, incriminating him forever. They were probably listening right now down in Texas. But of course; they had already listened multiple times and made notes for Petterson.

"One small thing," she said. "When you talk about the chemistry, it's too much to try to explain all that carbonate and bicarbonate ions stuff, especially without slides. Just say that carbon dioxide dissolved in seawater produces a chemical reaction that reduces the number of carbonate ions, making them less available for building shells and skeletons. An analogy that people understand is osteoporosis."

Ray was fixed on "when you talk." Present tense? Was he still talking? Was there a future tense for him, a future of talking?

She reached out and handed him a folder. "And this is the data you were asking for. The Gulf of Alaska. The oversaturation that's pretty startling, the change in the horizon since the previous fall. And under that is my thesis. It's still a draft, but I'd be pleased if you'd review it for me. I wish I'd asked you to be on my thesis committee, because it's all interdisciplinary, isn't it? I'm hoping to revise it for possible publication later."

He held the folder in his two hands, the precious weight of it.

"Did Oakley give you the OK?"

"What do you think?"

The only thing he could read in her face was seriousness, determination. Possibly there was a challenge there.

"You shouldn't, you know, put yourself in harm's way." He said this without a great deal of conviction. "He's your thesis advisor. You're his student. He can influence your future."

She stood up and was smiling again. "Oh, I've already taken care of *that*. I've already blown *that* future." She held up a hand. It was either a stop sign—*say no more*—or it was a high-five salute.

Later, when he told Nelda, she added a third possibility. Helen might only have been saying good-bye.

Chapter Eleven

Annabel had chosen to live in Fairbanks because people there, at least around the university, tended to be both well educated and freethinking. The populace embraced a nicely libertarian ethic of live and let live. You could have your wacko belief system. You were free to hoard broken vehicles and appliances in your front yard and to grow marijuana in the back. And, of course, you could join one of several self-defending militias. In general, people didn't hide opinions or prejudices, and there were few motives for lying, cheating, misrepresenting, or covering up bad behavior—at least outside the domestic sphere.

Perhaps, she thought now, she was naïve, but that was the Alaska she knew. If there were legislators who took bribes and were otherwise comfy-cozy with the industries they were supposed to regulate, those people operated in far-off Juneau or Washington, beyond her ken. So when she heard that there was monkey business at the university and that Ray Berringer had gotten slapped for exposing some of it, she was disheartened. *Of course* she leapt to his defense.

Despite their differences, it was clear to her that Ray stood on the side of truth, beauty, and the downtrodden. She forgave him the temper tantrum he'd had on the boat and for his lack of social skills that could be interpreted as unkindness. He would not have corrected her about pteropod eyeballs if he hadn't been passionate about pteropods and their true selves. He would not have convulsed so much when she'd showed up at his office with her frog-sword if he hadn't been relieved to see her. He would not have absolutely forbidden her to stage a protest on his behalf if he hadn't been concerned for her own safety—even after she assured him that no one was going to mess with a sixty-seven-year-old lady in neoprene.

But now the man had outed himself on the radio and been slapped back again—probation, she'd heard, as though he were a criminal—and, in general, the world was falling to pieces. Not just the natural world, which was a given. And not just the world of endless wars over oil and perceived Muslim terrorists. The whole one-percent thing, the return to robber barons with obscene wealth. Somehow a threshold had been reached, and even in tolerant, laidback Fairbanks—so far from all the hip places that had been protesting for years already—the citizenry had had enough.

Which is why Annabel was now occupying the university campus outside the science building named for a major oil company.

On a frigid February afternoon she strode back and forth across the quad in her purple snowsuit and bunny boots, in a line of protestors carrying homemade signs. Her very colorful cardboard sign read, on one side, *Free Ray Berringer,* and on the other, *Pteropods Are Dying for Oil Profits.*

"Hey, hey, ho, ho, corporate greed has got to go!" they chanted over and over in steamy clouds of breath.

The line—a dozen men and women—turned at the end of the quad and—*scrunch, scrunch*—headed back over the packed snow. The intense young man leading the march was wound in a red and black scarf and kept phallically thrusting his *Corporations Are NOT People* sign into the air.

"Hey, hey, ho, ho."

Annabel was feeling as righteous as a Baptist preacher. The colder it was and the more the protesters endured the curious or disdainful looks of underdressed students and the occasional taunt of "get a job," the more certain their mission became. The great ignorance needed to be repelled, truth told, corruption exposed. A citizen could not simply stand by, which was why Annabel felt she could reject Ray's wish that she not involve herself on his behalf. And why she could carry her sign. The local was essential to the global, and both the silenced Ray and the voiceless zooplankton needed others to speak for them.

A few more protesters trotted up from the parking lot. One, a regular, wore a polar bear outfit with a big black clown nose and matted faux fur, and another wore a mask resembling the head of a beluga whale. The two species were threatened by both the loss of sea ice and the State of Alaska, which kept fighting their endangered listings instead of doing anything to protect them or their habitat. "It's all the same forces," the polar bear girl had said to Annabel when they first met. "It's all driven by the fossil fuel industries that want to continue business as usual, the same industries that control our politicians." "And the university," Annabel had added. Another arrival was handing out stickers with the names of the largest oil, coal, and mining companies in slashed circles. There was a general milling about while the group fumbled with mittens and adhered the fresh stickers to their signs, parkas, hats, and insulated derrieres. Several of the new signs read, *Divest fossil fuels now!*

"More arrests in D.C.," someone commented.

"The State Department's wavering on the transboundary treaty again."

"Great band at the Arctic Fox tomorrow night."

"Any of you have notes for East Asian Civ?"

"Seriously, a moose stomped your homework?"

Annabel looked up at the top floor of the admin building, where she imagined the president's office was, in the corner where the low sun was glinting off a window. She imagined the man standing at the window, arms folded across his chest, looking down on the activity. She hoped he was really annoyed. And worried. Having serious doubts. So far, he had not tried to stop the protest, or even to remove the tents that a couple of the students had pitched in the quad. He had said something in the paper about "most students are taking their studies seriously and attending class" and something about "misplaced nostalgia for a worn-out national dissent." He had no comment about the university's corporate ties or what connection Jackson Oakley had to the Council for Science Integrity, which several letters to the newspaper had blasted for its bogusness. Nor did he have a comment about Ray Berringer's conduct, which he said—sharply, according to the reporter—was a personnel issue. She hoped he kept a pair of binoculars on his desk and could read the signs. *Don't pollute science. Real integrity starts here!!!* A red and white for sale sign with *University of the North* written on the white space. *I can't afford my own "think tank" so I made this sign. SOS* in huge black letters and *Save Our Seas* in smaller red ones. The divestment ones. Perhaps her favorite, *Real scientists love their Mother (Earth). Marijuana, it's a PLANT!* with a peace symbol.

OK, so most of the group was kind of ragtag. She didn't guess they had any Young Republicans among them. At least a few were legitimate science students. One was a poet. One worked in IT, helping reset passwords. One older man ran for the state legislature every other year on an antifascist platform and never got more than a few dozen votes. Two women dressed entirely in black had migrated over from a lonelier antiwar vigil they'd been keeping for years. Ed, Tony, Deborah: Annabel was getting to know names.

The new stickers were stuck, the mittens back on, signs lofted high once again. Annabel stepped to the front and sang out the first words to "Hava Nagila," then vined and scissored and scuffed her way, snow shards and sparkles flying, back across the quad. All the rest, singing out or at least faking the ancient Hebrew words, danced joyously after her. The well-padded security guy in front of the library, with his holsters full of radios and mace, set down his steaming cup of coffee and twinkled his fingers. He might have been mocking them, but Annabel chose to think otherwise.

Another day, and Annabel was back, singing "This Land Is Your Land" with a fingerless-glove-wearing guitar player and a druid drum circle. The signs planted around them tilted in the snow like a drunken forest.

On a break, she marched into the science building to use the restroom. It was one of the newer buildings, attached to an older one and funded by oil industry "philanthropy"—as opposed to other infrastructure paid for with state money that came from taxing the oil industry. Annabel understood that this was Alaska's conundrum: how much to tax, how much to "incentivize" to keep the industry happy. The oil corporations were sophisticated; they could afford the best public relations people. A few million in goodwill dollars— a corporate name on a shiny building with computerized whiteboards and well-ventilated bathrooms—could win over the public and repay them with a few billion dollars of profit. That was a minor part of their strategy, of course, The major part had to do with campaign contributions, platoons of lobbyists, and threats to pack up and abandon Alaska to a graveyard of rusting pipes and barrels. *Wink-wink,* the bright lights signaled to Annabel. *Let me let you enjoy this "gift," and let you return to me favorable (to me) leasing schedules and conditions, self-regulation that avoids environmental oversight, and a generous (to me) taxation policy.*

I will use your bathroom, Annabel communicated upward, but next year I'm giving half my permanent fund dividend to the Arctic Environmental Center. If she needed the other half to pay bills—the same dependence that most Alaskans had come to have on the yearly payout of oil money from the state's savings account—well, that just made her a real and conflicted Alaskan.

Unwind the scarf, remove the beaver-fur hat, unzip the suit, another layer, another layer, down to the silk underwear: Annabel settled onto the toilet seat. There was not even any graffiti in the stall to read; the shiny steel walls were like egg yolk surrounding her. Sterile yellow egg yolk, like the ones that come from industrial egg farms. She was thinking about those poor hens and the disconcerting news that even free-range chickens weren't all that free when the door to the hallway wheezed open and heels clicked over the floor.

"I don't see the point," one female voice said. "What is it they want?"

"To change the world?"

The voices twittered together.

"You've got to admire them for standing out in the cold for hours every day."

"Oh, please."

They entered separate stalls and slid the locks shut. Annabel listened to the sounds of pantyhose snapping, streams hitting the water, a gaseous release.

"It's their right," the one on her left said.

"Oh, sure," said the other, "a right to free speech, to assemble, to annoy others with their singing."

"Singing? You can hardly hear it. You're sure you're not feeling guilty?"

"Hey, I just work here."

"Famous words of the SS."

"The who?"

"The *German* SS."

Shuffling of feet, rustling of clothes, flushing.

At the sinks, running water. Annabel could see through the crack in her door two women she didn't recognize, one with hennaed hair clasped in a silver barrette, the other with the over-muscled shoulders of a former swimmer and the kind of short curly hair that grows in after chemo. They were still talking, but she couldn't hear them over the running water. She thought she heard "Oakley." She might have heard "piracy" or "conspiracy" or perhaps "privacy" or "racy." The hennaed woman was looking at her teeth in the mirror. Annabel definitely heard "whitener," "bleach," and "I'll give you the web address."

And then they were gone.

Secretaries? Annabel had the sense that the university, like most bureaucracies, had a vast web of mostly unseen women who typed, processed, filed, copied, sent and received, reminded, and generally held things together.

She couldn't help herself. She took her Subaru key from her purse made of recycled plastics in a third-world country and applied it to the blank surface in front of her. CHANGE THE WORLD, she scratched in capitalized Herculanum lettering with exaggerated serifs. Graffiti, she reminded herself, came from the Italian "scratched" and had a long and reputable history as an art form, often revealing what lay beneath added pigments. If it had become associated with vandalism, that was unfortunate. Her design was both lovely and revealing, and she hoped that those women would each, one day soon, enter that very stall, turn around with descending pantyhose, and recognize part of their conversation. They would have to think about that. She scratched two finely shaped exclamation points after her "D."

The gatherings grew. More tents were pitched. People brought food and finger puppets and a sculpture of a spavined bull carved in ice, delivered by dogsled. A propane cooker boiled water for cocoa and warmed pots of vegetarian chili. The burn barrel and the armloads of construction scraps and brittle branches beside it reminded Annabel of skating parties when she'd been a child, back when New Jersey winters were predictably cold.

There were the regulars, and there were people who were regular for a while and then disappeared, to be replaced by new regulars for another while, and there were the occasionals and then the merely curious, drawn by the fire or the molasses cookies or the singing and drumming and exchange of information. Annabel occupied the quad at least twice a week on her way to swimming and showering, and she nearly always brought food, a log for the fire, and a Buddhist teaching or a poem.

On a Thursday, she recited a translation of an Anna Akhmatova poem about betraying one's native land and abandoning its songs. Akhmatova was a personal hero of hers, for staying in Russia when her friends were fleeing, and writing passionate poems that were often oblique and still got her in trouble with authorities.

There was a lot of nodding around the burn barrel, and then they talked again about the university's failure to respond to the recent petition from the ad hoc committee. Was it too much to expect the university to be transparent about its funding—what portion came, for what purpose, from the legislature, from tuition, from corporations and other donors, from what investments?

"I'm afraid they'll raise tuition even more," someone said. "They'll use it as an excuse."

"The regents decide the budget."

"Then maybe we should be talking to the regents."

Annabel studied her *Free Ray Berringer* sign, now losing a little of its sparkle. She was distressed by how many people kept asking her who Ray Berringer was—more than asked her about pteropods. When she told them, they usually remembered, *oh, yes, the professor who was censored for something he said,* but Ray's name and the details had been lost in the general noise, and the more she filled in for them the more their eyes darted around. It was, of course, all one thing, all connected: the corporate control and misinformation campaign, the loss of democracy, the destruction of the environment, the silencing and discrediting of those who challenged the status quo, the manipulation of science, the wanton way of American life, the banks, the perversion of education. The movement had to speak to it all.

"Annabel!"

And there before her stood the bundled shapes of her shipmates, Tina and Cinda. Tina was wearing a knit hat with reindeer antlers, and both of them clutched overfilled daypacks. "What's happening!?" Tina shouted at her.

Annabel pointed at her sign, then flipped it so they could read the other side.

"Awesome!"

Annabel introduced them to the circle. "My marine science friends. Some of Ray Berringer's students. How is he, anyway?"

"Good. He's good," Tina said. When she moved her head the tiny bells on the points of the reindeer antlers tinkled. "Quiet. Teaching. Writing zooplankton reports. Reading our shit. You should go see him."

"I kind of did that. He kind of didn't appreciate it."

"Oh, I don't know. He was kind of laughing about it the other day. Something about a sword?"

"He doesn't really get performance art."

"Things are happening, though," Cinda said. Her head was down, texting, bare hands reddening in the cold.

"Really? What?"

Cinda and Tina exchanged a look.

Tina said, "Let's just say that what happens in Texas doesn't stay in Texas. That's really all we can say right now." She looked toward the science building and Annabel followed her gaze. Classes were getting out, and students were surging through the doors and into the quad. What now? They were unfurling banners. They were unfolding pieces of cardboard. They were blowing on kazoos.

"Flash mob," Tina said.

And then there were a hundred sunny-faced students surrounding them, holding signs and photos of fish and stretching out a white sheet with words painted in indigo blue. Annabel strained to make out the writing; the students holding it were jerking it so that it billowed in a sequence of waves. The middle word was "OF." The first word was longer. The last ended with "AY." Ray. It said Ray. It read FRIENDS OF RAY.

There was Colin, flapping one end of the sheet and grinning like a mad scientist. The Russian girl was parading a picture of a pink octopus shellacked to cardboard and attached to a wooden yardstick. Cinda was digging into her pack for more kazoos, and Tina had opened a kid's bubble jar and was blowing formations of soapy bubbles into the gray sky. Alex and Robert were there, and Helen, with a group of Native students. Marybeth was one of many handing out squares of paper with FOR printed in black letters. "Friends of Ray," she explained to Annabel. "But also 'for.' We're not against things, we're *for* them: academic freedom, science, truth. You know, *positive* things."

Someone positioned a wooden crate, and they took turns stepping up with their statements and speeches. They explained the scientific method. They explained the peer review process. Robert summarized the dastardly effort to confuse the public about global warming and, now, ocean acidification. A woman with Helen, who said she was from the village of Kivalina, spoke about the village's lawsuit against oil and coal companies. "It's just like with tobacco," she said. "They conspired to question the science and prevent any action to reduce emissions." There were lists of questions the university should answer. There were demands: *Fund research, not bullshit!*

Show some real scientific integrity! Stop the war on science! A young man who looked like he should still be in high school bitterly excoriated those who would steal his future.

Colin, when he took his turn, was shaking. He looked around and said, very seriously, "This situation cannot stand. While the Office of Ocean Acidification Science is withholding devastating evidence of trouble in our northern waters, the head of the office is pussy-footing around with corporate deniers. In fact, we've learned that Jackson Oakley just coauthored a paper for an industry-funded organization, promoting geoengineering as the solution to acidification. On the one hand, this group says acidification is not a problem, and on the other they want to fill the ocean with calcium oxide."

There were at least a few people taking notes and photos. One woman, standing beside a rumpled man with a camera, was scribbling into a long reporter's notebook. Another scribbler wore a hat with the school newspaper's logo. Someone in headphones was holding out a foam-covered microphone. Annabel turned to see how many people were standing behind her: dozens. Someone there was busily snapping photos—of Colin, the crowd around him, Cinda and Tina and Marybeth next to Annabel, Annabel. When the woman lowered the camera, Annabel recognized the short curls escaping a knit cap, the wide swimmer's shoulders, the face as seen in a mirror.

Early the next morning, when the fire in the burn barrel was out, campus security hauled away the barrel and the woodpile and the propane heater and tank. Officers woke the people sleeping in tents and told them they had to be packed up and gone by 9:00 A.M. or their tents and belongings would also be confiscated. They left the ice sculpture of the spavined bull with the rubber mermaids (Annabel's contribution) riding its back, but they took away the red and black anarchist flag that had been flying beside it.

Later, in the local paper, President Petterson said that it was a safety issue. "We're concerned about the safety of students in the cold, and in the proximity of fire."

"Two things we never have in Fairbanks," Annabel remarked to her elderly neighbor Yvonne when they met at the mailboxes. "Cold and fire."

"And yellow snow? I heard there was some unregulated peeing."

Annabel tossed her mail onto the seat of her Subaru. She had a concept for a new work, multimedia with slabs of rust and corroded metals. She would gather objects and think about rust and rot as metaphors. But first she needed to learn about the proposed geoengineering Colin had warned of. The geoengineering she knew about was Project Chariot, a crazy idea back in the '60s to blast a harbor in northern Alaska with an atomic bomb. Then ships, of which there were none, moving nonexistent freight from nowhere to nowhere, would have a place to park. It was meant to be a trial project, before being scaled up to improve the Earth in many more ways. There was to be no end of convenient harbors, canals, reservoirs, mountain passes. Rivers could be made to flow where the water was needed—backwards if necessary.

"Hey," she shouted from her window to Yvonne, who was still standing by the mailboxes with a clutch of catalogs. "Remember Project Chariot?"

"Of course."

"Besides blasting a harbor, wasn't there some idea about busting up the sea ice?"

"Oh, those nutcases kept coming up with more and more ideas they thought would be good for somebody. They said we should *warm up* the Arctic, make Alaska more suitable for agriculture and less expensive for home heating. They said if they broke up the ice, more solar heat would be absorbed and the climate would warm." Yvonne scoffed and shook her earmuffed head. "Funny how we didn't need nuclear explosions for that disaster. But those guys—

they had the politicians and the businesspeople convinced they could make a better planet than God."

Annabel was seeing in her future assemblage—in the flaking metal layers, dangerously sharp at their edges—a statement about human hubris.

Yvonne leaned into her open window. "And you know, it came too darn close to happening. Because they were the 'experts,' you know. Who were we to worry about things we didn't understand? They promised that no people, and no food, would be harmed. And it wasn't going to cost us anything. They were going to give Alaska a 'free' harbor."

She started at the science building, bypassing the quad—although she noted in passing that there were now more, and more colorful, tents plus a new fire burning on a piece of tin atop the snow. And flags everywhere—red and black, also the yellow one with a snake, earth flags, the old stars and stripes, at least one peace flag, a string of Tibetan prayer flags. It looked like the United Nations. The day was clear, and a breeze was rippling the whole scene most beautifully.

Annabel walked determinedly past the lounging security guard and right through the gilded gateway to the Office of Ocean Acidification Science to plant herself in front of the receptionist's desk. The receptionist was neither of the women she'd seen in the bathroom—which ascertainment was part of Annabel's mission. "I'm seeking some information for an art project," she legitimately stated. "Do you have some reports or anything that would tell me how ocean acidification can be affected by adding calcium oxide to the water?"

The woman looked alarmed. "For an art project?"

"Yes." Annabel presented her most fawning smile.

"And who would this be for?"

"Myself."

The woman blinked twice before asking, "And you are?"

Annabel gave her name.

"Are you on the faculty here?"

"No."

"Student?"

"Always."

"I don't know that we have anything on that subject. Have you tried the library?"

"I thought I'd come to the source." Annabel exaggeratedly craned her neck back toward the doorway and its signage. "I think this is where you do ocean acidification science?"

The woman pointed at a card rack just inside the door. "We have a few handouts there. Feel free to help yourself."

Annabel looked at what was on the card rack. There was a glossy flyer about the OA office and additional flyers about the university, the School of Marine Science, and student aid. There were campus maps. There was one "fact sheet" about ocean acidification, with colorful diagrams of the carbon cycle. Annabel took this and the glossy flyer. She turned back to the receptionist. "Maybe I could speak to the director?"

"Oh, I'm so sorry," the woman said. "I'm afraid he's in a meeting all day."

"I'm afraid he is," Annabel said.

The woman didn't react.

"How about another person? Who would you recommend I speak to if I have questions about effects of adding chemicals to seawater?"

The woman took a pad of yellow Post-it notes from her desk and passed it to Annabel with a pen. "If you write down your name and your contact info, and what it is you want, I'll see if someone can help you. I'll pass it along. But as I said, I don't think we have anything on that. You should go to the library."

"I'll tell you what," Annabel said. "I'm going to go to the library, and I'll come back another time with some more precise questions." She drew a shelled pteropod on the sticky note. The quick and impressionistic drawing, perhaps unfortunately, resembled a toilet bowl being engulfed by giant labia. The receptionist looked at it with neither recognition nor expression and set it to one side of her desk.

Annabel walked through the rest of the building, hoping she might spot one of the bathroom women, but there were mainly closed doors forbidding entry and, on each floor, a security officer who guardedly offered, "Can I help you?"

She had always intended the library. There, she first checked the student newspaper. There was a photo of the Kivalina woman on the crate (described as a "soapbox") and a reasonably factual account of the flash mob. The reporter (no doubt concerned with "balance") had found someone to say, "They're all wearing clothes made from petrochemicals. They're a bunch of hypocrites." She'd also gotten through to Jackson Oakley himself, who was asked whether adding chemicals to the ocean was a possible solution for ocean acidification and who responded, obliquely, "The protesters are just misinformed." Annabel absorbed all that and then settled in at a computer.

In general, she quickly discovered, the term "geoengineering" referred to globally-sized engineering projects intended to counter the effects of the anthropogenic carbon dioxide in the atmosphere. There were two major proposed techniques. One addressed reflectivity —trying to block the sun's heat with "enhanced" clouds, sulfur aerosols, or space mirrors. The other involved trying to remove carbon dioxide from the atmosphere through some kind of capture. The first, even if it were possible, would do nothing to combat ocean acidification (except, of course, to postpone actions to reduce carbon emissions, which would allow acidification to worsen). The second included fertilizing the ocean with iron to increase the growth of plankton—which, in theory, would take up more carbon. Annabel read until she understood that the plankton thus encouraged sooner or later (mostly sooner) released their carbon back into the cycle—and that there were also grave concerns about messing with the ecosystem on such a scale. There would not be, from what she could decipher from the highly scientific paper she muddled through, any appreciable change to ocean acidification; that would depend on complicated calculations about what percentage of anthropogenic carbon ended up, for what periods of time, in the atmospheric, terrestrial, and oceanic sectors.

Annabel checked her e-mail. There, in a blast to undisclosed recipients from an address she didn't recognize, was what looked like a press release from the Council for Science Integrity. "New Geoengineering Possibility Tackles Ocean Acidification." The idea was that something called quicklime, made from limestone, could be added to seawater to absorb carbon dioxide. This could both sequester carbon and also make the ocean more alkaline. "A promising technology," the one-pager said. "Alkalimization can be the answer to acidification." Chemical oceanographer Jackson Oakley, of the University of the North, was directly quoted: "The simple ocean chemistry works."

Annabel read farther down. At high temperatures, limestone broke down into quicklime and carbon dioxide. In seawater, the quicklime could absorb more carbon dioxide than the limestone heating produced—thus "sequestering" carbon. A key factor was the extreme heat needed to "cook" the limestone; this demanded a lot of energy. Oakley was quoted again: "This can be accomplished by using 'stranded energy' that isn't easily accessible for other uses. In northern Alaska, we have tremendous natural gas resources without a market, and these reserves happen to be right next to the Arctic Ocean. We've been given a perfect opportunity."

Annabel sat back on her chair. Seriously? An opportunity to

burn up more fossil fuels for no other purpose than breaking down rock into something that could absorb carbon dioxide? And then dump enough of that rock dust in the ocean to affect its chemistry? *Seriously?*

In a way, the plan made perfect sense. The oil and gas industry would get to exploit more fossil fuels while the need to reduce carbon emissions would be obscured by the suggestion that there was a global "fix" in the works. It was a perfect plan to go after more oil and gas in the Arctic and make more money for Big Oil—and Alaska.

Breathe in, she told herself. Breathe out. Breathe in. Think like a pteropod. Your life depends on what happens. Breathe out, in, out. Flag the mystery e-mail. Use your *ujjayi* breath. Breathe again. The victorious breath. The palate. Pteropods united, pteropods swarming. Be one with the pteropods.

Chapter Twelve

Megan was the girl's name. Ray was unlikely to forget it again. She'd gone to Dean Morris with an accusation that Ray had stared at her breasts and implied that she could help her grades by being "available."

From the far side of the dean's supersized desk, Ray racked his brain to try to remember if he'd used the word "available." It was very possible that he'd suggested that *he* was available to help her review material and catch up on what she missed. He couldn't deny noticing her breasts, the frightening fleshiness of them.

The dean was telling him that "they" had done an investigation. It had been suggested that Ray had a drinking problem. It was reported that he'd joked about being in a bar with female students and "eating their cherries."

Ray felt his face flush. *Oh, great.* How could breaking out into a red-faced sweat not look guilty? But how had that ridiculous story gotten to the dean? He'd been among friends, all men, waiting for a tedious meeting to begin. Someone had started, a crazy thing a student had said, and then they'd all had stories—a sort of "kids say the darnedest things" colloquium. He flushed again to think of Marybeth, her innocent face, how quickly he'd turned away, not wanting to embarrass her. What if the charges against him were made known—and she recognized herself? And—*God*—did that sound awful, put that way! He hadn't been joking about eating women's cherries! The story had been about his own embarrassment, the recognition that language changed and carried different meanings. He'd told Nelda the story! Nelda hadn't been offended! She hadn't thought it was funny, but she hadn't been offended.

The dean was going on. A review of Ray's grade postings had revealed that he had a history of giving slightly higher grades to women than to men.

An investigation? Because a girl said he looked at her breasts? It seemed to Ray that this was all out of proportion, and that someone should have spoken to him before going hunting for unfortunate remarks and potential grade disparities. He couldn't help thinking that there was something more behind it. He gathered himself. "Could it be," he said, in a carefully modulated voice, "that female students on average might work harder than male students and might deserve slightly higher grades?"

The dean didn't want to, as he put it, "engage in a generative debate," but he did admit that no one had looked at grades across the board to see whether there was a gender difference and whether Ray's grades were statistically different from the norm.

Ray threw himself on the dean's mercy. "I don't want to seem paranoid, but is it possible that I'm being investigated because I've been otherwise inconvenient?"

The dean seemed to be repressing a smile. "I don't think you want to add 'paranoia' to your list of problems."

He had a point there.

Ray said, as flatly as he could, "You and I both know that some people weren't happy when I spoke out about ocean acidification and its effect on organisms."

"Its *possible* effect. I think your lack of nuance, among other things, is what's gotten you into trouble. And of course, you've previously been reprimanded in this very office for speaking carelessly and roughing up a colleague."

"I did *not* rough up a colleague. I only *wanted to* rough up a colleague."

"Be that as it may." The dean glanced at his notes. "As I'm sure you know, we treat sexual harassment very seriously at this university."

"Yes, and I'm ready to give you my account of what happened with that girl. There was no harassment involved. Unless it was *she* harassing *me* about having to do the expected classwork."

The dean frowned. "That won't be necessary right now. We'll get to that when we schedule a disciplinary hearing. And I suggest that you don't, *ever*, speak about women harassing you. That doesn't go down well. We could use a little more respect around here. A little more lip-buttoning, if you know what I mean." He gave Ray a long look, the kind a person might give a moose he was trying to get by on a trail—part effort to judge what the other might do, part stare-down, a warning to stay put.

"Pick your battles," the dean said.

Ray knew they were talking in code now. Or the dean was. Ray was feeling like a comb jelly out of water, collapsed and stranded. About to be stepped on by a giant foot. The dean was going to tell him to forget about attending the marine science symposium in Hilo, just a month away. He was going to revoke his authorization. Ray could see it coming—he was going to be punished, scheduled for sexual harassment classes, shoved back into silence.

"So," the dean said, opening a file folder, "our business today, regrettably, is for me to tell you personally that, based on the evidence of sexual misconduct, you are suspended from your position, as of now." He handed Ray a letter. "This tells you that and lays out the hearing and appeals process. But as of this afternoon, you will no longer be teaching or doing research here, at least not until the completion of the hearings. You won't have access to your office, etcetera. Your classes and advising are being reassigned." The dean stood up. "I'm sorry," he said, unconvincingly.

Ray read the letter before he got up. "Pick your own battles," he said to the dean's staredown face. He didn't know quite what he meant by that, but he had reached for it as an alternative to "fuck you." What he knew for certain was that Jackson Oakley and his oleaginous council-for-the-opposite-of-integrity had got what they wanted.

The days after were barely better.

His e-mail account had been immediately shut down, set to send an automatic message that he was "on leave." Sam helped him open a Gmail account, but he had not even attempted to reconstruct his network. When he checked, he found only ads for penis enlargement pills and pleas from non-English speakers for his bank account numbers. He started looking instead at YouTube videos of talking dogs. Helen had called, briefly, to let him know that she'd been one of several students interviewed by someone with the university's legal team. The questions were about his relationships with students and whether they'd ever heard him make offensive jokes and comments. "Everyone wants to know what the heck's going on."

That woman, Annabel, had called to tell him with considerable excitement that she'd made an important discovery. In his desperation for any good news, he'd allowed himself to hope.

"*Clione,*" she said, as though that were an answer.

Pteropods were not exactly his main concern at the moment. "What about *Clione?*"

"The name comes from the Greek sea nymph Kleios, with a 'K.'"

"Yes?" He'd drawn away from the phone's receiver at the word *nymph.* It reminded him of *nymphet,* from a book Nelda had made him read long ago, about an old man fondling young girls. That was all he needed, a link-up to more perversion. The girl with the complaint had been no prepubescent Lolita.

Annabel's voice was almost shrill. "Why didn't I know that?"

"I have no idea why you didn't know that. Are you an expert in Latin, Greek, and mythology? You're telling me this because . . . ?" He was still holding on to hope that there was a life ring somewhere at the end of the lengthening rope.

"Kleios," she said, with exaggerated annunciation, as though she was the word presenter at a school spelling bee. "The daughter of Oceanus. Kleios is the muse who protects *art and science.*"

She had delivered that profound news, and then signed off with another intake of breath, as though she might be toking up.

His teaching colleagues, a fair number of them, called with expressions of sympathy and support, but he could hear in their voices their commitments to self-preservation, to hunkering down, circling their wagons. They were not going to risk their own careers. Their questions, he could tell, were aimed at learning enough of what had happened to prevent their own missteps. Their offers were vague: "Let me know if I can do something." Or cynically hopeful: "I'm sure things will work out." Someone else would do something: "The union will be all over this."

The union, in fact, was not helpful. Charges of sexual misconduct were so sensitive, he was told, the union had its hands tied. "We can't look like we're defending predatory acts," his union representative told him over the phone. Ray, stricken by the word "predatory," had gone down to his basement and thrown darts at the long-ignored dartboard for an hour.

Before all that, of course, there had been his family.

"What!?" Nelda had fallen into a chair and clasped her hands over her heart. "What?" she repeated. "Sexual misconduct? With a

student? *You?*" Her face had looked like it half wanted to laugh at the absurdity of the accusation, half was deeply alarmed. Then it turned to one hundred percent alarm. Then a few other emotions ran across it, including fear and anger, possibly doubt. He could see her wondering about the Hawaii conference, which she was planning to attend with him. Ray recalled—he'd read this in a magazine, maybe at the dentist's office—that there were stages to suffering: denial, anger, depression, etcetera, and it came to him now that his news was soliciting something of the same, except in rapid order. Nelda flew through an emotional cyclone before cycling through again and settling on anger. She uncurled her hands. She shook her head and lined her mouth like a sharpened blade. "How could you," she spit out. It was not a question.

Now it was Ray's heart threatening an aortic blow-out. He shouted his innocence, but he was thinking, *My God! What shithole have I fallen into, that even Nelda's against me?*

It soon became clear that, while she was indeed directing her anger at him, Nelda didn't believe a word of the accusation. Her anger was simply about him (once again) being the person he was, a person who would so persistently annoy another person (and now multiple persons) that people he should just avoid would feel the need to respond to him in, now, multiple negative ways. Had he not brought all this on himself by harassing that man for his data and then going on the radio and doing his truth thing?

His truth thing? He looked at Nelda's hardened jaw and felt wounded all over again. He could bear being an annoying person. But truth? Was truth to be belittled? Was standing for truth and honesty something to be avoided, regretted? He turned away, walked to the end of the living room, stared down at the worn edge of the Persian carpet that had come from Nelda's parents' house.

"I'm sorry," Nelda said. "It's just that I'm upset. Of course I'll help you fight this. Of course the truth is important." She tried to smile. "That must be why I like you. You're honest to a fault."

Ray noticed that she'd said "like," not "love." And then qualified his honesty. He would take what he could get.

"This won't be easy for any of us," she went on, and he could see her very organized mind clicking through myriad ways in which he was disrupting his family's lives. "You can bet some cruel child will tell Aurora her father's a pervert. Do we need a lawyer?"

From there, what had followed was a family meeting, in which he and Nelda outlined for Sam and Aurora, as simply as they could, the situation and what might happen next. Nelda did most of the talking.

". . . So what your father's accused of could be the result of a very confused young woman, and we don't want to condemn her, but we also can't let her confusion hurt your father's reputation and his ability to do his job. The other possibility is that the misguided young woman is being used by others to get back at your father for being outspoken about ocean acidification."

This had not actually occurred to Ray—the distinction between the accusation being used and the girl herself being used, that is, recruited to the cause. Making a big deal out of a loony charge, yes, but recruiting the girl, orchestrating the event? He thought *he'd* been the paranoid one.

Sam, who had been looking like he wanted to be somewhere else, lit up. "You mean Jerk-off Jackson? Oily Oakley?"

"Sam!" Nelda gave her son an exasperated look, then turned to Ray with an almost identical look that screamed *the apple falls near the tree.*

"We don't call anyone jerk-offs around here, Sam," Ray lied. "But it's no secret that Jackson Oakley and some other people at the university have been unhappy with me for speaking about acidification. We're not saying they set up that young woman to file a complaint about me. More likely"—he shot a look back at Nelda—"they're just using it to their advantage, to silence me. Or perhaps"—he thought he should fudge—"it's entirely a coincidence. I'd like you to *not* comment about any of it if anyone asks. Anyone says anything to you, you say you're sure your dad will be cleared and back to work soon because there's nothing to the claim. Don't get into it with anyone. Both of you." *And please*, he prayed, *don't let there be any talk of cherries.*

Aurora, pulling at her hair, asked her mother, "What confusion?"

Nelda stepped right back in. "We don't know. Some girls don't learn appropriate behaviors, and then they misinterpret or try to manipulate other people. Some people act out sexually. Or something scared her."

"Something made her lie?"

"We don't want to say she lied. She may have been confused about what happened. Her sense of reality might not have been very real."

Ray said, "She lied. If anything, I was *avoiding* looking at her exposed chest."

"Gross," Aurora said.

"No busty women ever try to seduce *me*," Sam said with a sigh of regret.

Nelda frowned again. "Sam, this isn't about sexual attraction. This is about someone wanting something—whether it's a good grade, attention, or—whatever."

Ray guessed he was glad to know that Nelda didn't think he could possibly be sexually attractive.

"On the upside," Nelda said, trying to smile, "your father will now have more time to spend with us and for special projects like cleaning up the garage and fixing that shelf in the refrigerator. And he and I"—she shot him another of her sharpened looks—"are still going to Hawaii."

———

In penance for his miserable life, Ray did partially clean up the garage. He washed bacon grease off the tea kettle. He made dinners, including a chicken marsala that no one in the family seemed to like, and was resolute about drink limits—two with dinner, never alone. He reread his favorite Isaac Asimov stories and some of a book about mindful living that Nelda forced upon him. He found the coin collection he'd had as a boy but discovered that Sam—or maybe Aurora—had raided it for spending money.

At the hardware store, his fellow shoppers talked, as always, about the weather. After a couple of winters of record-breaking warmth and even rain, the cold was back. (So was, in certain circles, the "so much for global warming" refrain.) The cold talk was not complaints; Fairbanksans liked to brag about their hardiness. This is how tough we are: when the fuel oil congeals, we use hair dryers to thaw it out and then shovel more insulating snow around the tank. And this is how cool we are: for fun we drive on our square tires to the darkest places we can find and look at the northern lights. On his way home, Ray drove on his own frozen tires past the university, where students were photographing themselves in their underwear in front of the big digital campus thermometer that read minus forty-one degrees. Ray had to look away. He thought instead of Hawaii. Soon.

He took another phone call from Annabel, in which she apologized about Kleios and explained that she'd gotten bad information from an Internet forum and the truth was that Kleios was not related to Oceanus at all and was not a sea nymph. Kleios was also known as "Clio," and was a Muse, one of the nine Greek goddesses who presided over the arts and sciences. She was specifically the Muse of history. "People just make things up," she complained.

Yes, Ray had to agree. People do just make things up.

He decided he needed a new hobby, one that would take him out of the house and among other, perhaps mindful and nonalcoholic, people. In the newspaper's listing of community events, he found an announcement for a drawing class sponsored by the local arts association. Why not? He had a great photographic eye; why not train his eye to direct his fingers and learn to illustrate his articles with drawings as well as photographs? Sometimes photos just didn't show what he wanted to show, or journals he submitted to preferred drawings. If he could learn to draw apples and pears, he could draw copepods and ostracods.

On a Monday evening he went off to the arts center with his sharpened pencils, charcoals, and a new giant pad of art paper. He was feeling adventurous—ready to try something new, even to *be* someone new.

"Embrace your wild mind," Nelda intoned as she saw him out the door. The more he was around her, the more Buddhist she was becoming, and the more grateful she seemed to be whenever he went off to the store, the library, the post office.

In the car, he listened to the Backstreet Boys and went over the phone conversation he'd had with Helen the day before. She'd called to tell him that Oakley was going to be the lead scientist on the spring cruise, in May. She would be going again, and at least several of the others who'd been on the fall cruise. Oakley was handpicking the students. No, she didn't know exactly who would be doing the plankton work. Alex and Tina were going. She wasn't sure about Colin. Nastiya, she'd heard, would be fishing with her boyfriend as soon as school got out and wouldn't be available. *Available*—the word stung. Helen thought there would be some undergrads.

The coming cruise would be the first in nine years that Ray would miss. He'd written the grant proposals; he'd gotten the money. He'd trained the students, assembled the equipment, made it all happen. And now he wasn't invited, wasn't even consulted. Insult to injury, the cruise had gone to Oakley. Oakley—who had been too busy to participate before, too busy to submit his data or help with the grant proposals and reports. Oakley—who didn't believe there was a problem that dumping quicklime into the ocean couldn't solve.

He and Helen had talked, briefly, about that as well. A number of politicians had been quick to jump on the quicklime thesis, particularly the part of Oakley's paper about using "stranded energy." "One thousand five hundred seventeen degrees Fahrenheit," Ray had told her; that was the temperature needed for lime-burning. Ray didn't believe for a minute that anyone truly believed that such a process could work on any scale beyond a fish tank. Talk about quicklime was just one more float of a phantom "solution" to instill more confusion and delay any real response to the climate and acidification crisis. The oil and gas industry was no doubt hoping to get some new subsidies or a gas line paid for by the government out of the deal before the whole idea was debunked.

Ray didn't want to ask, but Helen told him about the campus occupation anyway. It had changed, she said. The only ones still out there were the anarchists. They were smoking pot and passing out hand-copied quotations from Emma Goldman and Noam Chomsky.

Downtown, Ray parked in ice fog at the art center and hurried inside. He had planned to arrive early to meet the instructor, but there were already a few others taking seats in a circle around a table covered with a thick, rumpled brocade. He found the instructor, an older woman with paint on her smock, who told him to sit anywhere and that everyone "just did their own thing." She would circulate with comments and occasional technical advice, but the class was mostly just an opportunity for people to get together and draw, and everyone chipped in a few dollars each time. There was coffee and tea in the corner; everyone helped himself.

Ray sat on one of the folding chairs and waited for further instructions and the arrangement of whatever was to go on the table. He found it somehow comforting that the others, as they collected and greeted one another, were mostly women, and mostly middle-aged or older, not unlike a group he'd imagine meeting at the fabric store or the dress shop that catered to plus-size women (not that he'd ever been inside either establishment). There were very few men and very few younger people, none of them with facial tattoos. The room, like most public buildings, was overheated, and he stripped to his T-shirt and settled his pad of drawing paper on his lap.

Another woman had come from somewhere and was now stepping up onto the table and taking off a bathrobe. The instructor moved in front of Ray and helped the woman position herself on the brocade. Ray registered: *Naked woman. Very attractive young naked woman with a golden tan and whiter parts from under a bikini. This is a class to draw naked people. The newspaper had said "Life Drawing." Not "Still Life."*

Ray stared at the pad of paper in his lap, pencil poised over it. He had come to a class where he would be closely studying a naked young woman, someone who was no doubt a college student earning a few dollars as an art model. He was expected to draw her body. The instructor moved away, and he saw when he lifted his head that he had a perfect front-on view of the model's pubic area, complete with red hair. He lowered his head again and thought how completely inappropriate it was for him to have taken up a hobby that involved young women's bodies. He had to escape, but he couldn't very well just get up and leave, not at the moment when everyone was settling in to draw. The pencils and ink pens were scritching into paper now; the room was quiet and unmoving except for heads looking up and down, to model and paper, model and paper.

And then, a flurry of movement behind him, a slap to his shoulder. "Ray! OMG, how amazing to see you here! I just got here, and I couldn't believe it was you. It's you, *bell'uomo!* The artist-scientist!"

She chattered on, Annabel in a gypsy dress and peacock earrings that swung wildly with her also swinging beaded dreadlocks. She was so glad to see him. She couldn't believe he was at an art class. This was so *fantástico!* She was so eager to see his work. Some-one had given her a birch burl she was going to carve to honor Kleios, the Muse she'd decided after all could be their Muse, even if she was supposed to be about history. History was everything, wasn't it? The history of the Earth was geology. The history of human endeavor involved the arts. She would be referencing his photos, which captured such infinite beauty. After awhile he couldn't hear anymore. After awhile he had to put his pencil tip to paper. He drew a toe. He drew a badly proportioned foot. When it was time for a short break, he left.

Since art was not going to be Ray's new hobby, he decided to take up bird-watching. The fact that it was still winter might have deterred a more reasonable person, but Ray figured that the small number of cold-weather birds just made it easier to identify what he saw. Ravens, chickadees, the gray jays he knew as "camp robbers," magpies, grouse, a couple of owls, a couple of woodpeckers, redpolls, crossbills, pine grosbeaks, ptarmigan on the ridges and domes—that was about it. For Ray, given present circumstances, a solitary, simplified, and largely uncomfortable pastime seemed like a good idea.

On a darkening afternoon, Ray tromped through birch forest in his big boots and puffy parka, binoculars tucked against his chest and his *Sibley's* and a thermos of coffee in a daypack. The woods were lovely, dark and deep, as the old poet had romanticized. (Ray knew the Frost poem because Aurora had memorized it for school one year, and he'd had to listen to it repeatedly at the breakfast table, the little horse thinking it queer and all.) There had been no wind for days, and the crystalline snow and frost were layered thickly over all the branches, dazzling in the low-angled sunlight. Snowshoe hare and squirrel tracks crisscrossed the one packed trail that Ray followed.

The only sounds were the scrunch of his boots and the huff of his breath, a tree creak and then the sifting of snow as a dislodged handful floated down. From far off, the rumble of traffic on a rutted road.

Ray stood and waited, thinking small thoughts about snow—the metallic taste of it in the cold, and the many words the Athabascans had for its kinds: dry and fluffy, old and compressed, good (or not) for building a snow shelter, the dangerously hypothermic wet kind. His thoughts went from there to an Athabascan story about two old women left behind by their tribe when times were tough. The women were mentally strong and worked together to survive the winter and eventually rejoin the tribe. It was a story, he thought, more about women than about age or Nativeness. He was pretty sure that if two old men were left behind, they would have fought over the last piece of fish, and one would have killed the other for it. Darwinism, of course. Men were made to fight over women and be the successful breeders; women took care of others, cooperated. This thought led to the next, unwanted one: that girl and her accusation. He shook it off and kept walking, attending to the feel of the frozen mucus in his nose and to a litter of powdery, pecked debris on the snow.

And then they arrived, tearing up the monochromatic stillness with their flitterings of wings and blood-red spots of brilliance. The lovely redpolls: his new favorite birds. A flock of twenty or more darted in and out among the birches, pulling at old catkins. *Chip-chip-chip-chip.* With their feathers all plumped out, they looked almost round, like small decorative snowballs, the males with blush chests and red forehead patches. They were all around him now, so close and so fast-moving that his binoculars were useless. They were mostly common redpolls, but he was learning to see among them the less common, less streaky hoary redpolls, described in his book as "frostier," with a slightly smaller bill. They were finches, like Darwin's—and, like Darwin's, adapted for discrete environmental niches, the right-shaped bill for the particular seed on its "island." Acrobats, they jostled upside down and sideways among the branches. It was hard to imagine such a small bird, needing all that hopped-up energy, staying warm through a Fairbanks winter. Another supreme bit of evolutionary adaptation: the enlarged esophagus that stored seeds gathered during the day for fueling through the darkness and cold.

Ray was priding himself on his patient and keen observations, his attentiveness to detail, the differences among individual birds of the same species; more and less streaky, more and less blush, bigger and smaller. After each of his outings he looked in books and on the Internet to learn more about bird physiology, feather construction and insulating value, taxonomy. He pondered the familiar debate between splitters and lumpers, this time regarding the number of redpoll species. He read about the esophagus and another cold-weather adaptation—in legs, the placement of arteries (carrying warm blood from the heart) up against the veins, returning cooled blood back to the heart.

In general, Ray had given over to entertaining himself with figuring out the connections in his new, avian world. He was doing it mostly alone, although he sometimes called in observations to the local bird hotline, and once someone named Bud had called him back for an engaging conversation about irruptions. Some years— like this one—there were thousands of redpolls in the area, and other years very few; the birds seemed to respond to the plenitude (or scarcity) of birch and alder catkins.

Birds and their habitats: migrating birds, at least, had some ability to adjust to changing conditions, to fly to new areas. Ray had read about a study that showed that a majority of North American bird species—especially seedeaters—had moved significantly northward in response to climate change. Just the week before he'd spotted an American robin puffed up on top of a spruce tree— unheard of in an Interior winter until recently. He couldn't say that the robin looked very happy.

Many marine organisms could also move to find water temperatures to their liking; his crew had certainly seen that in the Gulf. But how could they flee an acidifying ocean?

Ray forced his thoughts back to the here and now, to birds. The redpolls, as quickly as they'd come, departed in a whirl. A raven cawed from deeper in the woods. He brushed off a fallen log and sat on his extra gloves to pour himself a cup of lukewarm coffee. Now a pair of chickadees swung through a spruce, and he tried to follow them with his binoculars. He was looking in particular for deformed, overlong beaks—a disturbing affliction thought to have something to do with chemical contaminants. Ray had not yet seen a bird with the condition, but until recently he hadn't been looking, and if he knew one thing for sure, it was that, in general, not looking was a good way of not seeing.

CHAPTER THIRTEEN

March came, the usual bear. The only word about Ray's status was that someone working on the investigation had left on maternity leave. He and Nelda flew to Hilo, to the symposium on marine science and technology, where he delivered his paper on the annual cycles of zooplankton abundance and biomass. He got a nodding response to his findings of southern species and his cautious conclusions about variability, and he attended several other sessions that provoked lively discussions. He was glad to reconnect with various colleagues that he only saw at an occasional conference or corresponded with in reviewing one another's papers, and he'd had a drink with a former grad student who was now at Scripps doing something with giant xenophyophores in the Mariana Trench.

"Your tribe," Nelda had said, approvingly.

A central theme at the symposium was ocean warming and acidification. There was a lot of talk about the Big Three—those two plus low oxygen—in combination with other human-induced stresses. One presentation he found particularly relevant was about species-specific pteropod sensitivities to hypercapnia and hypoxia, and he had a good talk with the German biologist afterwards.

His name badge still said University of the North, which was problematic. When someone came up to him, stared at his badge, and then peppered him with questions—how long he'd been there, what was happening in such-and-such program, would it be a good place to send a doctoral student—was he required to explain that he was not, actually, representing the university? Should he be surveying other tags to try to find another school—or an obscure government agency—that might need a zooplankton expert of dubious character? Weren't there some people here from Siberia?

In a hallway outside the meeting rooms, little girls were charging five dollars to color name tags; the money, their sign said, would go to protecting sea turtles. "A very good cause," Ray complimented them while handing over his donation. He asked them to create a dark blue sea over and around *University of the North,* essentially obscuring it, and then to fill the rest of the white space with whatever they desired. (He had noticed that flaring suns and rainbows were favorite designs.)

The dark blue sea, it turned out, only caused people to peer at his badge more closely. "Unaffiliated," he started saying.

There were, of course, colleagues who'd heard about his situation and felt the need to question him. "What the hell's going on in that icebox of yours?"

He still had not formulated an answer appropriate to the generally jovial line of questioning. Everyone seemed to have his or her own issues with funding, university politics, corporate sponsorships, dealing with the denier crowd. About the Council for Science Integrity, the fellow who did otolith analyses blew a raspberry. "That's what we get for giving this country over to corporations. What're you gonna do?" The question was rhetorical.

The last day of the symposium was set aside for field trips, mostly water-based recreation, mostly for families—snorkeling, fish viewing from a glass-bottom boat, swimming with dolphins.

"I can't do it," Ray said to Nelda, as they lay atop the pineapple-design quilt in their hotel room, pillows piled behind them. The coquí frogs in the garden outside were well launched into their ear-splitting mating calls.

Nelda lifted her eyes from her book. She was reading about Captain Cook, who was thought a god when he arrived in Hawaii. Everyone knew how that turned out for him.

"I can't look at another dying reef," Ray said. "It's just too depressing."

"Then do something else."

"The turtles are just as pathetic. There's a little roped-off beach where they try to protect their nesting sites, but the beach is eroding. They've got people digging up turtle eggs and moving them to higher ground, and then rescuing the hatchlings and carrying them to the water. It's feel-good for the people, but hopeless for the turtles."

"Isn't there some kind of boat thing?"

"I've been on boats."

"We could just do something by ourselves. There's a botanical garden."

Ray could not see himself walking around a botanical garden, drenched with humidity. Native plants might be interesting, but he knew that battle was already pretty much over, too. Nearly all the vegetation on the island was nonnative, invasive, alien. Even the food plants that Hawaii was famous for: pineapples, papayas, mangos, bananas, coffee beans—all of those had been brought from elsewhere. Just like the deafening coquí frogs, accidentally introduced from Puerto Rico. Now they were taking over the island, eating up the insects needed by native birds, which were also rapidly going extinct, replaced by mynas and other exotics. And then there were the feral pigs, mucking up everything. "I don't think so."

Nelda was wearing her I'm-trying-to-be-patient face. "Well, I signed up for snorkeling. I'm going to stick with that. You do whatever you want." She turned back to her book. "I don't need to know that the coral and the reef fish used to be more plentiful to enjoy them now. I like looking at them. I can see the beauty in them." There was the slightest emphasis to her "I" in the last sentence, which Ray took as a rebuke: *she* could see the beauty; he, given his crappy character and degenerate state of mind, apparently could not.

"OK." Ray watched the room's fan circling, listened in the spaces between the coquí calls to the mini fridge humming. The main source of electrical power in Hawaii, he'd learned, was imported oil—90 percent. Hawaii could not be more blessed with sun, wind, and geothermal resources, and yet even here humans couldn't manage to set a course that wouldn't destroy the planet. He felt the urge to pull the plug on the refrigerator (which was empty, in any case, except for bottled water) but instead snapped off the light on his side of the bed and got to his feet.

"Going somewhere?"

"Downstairs."

Nelda gave him one of her looks and pushed her glasses back up her nose.

"I'm on vacation," he said. "Or pretending to be."

In the bar, Ray found the part of his tribe that, like him, was in need of a chemical adjustment. He was introduced to a technician who monitored the Mauna Loa Observatory.

"That's got to be like a shrine," Ray said, freshly enthusiastic. He admitted his hero worship for Charles Keeling and told the man about using him as an example with his students: the virtues of inventiveness, long and methodical data collection, persistence in battling for funding, conviction. He might have gone on a bit long about some of this, but the technician, Rob, seemed to be a tolerant fellow. Ray asked, "Do people drive up there to see the home of the Keeling Curve?"

Rob said, "We've still got Keeling's original black box. Occasionally someone wants to see that."

It turned out that Rob would be driving to the observatory the next day and would be glad to take him along. "You wouldn't want to take a rental car," he'd warned Ray, who already knew—because Nelda had read him the small print—that their rental contract forbade travel off the main, properly paved roads. Ray tipped the bartender too much and returned to his room with an improved attitude.

Nelda was still reading. "Listen to this," she said. "'The islanders thought the English had volcanoes in their mouths, and treasure holes in their sides.' They'd never seen anyone smoking or imagined clothes with pockets."

"Paradise," Ray said. "No mosquitoes either back then. No missionaries. Who needed clothes?" He unbuttoned his aloha shirt, the one swimming with bright-colored fish, which Nelda had bought for him the day they arrived and she discovered that he'd packed mainly T-shirts illustrating the sexual behaviors of salmon and ratfish. "I'm going up Mauna Loa tomorrow, with a NOAA guy, to the observatory there. I don't suppose you want to join us?"

She was back to her book. "I suppose not. I'm pretty sure I didn't come to Hawaii to be in snow."

"There's no snow in March." Rob hadn't mentioned snow, though he had said to bring a jacket.

"I saw pictures of skiers."

"That's the other one. Mauna Kea. This is Mauna Loa. It's where Charles Keeling did all that pioneering CO_2 measuring."

"That's not depressing."

"No." Ray went into the bathroom to brush his teeth. She was right, of course, in her ironic way. Over fifty years of incontrovertible data establishing the unprecedented rise in carbon dioxide—and still no acceptance of what that meant, only lethal inaction. Tomorrow he would spend three hours in a car, burning up gas, and the next day he'd get on a plane to trash his beloved planet even more.

It was a long drive up the mountain, on a one-lane road with jagged holes and stretches of sharp volcanic rock. In the government jeep, Rob swerved and accelerated and bounced over cracks and across edges, apparently knowing—or trusting—that no cars would be coming the other way. He was a congenial fellow, full of detailed information about the various lava flows that had built up the mountain.

Ray had to admit, the landscape through which they were moving was amazing. Some of the flows they intersected were hellish piles of sharp *a'a*, the kind of debris one might imagine at the end of the world, when all the roads and sidewalks and plastic junk were blown up and scattered. Some were the smooth-surfaced snaking and coiling *pahoehoe* that Ray could easily imagine oozing down the slope, building up new layers. Different flows had run over each other, and were of different compositions, different colors: black, gray, brown. The older ones sprouted single colonizing plants: a few blades of green here, a flutter of yellow flower there, explosions of color against a background of molten lead. Up and up: the gradual rise that was the long sloping shield of the volcano, its actual top somewhere in clouds. He wished Nelda had come. He wished Sam and Aurora were with him. He'd be pointing out plant succession. He'd be praising resilience.

Rob had not asked him a single thing about himself or his work. Ray found this lack of curiosity, under the circumstances, oddly pleasing.

Finally they were approaching the gate, with the suite of buildings, domes, and towers hovering in sunlight beyond. Then they were through, and parked, and Ray stepped out into chill air. He noticed immediately the bronze plate on the side of the smaller building: the Keeling Curve, its sawtooth graph rising steadily across the years. Reverentially, he read the signage: *Keeling Building, 1997, in honor of Charles David Keeling on the fortieth anniversary of his first CO2 measurements at the site.*

"People think he worked here," Rob said, jangling keys. "But he only came up here a few times. He was at Scripps. He died in 2006, before my time."

Inside, the one room was crammed with floor-to-ceiling metal frames holding the various analyzers, with their screens and print-outs and clipboards. Rob pointed around the room—CO_2 and the other greenhouses gases, ozone, particulates, mercury. Cables and duct tape–wrapped piping descended through open ceiling tiles, and the gas cylinders—key, Rob said, to calibrating the equipment for accurate readings—stood in rows.

Ray felt an unreasonable envy. It was so *easy*, really, to collect all this data. CO_2 in the atmosphere kept to its own molecular struc-ture and was evenly spread around. Nothing was so simple in the oceans. He glanced at a wall poster, and his envy extended to all the dots and squares, all those stations around the world where clean-air samples were collected. Even ships far out at sea collected air sam-ples. All a person needed to do was open a flask and let it fill with air.

Rob was holding up one of those stainless steel flasks, like a fat pigeon in hand.

In the other building, Rob took him to Keeling's original ana-lyzer, stored in the hallway as a bit of historical detritus. Behind its door the typed component labels were peeling off: amplifier, sample cell, reference cell, detector, chopper, scrubber. Simple enough, Ray thought, *and* the work of a genius.

Rob was giving him the tourist talk. "Why did he do it? He always said, 'I was having fun.' The man loved his work. He loved figur-ing things out."

"He didn't love having to constantly defend his work and beg for money," Ray said, more forcefully than he intended.

Rob nodded. "He called what he did 'an activity with almost invisible benefits.'"

Almost invisible benefits. Ray was going to remember that. Hard enough to justify to agencies and funders, harder still to defend against massive disinformation campaigns.

Rob was reaching into a cabinet. "Here. We have these for tourists." He took out a small glass vial and led the way back down the hall.

Outside, he waved the vial around. "Like I said, for tourists. This is not scientific. But we give them a little sample of air as a souvenir." He capped the vial, wrote something on the label, and handed it to Ray.

The label circling the vial was printed with the Keeling curve and the words *Mauna Loa Observatory–Where It All Began.* Rob had written in the date and the current CO_2 level—405.3 ppm.

Ray clutched it in his hand. "I bet swarms of tourists are begging for these."

Rob shrugged. "School groups from Hilo mostly. But we have other visitors. Last week a lady working on a murder mystery. She wanted to imagine someone poisoning a competitor by releasing certain gases in his workspace."

"I should have thought of that."

The two men stood looking at the clouds below them until Ray said, "I'll walk around for a while."

It would take a couple of hours, Rob told him, to check calibrations and do routine maintenance. He pointed the way to a trail that led to the volcano's summit. "You won't have time to get near the top, but it'll get your heart going."

Ray was happy to stretch his legs after jamming his foot against an imaginary brake pedal for so much of the drive. The trail was cindery, not an easy go, and the altitude was something to consider: the air might have been among the purest on Earth, full of the standard 21 percent oxygen, but at 11,000 feet, the lower pressure made the air "thinner."

Happy, with Ray, was relative. He was happy to have seen "where it all began," no matter that Mauna Loa wasn't Mount Ararat and would never be acknowledged as a place of significance by the Genesis folks. He knew very well that numbers, percentages, scales, and other measures were more mysterious than God to even ordinary, otherwise perfectly sane people. Atmospheric carbon dioxide had increased from 0.031 percent to 0.0396 since Keeling started measuring in the 1950s? Such small numbers! How could that be a big deal? Ocean pH decreased by 0.1 in two hundred years? So what?

Ray, watching his feet and, now, breathing hard, gave himself over to the conundrums of his life. The ocean was so complex, its chemistry variable, its life forms so numerous and so incompletely understood. What could a couple decades of data prove? What "discoveries" would justify continued funding? What if the people in charge didn't really want to know what was going on, if they preferred to turn away from the implications? That last question, it was now apparent, wasn't the least bit hypothetical.

Stopping to catch his breath, he looked down at the station—a lonely outpost on a parched lunar landscape. A small, unimposing, functional building named for one small, determined scientist. Year after year after year, technicians filling flasks, taking measurements, compiling data, reporting.

To the west, on the Kona side of the island, the clouds had settled. He couldn't see the coastline, but over the tops of the clouds, far in the distance, two blues met at the horizon. Sky and ocean—his Pacific Ocean, extending all the way to Alaska.

He dropped his eyes back to earth. Off to one side of the gray cindery path lay a single piece of *a'a,* its color shaded from blood-red to plum-purple. It was the size of a ping pong ball and, when he picked it up, not much heavier. It was as much air as mineral, as porous as a hexactinellid sponge. And as beautiful. He turned it over in his hand and felt like he was being pulled under a wave. He sat down on the trail.

Lack of oxygen was supposed to muddle one's mind—all those stories of mountaineers confusing directions and walking off cliffs—but for Ray what might have been a muddle seemed like its opposite—a moment of clarity. He was imagining the ocean around him, its darkness and its cold, and the drops of water with their microscopic protists and then the Earth from space with the plankton blooms spraying out like green banners, like the northern lights, and then he too felt expansive, like *Neocalanus cristatus* hatching out the eggs to which it had given over its entire body. How alike hatches and blooms and consciousness were to an exploding star which, one day, would begin things again.

After he sat with that for a while he thought that it might be a good idea to get into better shape. Maybe he should take up running with Nelda; she'd stopped suggesting he do that, so it would be of his own impressive volition. Then he thought about the rock, warm in his hand. Its fire origin floated him an image of the artist, Annabel. He hated to admit it, but her pieces of ice disappearing into the dark, with the flames and then the embers reflected by the ice and the water, were memorable. The diminishing light and the blinking out into darkness—he guessed you could take whatever meaning you wanted from that.

For a moment he considered pocketing the rock—a small gift should he ever see that woman again. She would appreciate every molecule of its being. She'd find some way to extract its energy and apply it to healing the world, even if that healing and that world existed only in her mind. Most likely, though, she'd know— and believe—the story about Pele the volcano goddess cursing anyone who took lava rock from the islands, and that would only cause trouble between them. If there was one thing he didn't need, it was more trouble.

He tossed the bright rock back to its natural environment, like returning a fish to water. He looked at it lying there—an oxidized fragment of Earth's center among the preponderance of gray—and felt much as he did when studying the curves and cilia of his micro-fauna. He didn't want to name that feeling. He didn't want to be an old goat weeping with sentiment. Instead, he brought back to mind his picture of Annabel, imagining her in this place, clinking yellow hair and folds of parachute swirling around her as she danced over *pahoehoe*. She'd be playing with rock and light, inventing possibility, having fun. Perhaps she wasn't really, in her spirit, that different from Keeling.

Ray wanted to have fun. In his case, fun would involve destroying the damned liars at the damned Jackson Oakley's damned center of misinformation. He wanted hot cinders to rain down on the lot of them. He wanted sulfurous clouds to steal their breath. Why couldn't he, Ray Berringer, think as creatively, even metaphorically, as anyone else?

He reached for another chunk of rock and threw it as far as he could across the lava field.

Chapter Fourteen

For Aurora, the winter had been especially hard—a hardness that had little to do with getting up in the cold and dark, freezing her feet in the shoes she wanted to wear (as opposed to the felt-lined boots that made her feet look like Minnie Mouse's), or having to help shovel the driveway. She was used to all that. But when your father gets fired from his job (well, not fired, but wasn't it the same thing?) because some girl said he looked at her boobies and wanted to sleep with her—there's not much that's more depressing than that. She didn't believe that her father had done anything wrong, but the whole thing was extremely embarrassing. Her parents had gotten to escape to Hawaii for a week, but she'd had to stay behind and suffer. She had stayed with her friend Jody, who let her wear some of her clothes and whose mother made french fries from real potatoes, but that had hardly helped.

"Kids can be mean," her mother had warned her, as if she didn't know that. "If they say things, just let it roll off your back. Don't even respond." Except for socking her ex-friend Molly in the stomach, she'd mostly let it roll. She'd become a hunched-over ape, dragging around and avoiding eye contact, stopping up her ears.

But now it was finally mid-April, with budding trees and a thawing, smelly compost pile. Her father had taken a new interest in gardening—to the extent of spreading wood ash on the last snow and nailing together some raised beds inside the moose fence, which he'd also repaired. The yard and the garage had never looked so good. A stranger might think that ordinary people lived in their house.

And then this happened: a leak from that phony organization. Some anonymous person had sent a whole bunch of secret Council for Science Integrity documents to newspapers, including both the *New York Times* and the *Fairbanks News.*

"Your paper? Really?" Aurora heard her father on the phone, talking to the newspaper's editor. "It says that? Really? They have a strategy? Yes, of course I want to see it!"

She had not heard her father so excited about anything in months.

He had apparently stayed up all night to read every word, because he was still excited early the next morning when he made them all gather around for yet another family meeting. "I know it's early," he said, "but as soon as the newspapers hit the driveways the phones will start ringing here."

"You could turn off the ringers," Sam offered.

The house smelled of coffee, which did not change Aurora's awareness that warmth was still in short supply—because the heat in their house mostly came from oil and their family was against burning fossil fuels and killing the planet. Bundled in flannel, wool, fleece, and down to make her point about being cold, Aurora roused herself enough to understand that the leaked papers were the kind that were usually super boring. Normally, only the people inside an organization would see and care about budgets, fund-raising plans, descriptions of how money would be spent. What was clearly revealed, her father explained, was that the goofy CSI organization was funded by oil, gas, and coal industries. Its programs included paying "scientists"—her father used air quotes—to promote those interests. Actual quotes from the documents said that goals were to "counter the alarmist message" of carbon emissions and global warming and to "prevent the implementation of dangerous policy actions to address the supposed risks." He read these out with great dramatic effect, like he was giving Lincoln's proclamation about freeing the slaves.

During the night her father had printed out the articles from the *New York Times* and then the documents that the *Times* had provided links to. Now his hands shook like a really old person's—maybe like Lincoln himself, if he was still alive—as he read from the gray, recycled, unbleached, cheap printer paper he always bought. "I'm not gloating," he paused to inform them, but he sort of was. "This is just what we suspected," he said, "but the dean and the president didn't want to know. Or they already knew and wanted to keep it under wraps. Most of the work of this front organization is about denying climate change, trying to convince the public that there's nothing to worry about. They're paying some weather guy to talk about how all the freakish weather is normal. They're paying someone else to develop a curriculum for teachers to teach that global warming is controversial. So here—listen to this."

He stood in front of their cold EPA-certified woodstove and, like the professor he was, read, "'Ocean acidification strategy: the theory of ocean acidification is based on the same assumption promoted by warmists—that increases in carbon dioxide are caused by humans and will have undesirable effects on the environment.'" He read out several parts of the strategy, all of which Aurora understood had to do with—one—raising money from those who would not want "dangerous policy actions" to be adopted and—two—using communication tools to confuse as many people as possible about what ocean acidification was or might mean for ocean ecosystems.

CSI and its partners would develop written materials that said that OA was controversial, ocean chemistry was complex, and that there was great uncertainty about whether there would be any ill effects. "Here's their message," he read with a sour-apple voice: "'Just as carbon dioxide is good for plant growth on earth, it spurs life in the oceans. It's natural, not harmful, and more can be beneficial.'"

He paused, to allow the three of them to think about that, presumably to think how disgusting those creeps were. Then he read through some of the specific ways the organization would promote its message. "OK, I'm getting toward the end here," he said. "'Strategy number six: funding for selected individuals. Our budget includes funding for *high-profile individuals* to assist us with communications and to publicly counter the alarmist OA message in other arenas available to them. At the moment, this funding goes to *Dr. Jackson Oakley,* director of the University of the North's Office of Ocean Acidification Science. We plan to expand this effort.'"

Now he was no longer gloating. He looked instead like he might throw up.

"Damn," her mother said, setting down her cup of coffee. "That's in the *New York Times?*"

"Not that detail, only in the links. The *Times* talks about the strategy memo more generally and says CSI responded that it wasn't official or adopted and they were pissed off that all those confidential documents were stolen. The story in the local paper is of course going to mention Oakley."

Sam was wagging his foot up and down. "They'll fire that guy's ass."

"Sam!" Her mother put her hand to her forehead, as though the whole thing was too much to think about.

Aurora, closing ranks, said, "You said 'damn.'"

"People will be talking about this," her father said. "The two of you should say all you know is what's in the newspapers."

"Is that true?" Aurora gave him a hard look, then shifted her gaze to her brother. "All we know is in the papers?"

"I'm not sure what all's going to be in the local paper, but probably just what I told you. Maybe a quote or two from university people. Not me. I told the editor I couldn't comment at this time, that I thought the university should have time to do its own research. The paper *might* say something about me being put on probation after criticizing Oakley's involvement with CSI."

Sam said, quietly, "After totally accurately calling him a fucking shill."

Aurora added, "And that that girl framed you because you wouldn't back off?"

Her father looked pained again. "The newspaper's unlikely to say 'framed.' But they may bring that up again, the fact that the university suspended me and hasn't resolved the complaint after more than two months."

"So someone got those in-house papers and leaked them," their mother said. "Do they know who? Does it seem funny that they got leaked to *our* paper?"

Aurora looked from the couch where she sat with her mother to her brother in the armchair. He looked back with narrowing eyes, like a rabid fox, and with the smallest upturn at the corner of his mouth.

OMG! Sam?

He caught her eye and shook his head, a slow *no* that could have meant any number of different things. But if she knew one thing about her brother, it was that he spent hours and hours with his computer.

Her father was talking again. "That's a really interesting part of the story," he was saying. "Apparently someone called the CSI office and pretended to be one of the board members. He—or maybe it was a she—said he'd changed e-mail addresses and needed the board meeting materials sent to the new address. And the secretary—or whoever—sent them to that address. No sophisticated computer hacking. Completely low-tech. Just a phone call, and an e-mail address that couldn't be traced back to anyone in particular."

Now *he* was the one with the fox smile, right when he said "anyone in particular." Aurora looked from her father to her brother and back again. Neither one was looking at the other. Sam was studying the carpet. Her father was looking at her mother. Her mother said, "Well, it *is* theft, I guess, or impersonation or something, but I wouldn't want to be that secretary right now."

In the lab, Helen was inventorying and assembling the materials and supplies they would need for the spring cruise. Jackson had put her in charge, to work from the previous spring's list. The larger equipment was in a warehouse; she'd sent Robert to make sure it was all there and ready to go, with spares of everything. She had the cases of sample bottles and the totes with the incubators. The microscopes. She was checking on the laptops and the new iPads. The hazmat chemicals were in the inventory, locked away for now. She was ahead of schedule, but she felt she needed to be. She was terrified that the ship would get out on the Gulf and they'd find she had forgotten something essential. One missing net, cable, or swivel, too few liters of formaldehyde or a misplaced package of chlorophyll filters—and they were screwed.

Ray had always managed the lists himself, doling out duties but double-checking everything and adjusting the lists from year to year, anticipating the study needs and any special projects that might be assigned. Jackson was much less involved. Since their "break-up," he'd been coolly cordial to her, and she wasn't sure whether giving her the responsibility for so much was a show of goodwill or a punishment. Whenever she had a question, his answer seemed to be, "Everything will be fine."

And now this.

Helen took a break to check her laptop. The blogs and commentaries, full of citizen outrage, were multiplying like snowshoe hares at the peak of their cycle. And, sure enough, CSI was full-on with damage control; now it was claiming its documents had not only been hacked but altered, and its allies in the denial ranks were screaming about what a terrible crime had been committed. They were claiming a conspiracy against them by those who couldn't accept other opinions. The *New York Times,* these same critics protested, had completely misrepresented the good work of CSI, and was complicit in illegal activity by publishing stolen papers.

Earlier, she'd read and reread the Fairbanks article, and she'd read the longer, more researched, double-bylined *New York Times* one. She'd skimmed through the strategy paper both mentioned. Now she read that Jackson Oakley had said he was misrepresented in the memo and that he'd only been consulting with CSI, providing scientific expertise and some ideas for "solutions" to ocean acidification. "How is that wrong?" he was quoted as saying. "Aren't we all for sound science and solutions?"

Alex swept into the lab carrying a box of beakers. "The Fairbanks economy just ground to a halt," he announced, as excited as Helen had ever heard him. "Everybody and their cats are online trying to figure out what just happened."

"I doubt all of Fairbanks cares that much."

"They care about scandal. We're in the *New York Times!* We're famous! It's like the Pentagon Papers all over again." She was pretty sure he was kidding now. "'The Pteropod Papers,' we could call them. Did you see where they said more CO_2 is good for the ocean? More productivity. And everything will adapt. That's the new message: 'evolutionary rescue.' Sounds scientific to me."

"Really? Evolutionary rescue?" Helen had missed that.

"It's in the paper Oakley coauthored. Didn't you read it? The theory that organisms will evolve fast enough to survive acidification. He didn't mention that the current rate of change is a hundred times faster than at the last great extinction." Alex picked up the plastic dippy-bird that lived in the lab, looked it over absently, set it down with a tap that made it "drink" from its glass of water, up and down and up and down. "What bunker is he hiding in, anyway? No one can find him."

It wasn't as though Jackson had ever spent that much time in the lab. Most recently, he and Helen communicated by e-mail and text. He'd finally returned the draft of her thesis as an electronic document with a very few tracked changes and comments. They were edits, a correction of a *which* to a *that,* adding a hyphen, taking out a comma. The comments had not been substantive, nothing like the thorough critique Ray had given her. Ray had been great—questioning her assumptions, pushing for greater clarity, suggesting she expand on the effects of melting ice.

"I haven't looked for him," she said.

"Well, I have. I was just in there. I need his signature, and his secretary said he was out for the day and she didn't know about tomorrow. She seemed pretty shell-shocked herself."

The door opened again, and Tina came in. "Dude! Dudette! What's happening?" She unloaded an armful of books onto a table.

Helen held up her list. "Just checking it twice."

Alex said, "You look suspiciously informed about something."

Tina made a show of clamping her hand over her mouth.

"What?" Alex said.

Tina released her hand, looked normal again. "Nothing. I'm just happy to see you guys. I've had, like, a thousand people today ask me who the leaker is. Like *I* would know."

Only in Fairbanks, Helen thought. Only in Fairbanks would people assume that the leak had come from Fairbanks. She said, "I'm sure there are plenty of people out there wanting to expose CSI. You saw their agenda—they're involved everywhere."

Alex and Tina both looked at her thoughtfully.

"Not that I'm suggesting anything, but I'd never tell if it was one of us," Tina said.

"Of course not," Alex said.

In the uncomfortable pause Helen's laptop pinged with new e-mail.

"I guess it's a mystery," Tina said. "The CSI board of directors is all men, so probably the leaker, if he was pretending to be one of them, is a guy."

Helen's computer pinged again. It could be her friend Jean trying to reach her. Jean was an old-school e-mailer; she claimed her fingers were too big for texting. "The board of directors is all men? Really? How do you know that?"

"You're really not keeping up," Tina said. "It's all there in the leakage, a list of board members, all CEOs and such. I guess they couldn't find any women who were corrupt enough to join them."

"Hey," Alex said.

"I know for a fact," Tina said, "that women care more about the environment and the future for their children. There's polling data. Well, I seem to be learning nothing new here." She gathered up her books.

"You already seem to be the resident expert." Helen meant this as a compliment, but Tina looked like she was being accused of something. She puffed up, defensive behind her stack of books, one of which, Helen noticed, was titled *The Republican Brain*.

"Maybe I am. If I wasn't following the news I'd have to be formatting my thesis, and you know how badly I want to do that. Hey, by the way, where's genius-boy Colin? He's been kind of absent in recent days."

Alex was fooling again with the dippy-bird. "Colin might actually be studying. He's got a big physics exam."

Helen opened her e-mail. It was Jean, twice. First, *WTF!?* and then a longer one, about being in a meeting but needing to express her fury about the idea of training teachers to teach that GW and OA aren't real. What idiot teacher would fall for that? Why was the university mixed up in this stuff instead of speaking out and defending science and education? She was one pissed-off alumna, and she was on her way north ASAP.

Alex and Tina were headed out the door. Helen called after them, "Someone needs to explain to me how people who teach creationism are also going to teach evolutionary rescue."

At the warehouse, Robert and Colin and two of Colin's band members were knocking back beers in celebration. "To truth!" "To exposing the bastards!" "To the whole fucking ocean!" This had been going on for a while.

Earlier, Colin had shown up to help Robert move pallets and rewind a cable. He'd brought along his guitar because he wanted Robert to hear his new song. Then his friends had called. And now they were here, with the bass and the fiddle and a trumpet that none of them really knew how to play. They were finding that the warehouse had awesome acoustics.

Angular Frequency had not yet made the CD that Ray and others had contributed cash to, but they were getting close. Colin was the principal songwriter, with a gift for marine-oriented rhymes. Now they all sang together, and Robert shook, like mariachis, a couple of plastic bottles loaded with screws:

> One fish, two fish, octopi,
> Won't you be my sweetie-pie?
> C-O-two just will not do.
> Give it up or you'll be blue!

In the library, Annabel was using a computer to look up sound patterning in Welsh poetry, something she had recently developed an interest in. But before she did that, because it would take just a minute, and because she was intensely curious about how things were developing, she looked to see if there was anything new about the CSI leaks. Somehow she was on a list to get updates.

The latest was a compilation of news links. The CSI people were working their spin: what a terrible crime had been committed, how "damaging" it was to the board members and donors whose identities and personal information had been made public. They vowed to learn the source of the leak and to see that the criminal was prosecuted to the full extent of the law. A British blogger had picked up the story, praising the anonymous leaker and saying "we have a right to know who's paying for public advocacy." There was a link to tune in live to an Anchorage radio show. She clicked back to the *Fairbanks News* website. Some of the very extensive comment thread had diverted into anti-university rants about greedy professors being paid on the side, moonlighting when they should be teaching. She read, "And what about the professor who was put on paid leave after molesting a student? Your tax dollars at work."

Annabel jerked when someone tapped her on the shoulder.

"Sorry," Nastiya said. "We see you here, we want to say hello." Marybeth stood beside her, the two of them in colorful, itchy-looking sweaters.

There was no one else at the bank of computers, but Annabel still spoke in an exaggerated whisper. "It's good to see you, my sweets." She was aware that the computer was exhibiting the comment stream, some of which was written in capital letters. She hoped that by turning to the girls she was blocking most of it, and maybe they were too polite to look over her shoulder.

"You know the news?" Nastiya whispered back.

"Which?"

"The leak. Professor Oakley is in, you know, hot water. He will cook up like a crab." Nastiya stifled her laugh.

"Yes, I heard all about that."

"And your friend Professor Berringer," Marybeth added. "He was right, everything he said about that place being antiscience. Now maybe he can get his job back."

My friend, Annabel thought. The last time she'd seen him, at the life drawing class, he'd looked mortified and left early. He hadn't acted friendly at all. Still, she could be magnanimous. "I hope so," she said. "Someone needs to protect the creatures great and especially small."

"I wish you were coming on the spring cruise," Marybeth said. "It's all just science people this time."

They were still whispering.

Nastiya was fidgeting with a pencil and looking around nervously.

Other students were streaming past, coming from classes. "Right here, from the library," someone said. "That's what I heard. But they can't trace it."

Annabel was trying to figure out if she could make a casual turn to the computer to return it to Google. Why this was even a concern, she wasn't sure, except that she felt a shadow of fear and suspicion falling across the campus. It might not be the best thing for her to be seen using a university computer to look at material leaked—was it true?—from this very library.

Nastiya said, "I'm afraid for the one who put those papers for everyone to see."

"It could be anybody," Annabel offered.

"I heard the e-mail was sent from the city library," Marybeth said.

Annabel was pretty sure Marybeth was looking past her shoulder. She shifted a little more into her sightline. Mention of libraries reminded her that, after talking to her neighbor about Project Chariot, she'd looked up some books about nuclear explosions.

No doubt some diligent protector of the homeland was, right now, getting a hard-on from her inquiry.

Nastiya arched her eyebrows. "You think it is a good thing, to steal papers?"

"Maybe not generally. But you know, if corporations and billionaires are messing with our democracy, maybe the only way to learn about abuses is by being a little tricky yourself. Maybe that way you level the field a little." She watched to see that Nastiya caught her metaphor.

"Someone tell me," Nastiya said, "those papers are in an envelope, put in the door at the newspaper. Some real person, not an e-mail."

"Hard copy?" Marybeth looked doubtful.

"I hear many things."

Annabel suddenly knew who Nastiya reminded her of—fiendish Natasha, from the old Bullwinkle cartoon. A terrible stereotype, to be sure, but there was a reason for stereotypes. Might the girl be planting information, or hoping for a fresh tidbit? Annabel was not getting a good read on her. Who would she be reporting to? Ray?

Marybeth rolled her eyes. "That Brad. I think he makes things up."

"I hear," Nastiya continued, "the president is very unhappy."

"That much is true," Annabel said. "The university's reputation just got trashed."

"The President?" Marybeth squeaked.

Annabel and Nastiya said at the same time, too loud, "*University* president."

"Oh."

"This is never happen in Russia," Nastiya said, and then added, in what might have been a non sequitur, "Brad and I are fishing soon."

Annabel's neck was hurting from her twist in the chair. So much for Welsh poetry. She'd killed her library time and had nothing to show for it. "Well, then, my little sea angels," she said. "*Dasvidaniya* until next time."

"Until we meet again until next time," Nastiya said, enigmatically. And then added, "Be careful when you play with fire."

Were her American idioms that good?

Annabel turned back to her screen and refreshed it. New news. Jackson Oakley had been threatened. Something about a mysterious package. She skimmed.

Uh-oh.

Cinda was glad she was going to be on the cruise again. At the moment, though, she was adding up credit hours, trying to figure out when she could get her damn degree. She'd had to defer a couple of grades, and she was way behind with her thesis. In fact, she'd lost interest in pollock parasitism and gotten much more interested in crinoids and their response to OA. Her thesis advisor—a lovely woman, really—had suggested she finish what she'd started with pollock. Pollock were important (i.e., studies about them were funded) because of their commercial value. But in Cinda's opinion, the crinoids, some species of which had survived the Permian-Triassic extinction, could have a more interesting story to tell.

Meanwhile, the kitchen garbage was stinking, there was cereal and dog hair all over the floor (why couldn't the dog at least eat the cereal?), and the report she'd been reading about threats to ocean-based food security had somehow gotten jelly on its cover. The newspaper was folded open to the continuation of the long article about the leak and the university's scramble to put a happy face on its involvement. The university had to raise money, the president said, noting the several years of budget cuts made by the legislature. The university had to go out and find grants from government agencies and "other entities" to fund its programs. This was not unusual; this was how it was done. Everyone agreed it was important to fund ocean acidification research. Blah, blah.

Cinda's undergraduate degree was in anthropology, and she was starting to realize that maybe it was anthropology she was most interested in after all. People had screwed up in the past. They'd used up or polluted their sources of fresh water. They'd broken up the prairie and let the soil blow away. They'd poisoned themselves with lead pipes and by dosing themselves with mercury. Humans were capable of learning and moving on, although it sometimes took them awhile to accept cause and effect. The ones who recognized the dangers first were heretics; they usually ended up persecuted, then dead.

Her phone, on the cluttered table, buzzed. Tina.

"Yes. No. Which letter? Of course. I can do that."

OK, so she had a talent for letter writing. The kitchen, the reading, the reengineering of her program and thesis—and, oh yeah, the kids—they would just have to wait.

Aurora returned from school that afternoon as a celebrity. All the talk had been about her heroic father, he who had unmasked a terrible corruption. Everyone seemed to have forgotten about the girl and her looked-at boobies. Even her ex-friend Molly had been nice to her and had given her a little heart-shaped lacquered box that she'd probably shoplifted from the store with the Russian nesting dolls.

Where was everyone? Not that she expected her parents or Sam to be home, but what if she had questions? She was still only a kid; they shouldn't forget that. She could still become a drug addict or a Fox News watcher. She should have supervision.

At school, everyone had kept asking her where her father had gotten those papers he gave to the newspaper, and she kept saying— per script—that she only knew what was in the news. Which got a lot of laughs. So then she started saying, "Maybe I stole those papers," and some of those dumb-ass kids, the same ones that would believe the Tooth Fairy gave you money, looked like they believed her. Or at least, you could tell, they wanted to think she was the one.

People could believe whatever they wanted. She would like to believe that her father had never done anything wrong in the first place. She would also like to believe that now he'd done something wrong that was also right. And that he wasn't making a juvenile delinquent out of Sam. But the more she thought about the situation, the more she suspected that she had only used her imagination, watching the two of them, that morning. Her father was smart in the way science people were smart. He wasn't tricky.

Since no one was home, she turned up the thermostat. When the furnace kicked on she pictured all that gassy stuff going up in the air, then coming back down to choke them all to death. Enough heroics. She just wanted, for once, to be warm.

CHAPTER FIFTEEN

Things happened quickly then, which suggested to Ray that "glacial speed" could be redefined, not just for actual glaciers sliding over their meltwater, but for bureaucracies like the university.

First there were all the defensive strategies, which included Jackson Oakley claiming to be a victim. He argued that he'd been misrepresented, and then that he'd been threatened.

Ray had his own suspicion about the mysterious package—the one for which Oakley had called in a bomb squad. This was confirmed when Annabel whispered into his phone. He might have had an oxygen-deprived moment on the mountain in which he'd thought of her with unreasonable sentiment, but he had really hoped he'd seen the last of her. But no, she urgently needed to meet with him. And no, it was not something they could talk about on the phone.

Thus he'd found himself on a snow-crusted field, pretending to watch the season's first sandhill cranes, while a small red-hooded woman with a sketchpad pretended to be drawing those same cranes. When they pretended to cross paths and stop for a casual chat, Annabel confessed to sending Jackson Oakley a piece of her art. It was *not* a threat, she emphasized. It was a gift. Perhaps it was meant to disturb him a little, because that was the purpose of art. It was both beautiful and disturbing. Now she opened her sketchpad and, in pretending to show him a drawing, disclosed a photograph of said object.

Ray's immediate reaction was intense jealousy. She sent *Oakley* a gift? Why him? Why not a deserving person, like, for example, himself?

His closely followed second reaction was, well, yes, it *was* disturbing.

What he saw in the photo were sharp pieces of rusted metal and wire mesh bent and rolled and riveted with more sharp metal. There was blue paint applied to some of it and flecks of brown, and lots of holes that looked like, and probably were, bullet holes.

He thought Annabel was waiting for him to admire it.

"Lovely," he said. "You draw a lovely crane."

"I guess I should have identified the package somehow," she said. "But I wanted it to be mysterious. I just wanted it to be this anonymous gift. Maybe he would start to see things differently. He'd look at a drop of seawater differently. He'd think about the meaning of corrosion."

Ray lifted his binoculars and watched a crane high-stepping across the field, its red crown blazing in the early light, then dropped the glasses back against his chest. "You're telling me this because . . .?"

She gave him a look as though he was being particularly dense.

"Because we're a team? Isn't that what you said on the boat? It's a team effort?"

Had he said that? He vaguely remembered the part where she'd announced her performance and he'd said something about how she couldn't just go off and do her thing without telling him.

Which is what she'd just done again—her independent, spontaneous thing.

She closed her sketchpad and tucked some of her wild hair

back under her hood. Her face was a circle of light. "So what do we do now?" she asked.

What Ray did was nothing, except to wait, after counseling Annabel to leave well enough alone and stick to drawing birds for a while. Privately, he was rather pleased that she'd terrorized Oakley. He enjoyed imagining a fearful Oakley backing away from the mysterious package to call security, then his face as he confronted what could logically represent shrapnel and firepower. No sense now in correcting that impression.

Meanwhile, the local paper was running a torrent of letters to the editor criticizing the university's involvement with CSI. Most of the letters were unusually well-informed, and even the ones from the conspiracy nuts were semi-appropriate—for once, there was an actual conspiracy for them to rant about. Both of his children were reading the newspaper with a heretofore-unknown interest, and the whole family had had a lively dinner conversation about the word "corporatocracy."

An alumna of the university, a Native woman from Anchorage, had apparently given the president a thrashing over the whole affair and threatened to lead a boycott of alumni giving. This was according to Helen, who was a friend of the woman and was now regularly reporting to Ray.

Nastiya's boyfriend was distributing OA information flyers in boat harbors, and the two of them were organizing something they called Ocean Witnesses.

Colin's band—with its "ocean sound"—was much in demand around town and had been invited to a couple of festivals and the state fair.

Maybe there was a team, after all.

Ray started working out at the new gym in town. Sometimes Sam went with him and they worked out together.

———

As they were leaving the gym one afternoon, Ray heard his name called. That voice, again.

Jackson Oakley was standing by a parking meter on the other side of the street.

A coincidence?

Why wouldn't Oakley just walk on by? Why call out to him?

Ray tried to read his face. Was there a hint of a condescending smile? A flicker of friendliness? Stoicism? He couldn't tell. Now Oakley was crossing the street toward them. His very expensive leather jacket hung on him like an oversized shell on a hermit crab. Had the man lost weight?

Ray introduced Sam to Oakley, Oakley to Sam. Oakley still had his tanning-booth tan but otherwise didn't look well. His face was almost gaunt, like that of a monk who lived on rice and prayer, and his Adam's apple protruded goiterishly. Ray didn't think that Oakley would try to deck him in front of his son. Humiliate him, yes, but not harm him.

Oakley said, "Call off your dogs, Ray."

Ray forced himself not to smile. "My dogs?"

"You know what I mean."

Ray guessed he was flattered, that anyone thought he had dogs and the power to call them on or off.

He had learned something from Nelda, though, and it was to phrase what you say not in terms of criticizing the other person but in terms of your own feelings. He said, "I'm sorry you feel threatened. I know how that feels." He decided to change the subject. "Have you been unwell?"

Oakley scowled. "If you must know, I was very sick with vibriosis. I'm just now getting over it."

Ray couldn't, for a minute, say anything. He suppressed another smile. "A bad oyster?"

"I'm afraid so."

Ray made himself have a sad face. "I'm so sorry. I hope you'll be feeling better soon. Well, son, we'd better be getting home." He put his arm around Sam and walked away.

"You never call me 'son,'" Sam complained as soon as they closed the car doors.

"Sammysam," Ray said, using the baby name they'd abandoned years ago. "Do you know what vibriosis is?"

Sam pulled out his phone. "I can look it up."

"Let me have the pleasure of telling you. It's a foodborne infection caused by the *Vibrio* bacteria. People get it from eating raw oysters." He let himself smile, just a little. "Of course we never want anyone to be ill, but *Vibrio*'s been spreading as the ocean warms. And oysters, you know, are some of the first commercially valuable seafood getting nailed by acidification. There's not a more perfect illness to take down Jackson Oakley. The oyster's revenge."

He grinned all the way home, as Sam read from the Internet the symptoms of vibriosis. Fever, chills, nausea, cramps, diarrhea. Rarely septicemia.

Sam looked up. "Septicemia?"

"I'm not really taking delight in this," Ray said. "I'm not really, right now, having fun. It just might seem that way to you." He was thinking of Hawaii, his lava rock flying through the air. "Blood poisoning can be very, very serious."

The very next day Ray was notified by the dean that the investigation of his bad behavior was coming to a close. On the phone, the dean sounded weary but not apologetic. No, Ray would not have to appear before the committee, and he would not have to line up character witnesses. Apparently they already had a whole file cabinet of supporting letters. "You'd think you were the Dalai Lama himself," the dean grumbled. The main "development," he said, was that the girl who'd made the complaint had retracted it. She was known to have personal and boundary issues and had withdrawn from school in order to receive proper medical care.

Ray jumped up from his chair. "So I get to go back to work?"

"Not so fast. We still have to close things out. We'll let you know."

The royal *we*. The disassociating *we* might soon set him free.

While they were still at the dinner table that evening, discussing Sam's interest in tropical diseases and their northward spread, there was yet another phone call. The kitchen answering machine picked it up, but they all stopped talking and leaned toward the doorway to hear a deep voice say he was the chair of the university regents and would Ray please call him as soon as he got the message; it was rather urgent.

They all sat there, spoons poised over ice cream, until Nelda said, "Couldn't he have given you a hint? Urgent *good* news? Urgent in some other way? I don't like the tone of his voice."

"Call him, Dad," Aurora urged.

Ray had met the regents' chair once at some reception. A banker, maybe? A nice enough white-haired fellow with, Ray remembered, a much younger wife and an overfilled hors d'oeuvre plate. They had had quite a pleasant conversation about polar exploration and scurvy. He couldn't fathom why any regent would call any individual university employee; there were entire hierarchies to do that, and the regents were only supposed to govern, which mainly meant approving budgets.

Now Aurora was handing him the phone. "Call him!"

Ray took the phone into the living room and hit the callback button.

The man was effusively thankful to hear from him, and then cleared his throat. "This is all very awkward."

Ray waited.

"I believe that Dean Morris has informed you that you'll be reinstated."

Ray prepared himself to hear that there'd been a terrible mistake, that the dean was wrong, he was not getting his job back, the regent chair was going to tell him the job no longer existed, the regents had cut its funding, sorry and good luck. He waited.

"It happens that there's been a new development. Very unfortunate, actually. Not for you, no, not for you."

Ray still waited. That word again, another "development." He was imagining that something terrible had happened to the girl with personal and boundary issues. What if she'd killed herself? Or what if his poorly considered cherry story had reached Marybeth's ears and the shame of it had made her jump into the river? His mind was racing. Not unfortunate for him, though. Then why was the regent calling him? What was not bad for him?

"Are you still there?"

"Yes."

"As I said, this is all very awkward. The administration needs to finish its process to officially clear you, but the president himself asked me to ask you right away if you could be the lead scientist on the May oceanographic cruise. You've had that role before, I understand, and we're in a pinch."

Oakley, then. He was bailing on the cruise. Again.

"So," the man was continuing, "I know it's short notice and I know this other thing still needs to wrap up—though I promise you it will, it just can't happen instantaneously. I understand that everything for the cruise is ready to go—that very capable young woman, you know. But for the university's lead scientist, there's no one else we can turn to." He seemed to think that hadn't come out right. "*I mean*, we need your particular expertise. The continuity from other cruises. The confidence of the funders in the data collected. The absolute—well, I was going to say *integrity*—of the whole effort."

"The essential time series," Ray added.

"The essential time series, of course."

Ray let that sit for a moment. "What about Jackson Oakley? I thought he was the lead scientist."

"I'm sorry to say that Dr. Oakley has just resigned his position. Personal reasons."

"That's what's very unfortunate?"

"For him, yes. And it's created a bit of a crisis for us all."

There was more after that, about cruise preparations and approval for two more positions on the cruise (researchers of Ray's choice from other institutions, and he should make those invitations right away so they could arrange their travel) and something about the regents' commitment to advancing Arctic studies and marine science and asking the legislature for funding of a new lab plus monitoring buoys and then something about recruitment for a new director of the ocean acidification office beginning immediately and Ray should be sure to get the word out to his networks and suggest candidates. Interdisciplinary and all that.

And all that.

Chapter Sixteen

From her stool at the kitchen bar, Aurora was taking it all in. "The cruise team," her father called them. The funny one, Tina, and the other one, Cinda, were by the table with the food, talking to the one with skinny arms and the guitar case. That was Colin. The tall one opening a beer was Robert; he was talking to the professor from the other school, something about OA and fish brains. Her heart sped up just a little when she saw Alex unlacing his shoes by the door, adding them to the pile. Her secret crush. He'd dressed up for the occasion, in a yellow shirt ironed on the easy parts but not the sleeves and shoulders. The others were in the living room—a whole bunch of women and Sam laughing.

So that she didn't have to look at Alex, she looked at the printout of the punch recipe she and her father had made: raspberry Kool-Aid, lemonade, orange juice, pineapple juice, two big bottles of 7UP, and a bunch of fresh raspberries from the store—a first in the life of her family, who believed it was wrong to buy expensive things imported from far away, even though the raspberries they picked in the summer were all mooshed in the freezer. You couldn't use those fallen-apart, de-juiced berries in a punch that was supposed to look "festive." "Festive" was her mother's word.

Everything was festive because tomorrow they would leave for the spring cruise and everyone was happy about it, so happy her parents had decided to have a "kick-off" party. Her father had to be the happiest. He was wearing his favorite T-shirt with a bug-eyed cod and walking around barefoot with his big gnarly toes. Now he was surrounded by students, and they were all being goofy.

"All I know," her father was saying, "is that the regents got interested. And yes, I'm finally reinstated. I'm back to my regular research—those activities with almost invisible benefits, as old Keeling used to say. Not that there's not something to be said for invisibility, ha ha ha."

Then they were all cheering, and someone yelled "Speech, speech!" and her father said how much he appreciated everyone's support and that they were going to have a great time on the cruise, and welcome to the new people joining them. They were a great multidisciplinary team, and everything was great, and so on. And please start eating, because Nelda had made a great chowder and also those little puff pastries that really came in a frozen box but give her credit anyway.

Everything *was* great. It really was.

Aurora was only sorry that she couldn't go along with them. She still had school—the end-of-year testing and all that to see if the teachers were any good. And, anyway, that other time had been by special invitation. There'd been a bunk for her then, but now there were the two extra experts her father had invited, plus some new students, and someone was even going to have to sleep in the ship's library.

Helen came and sat on the stool next to her. She was wearing a flowery Eskimo dress with curved pockets and bric-a-brac, and smelled like soap.

"Hey, kiddo," Helen said. "Your dad's telling everyone about the great jellyfish you made and that you're going to arts camp. He's bragging on you."

He was?

It was true that she was going to the arts camp in Sitka for three weeks in July and that she was more excited about this than she'd admit to anyone.

"Which art classes will you be taking?"

"All of them. Well, mainly marimba, ceramics, theater, and creative writing. We're going to write a play and then put it on."

"Sounds like a lot of fun."

"Sam's going to Montana," she blurted.

"Really? What's he going to do there?"

"Make shoes for horses."

There'd been quite a family discussion about this. All on his own Sam had found a job on a dude ranch in Wyoming, taking care of horses and city people who needed help getting on and off horses. His new goal in life, he'd announced, was to be a farrier, which was someone who heated and beat metal to make horseshoes and then nailed them to horses' feet, which sounded painful but apparently wasn't. When their mother had said, "That's a great career choice" in the voice that meant the opposite, Sam had said something about the "post-automotive future" and that had shut them all up. Their father made a few phone calls and found out the dude ranch was not some Internet scam to molest teenage boys or steal kidneys, and so Sam was going, for sure.

"Good for him," Helen said.

Her father, just outside the kitchen, was joking with Colin, something about what classic songs Colin should know and yellow submarines. Her father touched his paper punch cup to Colin's, like they were clinking glasses.

Robert was saying to Marybeth and some other girls, "My sources say that pre-oyster he was already looking at another job, something about the ground floor of a limestone mining venture."

Aurora knew that was about Jackson Oakley. She imagined a giant mine, several stories high, and Oakley on the ground floor. She imagined a very large earthquake. She knew she should not be pleased at the idea of someone—anyone—being crushed under a zillion pounds of rock, but imagining something was not the same thing as wishing it.

One of the new girls said to Alex, "Richard Corey. It's a poem."

No one was talking anymore about leaks and leakers. According to her father, all the publicity had been bad for the bad people, and they shut up about it. No one was going to be found out and arrested.

Now Marybeth was telling a story about a cherry. "I can't believe I said, 'Would you like to eat my cherry?!' I didn't even hear myself! And Ray was so cool, he just pretended I hadn't said anything weird." Aurora saw that her father was listening from across the room and that he didn't look particularly pleased by being called cool. In fact, he turned kind of pale. But then Marybeth and the others all laughed at what was apparently funny, and his mouth turned up, just a little, in the corners.

In the dining room, Nastiya was giving a lecture about the Brad-boyfriend. He was in Kodiak now, she said. He was organizing. Someone is going up in the air to take photos of fishing boats and kayaks lined up to spell "acid ocean," and "save our ocean." "He is a founder of fishermen watching." Nastiya herself had come back at the last minute to join the cruise. Helen's cousin from some village would fish with Brad while she was away, so it all worked out.

It was kind of confusing, so many people to keep track of, all doing something, different things, to help the ocean.

"C'mon," Helen said. Tina was motioning everyone toward the living room.

"First," Tina said, when everyone was ready, "we want to announce with great sadness that this summer our Helen is going to be leaving us and will not be, at this time, pursuing her doctorate." Pause. "She's going to Washington, D. C. to tell those numbskulls it's time to get to work on reducing carbon emissions!" There was a lot of cheering while Helen looked embarrassed, but then she said, not at all shyly, that she was really excited about her new direction. "Partly I'll be working for the Senate Committee on Energy and Natural Resources and partly I'll be going to school in public policy. I think I was headed there all along but didn't realize it until recently."

Her father gave a little speech about it being time to start "translating what we know into policy and action," and that Helen was the perfect person to do that, and something about "the world's gain is our loss." There were a bunch of other congratulations—docs and postdocs and Robert was going to Antarctica, paleoceanography this, biogeochemistry that, new recruits, the regents were very keen on providing funding.

Finally, Tina handed her father a wrapped package. He looked like a little kid at a birthday party, unwrapping it and pulling out smaller packages from inside. The first one was something plastic, with a blue base and a winged creature flying up from it; the creature was mostly clear but with orange and pink around its body and its head.

"Oh, my God!" her father shouted. "It's a *Clione!*"

Then there was a Hello Kitty key ring that had a cat's whiskered face but a blobby body with a pink heart on its front, blue points to its head and a pink bow, also, on its head. And wings. There was another winged toy, made out of felt, with a red heart and red horns and a mean-eyed face like you'd imagine on a devil. There was a small thing on a stick, with a little white body and bluish wings, a pink heart, and a face with a half-circle smile.

"Oh, my God!" her father said again, and she could tell he really liked his presents. "Where'd you *find* this stuff?"

"eBay," Tina said. "This, by the way"—she picked up the thing on the stick—"is an ear cleaner. Like a Q-Tip, but Japanese. Reusable."

Sam said, "Huh?"

"Sorry," Tina said. "I should explain. It happens that the Japanese are very big on *Clione*. In joint honor of our naked pteropod and our fearless leader, we hereby enter all who are present here tonight into the culthood." Colin started strumming his guitar, and he and Tina and Cinda and Robert stood together and sang a song about *Clione,* abalone, on my phone-y, don't call me a sea slug, and words like that that made everybody laugh.

Her father tossed Aurora the Hello Kitty key ring. It was for babies, but still, it was kind of cool. He handed her mother the felt devil, and there was a look between them that was gushy and embarrassing. You didn't really want to see that with old people.

When the doorbell rang, everyone looked up, because who would ring the bell instead of just opening the door? Sam went to answer.

Annabel, twirling in with an armload of packages, was wearing somewhat normal clothes—a pink skirt with black leggings, a green Carhartt jacket. Pink ribbons in her crazy hair. When she took off her jacket, the top underneath was also pink, with "Fire and Ice" written on it in sequins.

Everyone sang the *Clione* song again and showed Annabel the *Clione* gifts, which were very exciting to her. "*Formidable!*" she shouted in non-English. "*Magnificent!*" She especially liked what she called "the statuette" and wanted to know where she could order several, because she would melt them into ruined shapes.

Now her father was unwrapping the purple box Annabel had handed him and pretending he was a little afraid of it, as though it might be a jack-in-the-box or explosives. There was a lot of newspaper inside, and then he lifted out a wood sculpture.

"I know you like representational art," Annabel said. "I don't usually do that, but I made an exception."

Her father held it up—very carefully, Aurora noticed—so that everyone could see. He turned it one way and another to show the beautiful grain that was swirling and grooved to look like a shell, and the two sticking-out parts, one bigger than the other, like leaves but Aurora knew they were wings.

It was funny: everything tonight was pteropody, like it had been planned that way.

Her father stared at that piece of wood like it was the best thing he could ever have dreamed of, and he said to Annabel, "This is incredibly meaningful to me. Thank you." He wasn't even being sarcastic.

She said, "I made two of them. This is the healthy *Limacina helicina*. The second one just got accepted for the juried art show at the Anchorage Museum. It represents *after* ocean acidification."

Her father nodded and looked only slightly worried. He rubbed one hand over the swirling part of the sculpture. "You got the umbilicus almost exactly right, but there's a few too many whorls to the shell. *Helicina* has five or six."

There was a sucking in of breath, and Annabel put her hands on her waist like a mad schoolteacher on an old TV show. "It's *art*," she said, sounding the word "art" like a poisonous dart she was throwing right between his eyes.

"Kidding!" her father yelled, and then he set the beautiful object on the coffee table and gave Annabel one of his awkward hugs, and then someone turned up the music and everybody danced with everybody. Even Alex. Aurora even danced near Alex and looked at him while he was looking at one of the new girls. Annabel showed them all how to move their hips up and down, salsa-style, and Aurora learned that she *had* hips.

After awhile Aurora went back to the kitchen stool where she could be less sweaty and watch everyone through the doorway. Annabel, with her funny smell and glitter-sparkle, set a package wrapped in white tissue paper before her. "We're the two left behind," Annabel said. "But we have other work to do." Her lips formed a straight pink line.

Aurora's squeal was entirely genuine. She'd assumed the second package was the kind of thing grown-ups brought when they were invited to someone's house—a hostess gift. But she should have known. Annabel was not a normal grown-up. She unwrapped the tissue paper, carefully. What was this? Something bookish. The cover was her favorite color, purple, and bumpy like alligator skin, with stitched-on squares of birchbark that looked like windows. A small white bone, knobby on its ends, fit through a loop to hold the book closed.

Aurora stroked the bone with her finger.

"Deltoid tuberosity," Annabel said.

Huh?

Annabel pointed out a thickened part on one side of the bone. "You can tell this is from a mammal, because the deltoid muscle of the shoulder attached here, to the humerus, this upper arm bone. A small mammal, from the size of it, possibly a rabbit? Deltoid tuberosity," she said again, as though the words were so delicious she could eat them. "Go ahead and unlatch it."

Aurora slipped the bone free and opened the book. The inside cover was spackled with blue and gold, like a night sky with stars. She turned pages. Pastel blue, the color of a robin's egg. Yellow like daffodils. Pale pink. The lightest green. More blue, and swirling like the ocean. Every page was clean and soft, with fuzzy edges. Every page was blank.

She looked up at the shimmering Annabel, who said, "It's a beautiful world, girl of light and *duende*. And you get to write the next chapter."

Aurora didn't know what *duende* was, but she would figure that out later. In the moment she could only say "Thank you, thank you, thank you," ten times over. She meant the gift, and she meant everything.

ACKNOWLEDGMENTS

Ocean-deep thanks to all those who helped bring this project to life:

For their marine science expertise: Russ Hopcroft, Jeremy Mathis, Kris Holderied, and members of the Seward Line Cruise in September 2010;

The crew of R/V Tiĝlax̂;

COMPASS for a fellowship to the Ocean Science Symposium in Monterey, California, in 2012;

Valued colleagues and early readers Tom Kizzia, Rich Chiappone, Jo-Ann Mapson, Tamara Dean, David Stevenson, Laura Long, and Kathleen Dean Moore;

The late Eva Saulitis for her example and inspiration always;

Students and faculty in the University of Alaska Anchorage M.F.A. Program who encouraged my work-in-progress readings;

Those responsible for generous artist residencies at the Santa Fe Art Institute, Virginia Center for the Creative Arts, Madroño Ranch, and Mesa Refuge—and my fellow artists who shared work with me in those magical places;

Kathy Howard and the rest of the "gang" at Graphic Arts Books;

Ken Castner, proximity theorist (and my partner).

Author Q & A

Q: *Do you have a science background or did* pH *require much research?*

A: My academic science background is relatively weak. I've never taken a chemistry course. I am, however, keenly interested in the biological sciences and am largely self-educated in them, and I'm lucky to live in a hub of scientific (especially marine) research in Alaska, with access to many scientists. My research for this book included a great deal of reading, attending presentations and conferences, and spending a week on a research ship. I was committed to making sure that, although the characters and plot are fiction, the science is accurate. My biggest challenge was keeping up with the science; through the course of writing and revising the book, we were learning more and more about what's happening in the ocean—and the situation for marine life was becoming increasingly dire.

Q: *The three main point-of-view characters in the book are Ray, Helen, and Annabel. You are obviously very different from each of them; you are not a man, an Alaska Native, nor a flamboyant conceptual artist. Which of those characters did you find most difficult to imagine?*

A: What I love most about both reading and writing fiction is the opportunity to inhabit characters very unlike myself. I had a lot of fun exploring the worlds and personalities of Ray, Helen, and Annabel. Even with the gender issue and some of his questionable attitudes and behaviors, I probably felt "closest" to Ray, and I came to be very fond of him. The biggest challenge was with Helen, because of the cultural aspects—that is, avoiding cultural appropriation while recognizing that Alaska Natives live successfully in "two worlds." It would seem wrong to set a novel in Alaska and not include Alaska Natives in it.

Q: *What are some of the challenges of writing eco-literature? Why did you choose fiction instead of nonfiction to tell the story of ocean warming and acidification?*

A: I think the main challenge in any environmental writing is avoiding didacticism. I didn't want to lecture about the harm we're doing to the Earth. I've previously written about environmental subjects in nonfiction, and I hoped that a novel might be more fun and reach more and different readers. Fiction is about characters and plot and allows for both drama and humor. It can entertain while also presenting situations and, yes, factual information, that readers might find spark their interests and broaden their understandings. I hope that my book will, at times, make readers smile and even laugh out loud.

Q: pH *has been called a "cli-fi" novel. What is that about?*

A: Cli-fi or climate fiction is a sub-category of environmental fiction that addresses climate change issues. Some of it takes the form of futuristic or speculative science fiction and some (like *pH*) is set in the present or near-future. Of course there have always been novels full of science (think *Moby-Dick*), but we seem to be entering something of a golden age for what are now identified as "science novels"—that is, literary fiction involving science and the lives of scientists. In working up my book, I studied and tried to learn from examples that include Ian McEwan's *Solar*, Barbara Kingsolver's *Flight Behavior*, T. C. Boyle's *When the Killing's Done*, and Margaret Atwood's *The Year of the Flood*.

Q: *You cleverly open your story on a floating schoolhouse, and deliver much of the biology and chemistry details to the reader via dialog: the professor and students talking about their work. It's an effective narrative strategy that avoids blatant exposition. Even so, how did you decide how much science the reader needs to hear to understand what's going on?*

A: A wise early reader said to me, "The readers don't need to know why the science is important, only that it's important to the characters." But I did want readers to understand the science at a basic level and appreciate its importance. I tried to present it in small parts and pieces, organically as the need presented itself, and not to let it interrupt the story's drama. I tried to anticipate what readers would need to know to follow the story and to work the "information" into the action. I didn't want to bore readers who might not be that fascinated with the science or to talk down to those with science backgrounds. My working title for the book was *The Pteropod Gang*, because I wanted readers to learn right at the top what pteropods are; I would like, along with my character Ray, for pteropods to be the "poster animals" of ocean acidification in the same way that polar bears are the "poster animals" for climate change.

Q: *How aware are fishermen of increased ocean acidification and the implications it might have for fisheries? How about others who depend on oceans and marine life for their livelihoods? Are they involved in its study or in seeking remedies?*

A: Alaska's fishermen (and Alaskans in general) tend to be quite aware of climate change and ocean acidification and their threats to fisheries and coastal communities. I have less sense about the rest of the country, in which people may not feel the immediate connections. Commercial fishermen are adapting in various ways, from diversifying (so as not to depend on a single species or region) to moving their fishing effort (for example, setting crab pots in deeper, cooler water.) There are also several programs in which they help with sampling, and they've supported funding for technologies like monitoring buoys. The problem is that the ocean will be absorbing CO_2 from the atmosphere for a very long time, even if we stopped burning fossil fuels today. There's no quick fix to acidification, so the emphasis has been on research to try to determine how various species will react and what management strategies can help.

Q: *Helen is an Iñupiat scientist committed to both her cultural values and empirical data. What do you hope readers will learn from her?*

A: I hope that readers will see Helen and the other characters as complex, in the way that we all are—we're never one "thing" but are full of contradictions and continual change. Cultures, too, are alive and always changing, adapting. I hope that readers will appreciate that there are many ways of experiencing and interpreting our world. What we call Western science is critically important, but other ways of knowing, like those developed by Alaska Natives over thousands of years, are also legitimate and worth learning from.

Q: *Part of the conflict in the book occurs between the scientists and the artist, Annabel. What do you want the take-away to be about the relationship between science and art?*

A: Science and art are both creative pursuits and are driven by curiosity about our world. Both appreciate beauty, complexity, and the unknown. I wanted to show both the tension between the two and the ways that they complement one another and even use the same tools. I'm personally concerned that in our schools today we seem to value STEM (science, technology, engineering, and math) above the arts. Education in the arts is vitally important, and participation in making art is something that should be available to and encouraged in all of us, however "untalented" we may think we are. We can't all be research scientists, but we can all respect the work of scientists and artists and use their tools of inquiry to enrich our lives.

Book Group Questions

1. Part of this novel takes place at sea, aboard a research vessel, and part takes place in Fairbanks, at a university. Does the depiction of life on a boat and life in interior Alaska fit with your picture for each? What details made each setting vivid for you?

2. While this novel revolves around the scientist/professor Ray Berringer, many other characters play significant roles. Which characters did you most relate to? What did you learn about Alaskan indigenous cultural traditions from Helen? What role does Annabel, the environmental artist, play?

3. Were you aware of the issues of ocean warming and acidification before reading this? If so, what information was new to you? As a result of reading this novel, are you motivated to learn more, change your own personal actions, or get involved in activism to help address climate change? What changed in your understanding?

4. Some of the information about ocean acidification and the threats facing the marine ecosystem is conveyed by the students as they conduct their

research. Why do you think the author chose to do this rather than letting Ray convey all the information?

5. Since fiction is imaginative literature, it creates a different connection with its readers than nonfiction, which is based on fact. Do you think it's a deeper connection? What are the advantages of using fiction to write about environmental issues? How might fiction reach a different audience?

6. What are the challenges and potential pitfalls of writing about topics like climate change and ocean acidification? What literary strategies does the author use to avoid these pitfalls? What role do you think humor can play in writing about a serious subject? Where are examples of humor in this book?

7. In this novel, we observe a subtle tension between science and art, as suggested by Ray's initial distrust of Annabel and his skepticism about her art. How does Ray's view of Annabel change? What does the author seem to suggest about that tension? What do you think: how are science and art similar and how are they in opposition?

8. On page 188, Ray wonders, "Was truth to be belittled? Was standing for truth and honesty something to be avoided, regretted?" At what point should we risk personal security in order to uphold truth as a moral standard?

9. When Ray and Nelda are near the end of their Hawaiian vacation, Ray thinks, rather sardonically, that the next day he'll spend three hours in a car burning up gas and the day after that he'll get on a plane to trash his beloved planet even more. To what degree are individuals— not just energy companies—responsible for greenhouse gas emissions and other environmental damage?

10. In more than one passage in the book, the question arises about when it's appropriate to share "depressing" news of what's really happening to our environment. When is the appropriate time to educate, from a teacher's or parent's standpoint? From a listener's perspective, should we be more receptive to hearing things about our world that might not be pleasant but will further our understanding of it?

11. Corrosion is a real process in ocean acidification—the shells of organisms like pteropods are literally corroded by acidified seawater. How is corrosion also a metaphor in the book?

12. The internecine politics of academia have been chronicled in many literary fictions over time. How does this story make you feel about the uses of science and information by universities struggling to survive on dwindling funding?

13. This novel includes the perspectives of several generations, since it's also told through the eyes of Ray's daughter, Aurora. What is the significance of the final scene, when Annabel gives Aurora the blank book?